ARE YOU WATCHING ME?

SINÉAD CROWLEY

Quercus

First published in Great Britain in 2015 by

Quercus Publishing Ltd
Carmelite House
50 Victoria Embankment
London EC4Y 0DZ

An Hachette UK company

A CIP catalogue record for this book is available
from the British Library

TPB ISBN 978 1 78429 296 6
EBOOK ISBN 978 1 78429 049 8

This book is a work of fiction. Names, characters,
businesses, organizations, places and events are
either the product of the author's imagination
or used fictitiously. Any resemblance to
actual persons, living or dead, events or
locales is entirely coincidental.

10 9 8 7 6 5 4 3 2 1

Typeset by CC Book Production

Printed and bound in Great Britain by Clays Ltd, St Ives plc

For Andrew Phelan

AUTHOR'S NOTE

The name 'Tír na nÓg' means the Land of the Young, or the Land of Youth, and comes from Irish mythology. Although it is a phrase in common usage in Ireland, the centre described in this book is entirely fictional.

PROLOGUE

She had forgotten how to breathe. That simple skill, the one everyone took for granted, had deserted her. Again.

Opening her lips, she tried to inhale, but the movement felt forced, unnatural. What little air she did manage to squeeze into her lungs made her chest ache and left her feeling dizzy, unfocused. And all this, when it was too late to run away.

Looking straight ahead, she confronted the dark cylinder head on. The barrel tilted, glided slightly to one side and then settled in front of her. Her chest was aching now, and she exhaled shakily and tried to get a rhythm going. In and out. In and out . . .

For a moment, everything was silent. She reached out, swallowed water, and felt it chill the back of her throat as the blackness loomed closer.

The man beside her smiled, distractedly.

'You alright, Elizabeth?'

Instinctively, she nodded her head, lying with a tight smile.

'Thirty seconds.'

There was no time to concentrate on breathing now.

'Twenty seconds.'

She picked up the glass of water again, put it down when she realised how much her hands were shaking.

'Ten seconds.'

That familiar music. The man gave a brisk cough, then picked up some papers and practised a smile.

'Five seconds. And four, and three and two . . .'

'Hello and welcome to *Dublin Today*.'

It was wonderful, magical even, the way she had come into his life – just when he needed her most.

The doctor had told him to get himself a hobby, an interest.

'We all need a reason to get out of bed in the morning, Stephen. We all need someone to talk to.'

Well, now he had Elizabeth.

He had realised straight away, when he saw her in the newspaper, that she was special. And then, when she appeared on his TV, it was as if the world had paused around him. He was enchanted by her. She was beautiful, yes, but there was more to it than that. Her smile was aimed at him; her words meant for him alone.

After that, it felt like she was everywhere: on his radio, on the television news, in the newspaper again – and what a wonderful day that had been! An interview, and a photograph, and a little box beside the main article telling him everything he needed to know about her. Her favourite food. The films she liked watching. The books she liked to read.

To think he almost hadn't bought that paper that day. It had been one of his bad nights, the worst kind, and he had fallen into a jerky sleep sometime around dawn, waking again at ten with a foul taste in his mouth and the fear from the night before still fogging his brain. He had wanted to roll over, shut his eyes, abandon himself to the shame and not face anyone because, after all, why would anyone want to see him?

But Mr Mannion would be cross if he knew he was thinking that way. So Stephen forced himself to rise from the bed, splash water on his face and stumble the few steps to the shop down the road. Just to prove he could do it. Just to prove he was alive.

And there she was, waiting for him on the stand just inside the door. A small photograph on the front page, with the promise of so much more inside. He'd been so excited he'd almost forgotten to pay, just grabbed the paper, held it close and was halfway out the door before he'd realised what he was doing. The assistant, a young Chinese woman, didn't see him leave. He could have taken the paper all the way home and no one would have noticed the theft. But Stephen wasn't that sort of person. So he returned to the queue and waited impatiently behind the tall blond man in the yellow jacket, whose breakfast roll was sending sausage-scented heat out into the air.

Behind him, a young woman pushed the wheels of her buggy rhythmically into his heels. Jab, jab, jab. Maybe she was trying to quieten her child. She wasn't very good at it. The baby's wails made his ears buzz, but he didn't care. A whole two pages.

Sausage man wanted a lotto ticket too and Stephen had to wait for nearly five minutes while the clerk fiddled with the machine, but he was so excited about what the newspaper contained that he forgot to get his own money ready and was left scrabbling around in his pocket for change when his time came.

As the wails increased in intensity, he could feel waves of exasperation coming from the woman behind him and his neck reddened as his hand dived into his pocket, searching for a euro coin but unearthing useless coppers instead. By the time he'd counted out the money on to the counter, he was sweating and had to wipe his hands on his slacks to make sure the newspaper was protected from smears.

But his embarrassment didn't matter; none of it mattered. None of them mattered. He had Elizabeth now, and she was all he needed.

CHAPTER ONE

It shouldn't have been this easy. It was a Garda station, for God's sake. It should have been impossible to get something this volatile into a building where upwards of two hundred highly trained police officers were supposedly poised for action.

But Detective Sergeant Claire Boyle was a professional too and she had given this operation a lot of thought.

The first thing she had had to consider was clothing. Nothing too tight-fitting, obviously. Nothing colourful either. She needed to be invisible, to wear clothes and, most importantly, an attitude that would allow her to get to her desk, do what she needed to do and escape again without anyone asking questions. The dark navy rain jacket was ideal. Bought several months ago, it hung loose and baggy on her now, leaving just enough space to hide the bulky package that was securely strapped to her chest.

She had timed her movements well, arriving at Collins Street during a shift change, and managed to get past the front desk and through the doors leading to the main body of the Garda station without being spotted at all.

As she continued to walk, head down, along a windowless corridor, one colleague emerged through an office door, his face brightening when he saw her. But her glacial stare froze the smile on his face and he remained silent as she marched past him and up the stairs. She was moving quickly now, swaying gently from side to side as she walked. All good. It was all going to work out. Her desk was just inside the door, the document she needed lying on top of it. Brilliant. All she needed to do was walk in, grab it and she could be back downstairs without the explosion taking place. All she had to do was . . .

BOOM!

Across the room, Philip Flynn dropped his armful of hard-covered files on to the floor.

'Ah, Jay—'

Claire felt, rather than heard the intake of breath.

Then . . .

'WAAAAHHHH!'

Oh, Flynn, you muppet.

Claire's body shook as the baby in the sling battered her head against her chest, and roared.

Flynn caught her eye and mouthed an apology, straining to keep a grin off his face. She wanted to gut him. But before she could move across the room the army had formed, and then descended. It was everything she had been dreading, and more.

'Oh, you brought her in! Oh, give us a look at her! Ah, the dote. Oh, isn't she GORGEOUS!'

'Bastard.'

Reddening, she flung the word at Flynn, but the word never reached him as every female in the room, both members and civilians, fell on top of her. There was no way of avoiding it now. Unzipping her jacket, Claire shrugged her shoulders and unfurled a cross and red-faced Anna from her sling. The little girl scowled and her wails increased.

'She has her mother's temper, anyway!'

Sergeant Rita O'Farrell reached out and stroked the damp curls on top of the little girl's head, which only resulted in an increase in decibels.

'Ah, isn't she gorgeous!'

Garda Máire Tierney, thought Claire, would have to sit her medical again – in particular, the eye-test bit. Mouth open, snot mixed with drool on her reddened cheeks, not even Anna's mother considered her gorgeous right now.

'Ah, she's a dote. Congrats!'

Garda Siobhán O'Doheny came over and gave Claire a quick smile. From the corner of her eye, Claire could see Flynn redden and edge towards the door. She still wasn't sure what had taken place between those two on the night of the verdict in the Miriam Twohy murder trial. But clearly no effort had been made in the intervening six months to clear the air. A pity. Still, they'd get over it, whatever it was. They wouldn't be the first pair of colleagues to shit on their own doorsteps. Besides, she was finding it very hard to feel sympathetic towards Flynn right now. Claire had sworn she wouldn't be one of Those Women, who paraded their new babies around the office as if no one had ever given birth before. And up until this afternoon she'd stuck to her resolve.

'What in God's name . . . ? Oh, it's you.' Superintendent Quigley's voice rose above the cacophony of tears and cooing.

Miraculously, Anna gulped twice and then stopped crying, her big blue eyes seeking out and focusing on the super's face.

The sea of women parted as he approached.

'Give her here to me. Are they upsetting you, are they?'

Picking the child up, he laid her expertly against his shoulder. In one smooth movement, Anna wiped her nose on his shirt and then looked up, surveying the office happily from her new-found place of safety.

I'm grand now. This guy knows what he's doing, the big blue eyes seemed to say as her hand reached out to play with his collar.

'Boyle, a word?'

'Certainly, sir.'

She would kill Flynn later, Claire decided, and her husband too. And Matt's client who had turned up late for his meeting, leading to the delayed handover of the child. But all of that would have to wait. Throwing a final thunderous look in Flynn's direction, she elbowed her way through her colleagues and followed her boss across the room.

'Jesus, sir, I'm so sorry. Matt's on his way; he just texted to say he'd be late; he was supposed to pick up the kid at home but he's going to meet me here instead and—'

Superintendent Quigley looked at her, momentarily confused. 'Huh? Oh, the baby. God, no, she doesn't bother me. Surprised you haven't brought her in before, actually. Little pet.' He smiled down at the child who was now drifting back to sleep in his arms. 'No, I need you to go out on a job. Immediately. You're free?'

'Absolutely!'

Claire felt her pulse quicken. She'd been back from maternity leave for more than a fortnight and hadn't done anything more strenuous than filing the paperwork that had built up in her absence. Her superiors had said that, given the successful outcome, no further action would be taken about the unorthodox role she'd played in the resolution of the Twohy case, but she had been starting to wonder if she was in fact in the doghouse after all.

Now, however, it looked like things were going to improve.

Rifling through sheets of paper on his desk, Quigley grabbed a notebook and read out a few details. Body of a man; house in the north inner city. Neighbour let herself in when he hadn't been seen for a couple of days. Uniforms on the scene; assistant pathologist on his way. Would Claire take a look?

'And take Flynn with you.'

'Absolutely, sir. Thanks. I'm on my way.'

She was halfway out of the office before he spoke again.

'Boyle!'

'Yes, sir?'

'You might want to . . .' He nodded down at the child in his arms.

'Oh, God, yeah! Absolutely, superintendent. Give her here . . .'

Too happy to be embarrassed, she raced back, grabbed the baby and headed once again for the door.

CHAPTER TWO

'Will you look at you! You ride.'

'Shut up, Dean.'

The woman at the television station had caked her in make-up but Liz reckoned that not even the thick beige pan stick could mask the blush that was flooding across her cheek-bones. Turning away from her friend's intense scrutiny, she feigned interest in a basket of scones.

Sensing victory, Dean pursed his lips. 'Can I buy you a coffee? Or do I have to go through your agent?'

'Shut UP!'

Liz's voice squeaked at the end of the second word and a couple of people ahead of them in the coffee-shop queue turned around to see what was wrong. One woman narrowed her eyes, wondering why Liz looked so familiar. Good-looking girl, certainly, and she was sure she'd seen those green eyes somewhere before. Was she a friend of her daughter's, maybe? Or did she used to live at the end of the road? Unsure, she raised her eyebrows and flashed a quick, noncommittal smile.

Liz gave an embarrassed grimace in return and then turned

her face away. Dammit. That sort of thing was happening more and more these days and she'd have to come up with some way of dealing with it, a reaction that was more appropriate than turning purple and looking at the ground. Reaching for a scone, she picked up her tray again and looked out into the main body of the restaurant. She'd find a seat down the back somewhere and—

'Holy crap! It's *you*! And you're HUGE!'

Dean's yelp echoed around the restaurant and she looked past his outstretched arm to the oversized TV screen suspended over the cash register.

Balls, balls, balls. And she'd been so convinced she'd be able to avoid it. But there she was, resplendent in her charity-shop jacket, hair flopping over her eyes, glowering out from the massive screens.

Dean was still talking.

'Look at you! You're fab! I told you you'd be brilliant!'

There was a whisper spreading through the rest of the queue now, a ripple of gossipy enquiry.

'Do you think it's her? It is her. I knew I'd seen her somewhere before.'

'Sweet Jesus.'

Liz shuddered, but not even the basket of scones could save her now.

Dean grinned. 'Hey, you owe me, lady. I think I—'

But she didn't hear the second half of his sentence. This was bad; this was worse than bad. There was a buzzing noise in her ear and she was afraid she was actually going to pass out, right there beside the wholegrain muffins, thus guaranteeing that even the people who hadn't seen her on the big screen would have to notice her when forced to step over her body.

Dean gave one more guffaw and then realised her mortification was actually genuine.

'Jesus – you really do hate this, don't you? Here . . . there's a seat down there, look, behind the potted plant. You go on, I'll get your coffee.'

'Thanks.'

Shoulders hunched over, eyes locked on the floor, Liz made her way quickly to the far side of the room.

'So, what were you expecting?'

Dean plonked a decaff Americano down in front of her and took a slurp from his overflowing cappuccino.

'Dunno. Not that, anyway.'

Liz burned her tongue on her own drink and took a furtive look around the room while she waited for the stinging to die down. In fairness to Dean, he'd gone some way towards redeeming himself by steering her towards this alcove. Not only was there a huge potted plant between her and the TV screen, the banquette-style seat came with a high back, so she was protected on two sides. It was the perfect place to get her head together. And, good Christ, did she need that.

Her friend placed his smartphone down on the table and grinned.

'I don't know why you looked so surprised. I mean, it was

a telly interview. You did know you were going to be on telly, right? The big cameras must have given it away?'

Liz rolled her eyes.

'Yes, Dean, I was well aware of that, thanks. But I was in there at nine o'clock this morning, and the piece went out live. I'd no idea they'd show it again.'

'It's a twenty-four-hour station, you eejit.' Dean smiled at her patronisingly. 'There's no such thing as a one-off programme anymore. Especially not with that crowd. Sure, it'll go out four more times between now and the evening news. Anyway, I don't know what you're worried about; you looked fantastic. Totally hot, but, you know, serious at the same time? Trust me, you've nothing to worry about.'

'Right.'

Liz smoothed back her hair and then glanced down at her hands. They'd stopped shaking. At least that was a start. It had been pretty stupid of her, to think she could just sort of sneak on television and hope nobody would notice. But the whole situation was just so . . . bizarre. It wasn't like she was one of those people who wanted to be famous. That had been the furthest thing from her mind.

'You did well, anyway!' Dean poked at his phone for a moment and then looked up at her triumphantly. 'You're trending on Twitter again!'

'Don't wanna know.'

Liz took another sip of coffee and settled back into her chair.

'You know I don't do Twitter – can't be arsed. Or Facebook, or any of that crap. I've enough ways to waste my time, thanks.'

And there's nobody out there I want to connect with, she thought to herself, but Dean didn't need to know that level of detail.

But her friend was still poking.

'Well, your boss doesn't agree with you. We've set up a Facebook page, actually, for the charity. Nothing too elaborate, just a few pictures of the place, a few details about what you do. We've given bank account details where people can send donations—'

Liz shook her head. 'I told you, I don't want to know. You work away with Tom if you like – and since when did you two get so pally, anyway? But leave me out of it. I did you a favour, I did your bloody interviews, now—'

But she had lost her audience. Dean pulled his phone closer to his face, and grimaced. 'Sorry, hon. I just have to answer this, OK? Give me a minute.'

And he was gone, thumb flying, muttering under his breath about feckin eejits as he emailed.

'No problem.'

Liz knew that, as a freelance journalist, Dean couldn't afford to be out of contact at any time for longer than five minutes and the constant checking of his phone was sparked more by necessity than rudeness. She needed a moment to herself anyway. She liked Dean, enjoyed his quick wit and was even starting to admire the unashamed aura of ambition that hung around him like expensive aftershave, but hanging out with him was like being on one of those teacup rides at the fairground – great fun while you were on, but leaving you dizzy and a bit unsure when your feet touched solid ground again.

The producer at the TV station that morning had asked her how they'd met. 'In school' had technically been the correct answer, but they hadn't actually been friends back then. Dean had turned up in fifth year, trailing unconfirmed rumours about suspensions and expulsions, and hadn't bothered to join any particular gang. In fact, her strongest memory of him from back then was of a restless, too-thin boy at the back of the class-room, always twitching, always on the move, darting between classes, rooting around in his bag for a pen that never seemed to be there and, towards the end, asking and answering far more questions than the rest of them put together.

After the Leaving Cert, Dean hadn't brought his fake I.D. to the local pub with the rest of the lads; he'd just kind of evaporated out the front door. A rumour went around that he'd been accepted to Trinity College on a scholarship and, given everything else that happened to her subsequently, Liz hadn't thought about him again until they'd literally bumped into each other on the street outside her office, just a couple of months previously.

Her first instinct had been to ignore him, or pretend she couldn't remember his name – her default reaction when con-fronted with anyone from her teenage years. But he'd spotted her and marched straight up, arms outstretched as if they'd been best buds back in the day.

'How've you been? You're looking great. What've you been up to?'

Liz had felt the usual stomach clench at the question. But at least now, for the first time in ages, she had a proper answer to give him. Quickly, she'd filled him in on her new job, the grandly titled 'Communications Executive' at the building they were standing outside.

'It's called Tír na nÓg,' she'd told him, unconsciously rolling into the bland summary she trotted out ten times a day on the phone when looking for grants or trying to get help for the clients. 'We provide assistance and basically a place to go for men who are on their own. Some of them are homeless; we can't put them up or anything but we help them find temporary accommodation if we can. And some of them are just lonely and they can hang around our place, read the paper, have a chat, whatever. A bloke called Tom Carthy founded it – he's the boss. It was a one-man show, really, but he took me on a couple of years ago to help out.'

And don't, for the love of God, ask me where I was before that, she prayed silently.

But Dean seemed far more interested in what she was doing right now.

'Tír na nÓg – yeah, I think I've heard of it. That Greg fella – the guy who went missing in Dun Laoghaire a couple of months ago – he was one of your clients, yeah?'

'Yeah.' Liz had nodded, tried to mimic Dean's flippant tone, but even though months had passed, her breath still caught in her throat at the thought of Greg Butler. He had been her favourite client. Tom's, too, although Liz knew he'd never admit to having such a thing. But they had all loved him, the

16

tall, sandy-haired man who had been at the heart of their little community. At fifty-four, Greg had been far younger than Tír na nÓg's other clients, and that wasn't the only way in which he was different. Greg hadn't needed any of the practical help the centre provided – the hot dinners, the warm place to sit, the help with form-filling and other aspects of officialdom that Liz provided on a daily basis. In fact, on paper, Greg hadn't needed any help at all. He lived with his elderly mother in a large, comfortable house on the south side of the city. He'd a large family, brothers, sisters, nieces and nephews, and pulled out photos of them often, chatting about them to such a degree that, when Liz had seen them at the funeral, she had known all of their names. But, despite his seemingly comfortable life, there had been something a little off about Greg Butler, a little strange. He had never lived away from home, he told Liz, had never stuck at a job longer than a couple of months. An oddball is what Liz's father would have called him, without meaning to be unkind – a man who was just that little bit out of step with the rest of the world.

Greg had turned up in Tír na nÓg one Sunday afternoon, saying his mother had heard a mention of the centre at Mass and wanted to make a donation. He accepted, after some persuasion, a cup of tea and stayed for an hour. Two hours, the following week. Soon after that, he began to visit every Sunday from two in the afternoon until the centre shut, shortly before seven. Sunday was family day at his house, he'd told Liz; his brothers and sisters would call to see his mother and bring their kids with them, letting them climb on the furniture and mess with the TV. He loved the children, but found the noise difficult to bear after a while, so he'd head off on his own – to the pictures, or into town – wander around a bookshop, or take a train to Howth and go for a walk on a fine day. But he was happier now he'd discovered Tír na nÓg.

That was until the day Tom admitted he'd have to close the centre at the weekends. It had been a tough decision and Liz had seen him agonise over it. But funds were tight, the heating bill high during a particularly gloomy spring. The clients understood, or so they told him. But Liz had seen the disappointment in Greg's face when he'd heard the news, and something else. Fear, maybe? That first Sunday, Liz persuaded Tom to turn off his phone, head to the cinema, take the break he rarely afforded himself. When he turned it back on that evening, there were several missed calls from Greg, but no messages. The guards called round to the centre the following Tuesday. Greg's family had reported him missing, they said, and couldn't think of anywhere else he might have gone. They were a large family, the Butlers, well connected. Nieces and nephews circulated Greg's photograph on social media while his eldest brother persuaded a journalist friend to run a short article on an inside page of the *Daily Tribune*. His sister and her tall, handsome, glossy-haired sons even called around to Tír na nÓg to see if they could help solve the mystery of Greg's disappearance. Liz made them tea while they made polite conversation and waited for news. But Greg didn't come back. The note, when it was finally found, asked that no one be blamed. Loneliness, Greg had written, is a mongrel that bites you just when you think you have it tamed. The water off Dun Laoghaire pier would have been freezing, the guards told Tom afterwards. He wouldn't have lasted long.

So, yeah, Liz had told Dean, her eyes half closed. 'Yeah. I knew Greg Butler.'

Her old school friend nodded.

'I remember reading the story now. Very sad. So, is money an issue? Do you need more money to keep the centre open at the weekends, is that it?'

She'd shrugged, unsure of why he was interested. Money, sure. But money wasn't everything, as the cliché went. Greg's family had had plenty of it, but it hadn't been enough in the end.

'But you're stuck for funds?' Dean had asked her again, an eagerness in his voice she couldn't understand. Then he'd explained what was on his mind. He was working, he said, as a freelance journalist, had just landed a couple of shifts at the news channel, Ireland 24, and was filming a series on what charities and other similar organisations wanted from the upcoming budget.

'I've a few interviews lined up already,' he'd told her. 'But I need, like, an expert. Someone who really knows what they are talking about. Would you do it?'

Liz had almost laughed in his face. Her – Liz Cafferky – on TV? But Dean, it seemed, was deadly serious.

'You'd be perfect! We're mad to get, like, new faces on screen, not just the same heads we're all sick of looking at. So – will you do it? Would you do a short interview with me?'

Liz had said no, no and no again, had told her boss about it and expected him to back her up, but Tom had muttered something about it 'doing her good' and refused to dismiss it out of hand. And Dean – the all new, all persuasive Dean – had eventually worn her down.

A couple of days later, she'd found herself staring at a huge television camera wielded by a gruff, middle-aged man in a navy fleece jacket, who insisted on her being filmed in her ridiculously untidy office because, he said, it would look right in the frame. Dean's questions came too quickly for her and she'd sensed his disappointment as she stumbled over her answers, saying, 'Yeah,' and, 'No,' to most, and even, 'I'm not really sure,' when he'd asked her a direct and overly complicated question about government policy and funds.

Then he'd looked at her and his voice had dropped and he'd asked her, quietly, as if there was no one else in the room, 'What about Greg? What sort of man was he? He had plenty of money, a roof over his head, a loving family. Why did he need to come here?'

Liz had taken a deep breath and told him everything she could remember – about Greg and his kindness; the way he used to let the older men win at Scrabble; how he never turned up at the centre without a cake or a box of chocolates, but wouldn't eat any himself, claiming he didn't have a sweet tooth. About how he told her once how peaceful it was to be in a place where no one made any demands of you.

'It's not all about money,' she'd told Dean then, her hands

cutting through the air. 'Sometimes it's just about having someone to talk to, and I don't necessarily mean big long counselling sessions either, although we can help people access them, if that's what they need. But sometimes it's just about people having the time to sit and listen to your stories, or joke with you or just bloody sit in the same room as you while you both watch the same rubbish show on TV. Simple human interaction, where you can just be yourself and people accept you for it. This place is a refuge, in the true sense of the word. A safe place to be.'

When she finally ran out of words, Dean winked at her and said, 'See? Told you you'd be fantastic!' Liz had forgotten the camera was even there.

She'd been mortified then, and flustered. Her hands shook so much that she nearly broke the tiny microphone as she removed it from her collar, and she found herself sounding almost petulant as she insisted to Dean and the cameraman and anyone else who would listen that she'd been useless and how they'd hardly use that on the evening news.

But she couldn't have been more wrong. That evening, she sat with Tom and a few of the lads in the Tír na nÓg sitting room and watched the interview on Ireland 24. Liz had hated how she'd looked on screen. There had been something almost aggressive about her, her long black hair flopping into her eyes, her skinny wrists sticking out of the baggy wholemeal jumper, which was the only clean item of clothing she'd been able to find that morning. She couldn't imagine anyone taking her seriously. She was embarrassed by herself, by the way her hands jabbed the air when she got excited, her tongue grew thick as she fumbled for the right words to convey the loneliness and the isolation she encountered every day.

But, to her surprise, as soon as the news was over, the men gave her a round of applause. Hours later, the news clip had gone viral, being shared, Dean told her, across Facebook and Twitter by people claiming she was a 'fresh voice' with something 'truly interesting to say'. Liz had just nodded, accepting what Dean was telling her with a kind of wonder. Unless she needed to do so for work, she never went online. The lads she met at the centre weren't the type to use electronic communication. And there was no one from her old life who she wanted to get in touch with or, more to point, who she wanted to be able to get in touch with her.

Then everything went even crazier. In the past three months, she had been interviewed four times – once more on television, twice on radio and once in a newspaper, as part of a feature called 'Young Women to Watch'. She'd particularly hated that piece, as they'd run a massive photograph of her looking cross-eyed and frustrated and had run one of those awful 'what's your favourite food and earliest memory?' questionnaires alongside the main piece. But Dean encouraged her to do everything she was offered and, to her amazement, her boss, Tom, did as well. Donations to the centre had been pouring in since she'd first appeared on TV, he'd told her. Men were calling round who'd never heard of the service before. They might even be able to open on weekends again.

Dean put down his phone and grinned at her.

'Well, just remember, when you're famous, that it was all down to me!'

'I have no intention of being famous, thank you.'

Liz's sigh came out heavier than she'd intended.

'But there is someone watching me, anyway.'

Dean, picking up on her glum tone, leaned forward. 'What do you mean?'

She reached into her pocket and took out the envelope, grubby now from repeated opening and resealing.

'This came to the office yesterday.'

Dean opened it and pulled out a newspaper cutting. It was a copy of the 'Women to Watch' interview. There was a printed note clipped to it. He read the words out loud, but he didn't have to. Liz had memorised them already.

'Dear Elizabeth. I've been watching you too and I hope to see you soon. Stephen.'

Her friend threw back his head and roared with laughter.

'Ha! Lizzie has a fan! God – maybe we do need to get you an agent!'

'Shut up, will you?'

Dean's notorious cackle had made a few heads in the café turn around and the last thing Liz wanted at that moment was more attention. Finally, Dean picked up on her mood.

'I'm sorry hon, this has freaked you out, hasn't it?'

'I dunno. A bit, I suppose.'

'Ah, here, don't let it bother you.' He bundled the sheets of paper up and stuffed them back in the envelope. 'This shit happens all the time, honestly. Two minutes on TV and people think they're your best mate. Seriously, it's no big deal.'

'I suppose.'

Liz sipped at her cooling coffee. Tom had said the same thing when she'd shown the letter around the centre the previous day and some of the lads had taken the piss out of her, telling her she was a star now and wouldn't want to know them. But at three o'clock that morning, as she lay awake in her apartment, it hadn't seemed so funny. There had been something – she didn't want to use the word *sinister*, didn't want to go there – but there had been something a little unsettling about the letter. Something weird. And she didn't have room in her life for weird anymore. In a sudden, decisive motion, she reached out, grabbed the envelope, crumpled it in her fist, threw it on top of their now-empty tray and deposited the lot on to the metal trolley on the other side of the aisle.

When she took her seat again, Dean looked at her, head to one side. 'That was signed, wasn't it? Maybe you should hold on to it . . .'

But the look on Liz's face made him, finally, realise she didn't want to joke around and he shrugged.

'Don't worry about it. Jesus. It's just one of those things, you know? It's a compliment, really. Won't be the last one, either; you're a natural on telly; I told you you would be. Anyway, enough about you, yeah? Let's talk about me, and all the fabulous things I've been doing . . .'

Liz exhaled gratefully as her friend settled into a complicated story about web pitches and uncontactable editors. Perfect. That was just what she needed – to let somebody else take the spotlight for a while.

CHAPTER THREE

'Good Jaysus. There must be hundreds of them. Can you imagine the smell if—'

'Don't.' Claire raised her hand. 'Let's not think about it, yeah? Not now, anyway.'

'Sure.' Flynn shrugged, his gaze still fixed on the pyramid in front of them. 'Still, though. It must have taken him ages.'

'Yeah.'

Claire was staring at it too. It was a complicated structure, a pyramid. The most solid structure found in nature. Or was that an egg? She couldn't remember. That was the sort of fact Matt came out with, not her. There was no need for Google when her husband was around. She'd even slagged him about it the previous week, told him that Anna would be sorted for homework when the time came. No need for an iPad; she had an iDad. The comment had come out a bit sharper than she had intended, actually. A mine of useless information, that's what she'd called him. Not to worry. Matt had a sense of humour.

But this was no ancient artefact and there'd be no archaeologists queuing up to organise tours. This structure was made of milk cartons. Hundreds and hundreds of yellowing, thankfully unopened, milk cartons, which stretched in neat rows from the floor to the damp, stained ceiling of James Mannion's sitting room.

Flynn dropped carefully to his knees, dirt and dust puffing out around him. 'I can't read all the dates but – Christ! These go back years.'

Claire stepped back and surveyed the sitting room again. It was in darkness, the watery winter daylight outside almost totally blocked by heavy velour drapes and yellowing net curtains. Those curtains had told her a lot about the neighbourhood when she had first arrived. Her own home was located on a similar red-bricked terrace, but, where she lived, most of the windows were clad in wooden blinds. Interior design shorthand for 'young couple moved in here, thought it was just a rung on the ladder, now they're stuck but they've painted everything white in the hope you won't notice the size'.

On James Mannion's street, however, it looked like most of the residents had been in situ for decades. Here, the windows were dressed in net curtains, and in a couple of the houses a religious statue was sandwiched between fabric and frame.

From the outside, there was little to make James Mannion's home stand out from the others. Inside, however, there was one major difference. At least, Claire hoped his was the only one on the street where the owner lay dead in the kitchen.

A mouse scurried across her foot. She flinched, and then shook her head firmly. Time to focus now.

'Poor oul divil.'

The words were an exhalation. Claire didn't respond, but heard and appreciated the kindness in Flynn's voice. Too many guards would be putting on the 'Big Man' act at this point, swaggering, cracking off-colour jokes or rolling their eyes to let it be known that they weren't affected by what they were looking at. And that would, for the most part, be bullshit. Claire knew from experience that the lads with the broadest swagger were usually the ones with the smallest balls and she'd seen more than one face drain of colour when the reality of a crime scene presented itself.

But Flynn didn't do swagger, or off-colour humour. He wasn't as dry a shite as she'd first feared – far from it. In fact, while they'd worked on the Miriam Twohy case together, she'd actually started to enjoy his company. He also knew when to keep a lid on it, and this was definitely one of those times.

'No one should have to live like this.'

This time she nodded, and met his gaze. 'It's rough.'

And that was an understatement.

A library, that was the first word that had come to her mind when she'd looked around the small house. She was reluctant even to call it a home. There were books everywhere – on shelves, in boxes, stacked neatly on the floor. A warehouse had been the second word, because every object in James Mannion's cluttered sitting room looked like it had been shelved or stacked against a wall by a machine. The books were all arranged in alphabetical order, a clock stood precisely in the centre of the mantelpiece, the only item out of place was a heavy glass vase which had fallen to the floor and could be seen peeping out from under the sofa. And then there were the milk cartons. Jesus only knew what the stench would be like if anyone tried to open them, but the care that had been taken over the erection of the structure was unmistakable.

However, unlike any library or cash 'n' carry Claire had ever been in, this place was filthy. The objects might have been neatly arranged but every single item was covered with dust, inches thick in places. Although the furniture in the room looked like it had once been expensive, the two heavy green armchairs were almost buried under more books and only one side of a matching velour sofa looked like it had ever actually been used. The sickly sweet aroma of damp clogged her nostrils and, on any other day, she assumed, would have been the dominant scent in the room. Today, however, the iron-rich scent of fresh blood was overlaying it.

Claire moved back from the pyramid and walked into the hall. The long legs sticking out of the kitchen doorway were dressed in stained grey trousers. Slacks, her mother would have called them. She stepped gingerly over the body, tried to avoid leaning against the torn brown wallpaper, found a foothold on the sticky kitchen floor. She bent her knees, rested on her hunkers, began to examine the scene.

The top half of the man's body was dressed in a wine-coloured jumper, covered in balls of fluff and worn through at the elbows. The collar of a grubby white shirt peeped over its neckline and curls of greying hair clung to the leathery skin at the nape of his neck. Her gaze travelled upwards. James Mannion had a fine head of hair for a man who, she had been told, was in his late sixties, but the thick locks couldn't quite conceal the large gash in the back of his head. Claire thought of the heavy crystal vase, half-hidden by the sofa. It would have to be forensically examined, of course, but she was in no doubt that she was looking at a murder scene and that the ornament could be the weapon.

Claire looked up from the body again. The man had been assaulted in the sitting room, in front of his neat piles of books and his pyramid, and had crawled in here to the kitchen to die. That much she knew from the trail of his blood. He would have found little comfort here, however. The kitchen was smaller than the sitting room but no cleaner. Filthy plates were piled up on a scratched metal draining board; food was encrusted on a stained and ancient two-ring cooker. In the corner, an old fridge gave off an intermittent hum.

'Who called it in?' Flynn's voice was strong, and carried easily from the sitting room, its clarity cutting through the fetid air.

Claire found herself responding equally briskly. 'Next-door neighbour. She calls in most days with a dinner for him, apparently. Says he never lets her past the front door but always opens it. Only yesterday he didn't. She gave it a while and, when she didn't see the lights go on in the sitting room last night, she got worried. Called us first thing this morning.'

'Can we talk to her?'

'Yeah. Uniforms are sitting with her, next door.'

'Grand. I just need to give the super a ring and—'

'Dear God in Heaven!'

Claire's head lifted sharply. Flynn was still in the sitting room. This voice had come from directly over her head.

'Who . . . ?'

Her words trailed off as she struggled to her feet, but the man loomed over her, blocking the entrance to the kitchen. As she was finding her footing on the sticky lino, he made a sudden strangled sound and then lunged towards her, knocking her to the floor.

CHAPTER FOUR

The blouse brought out the colour of her eyes. Stephen had never understood what that phrase meant before. But now, as he paused the programme and stared intently at the frozen image on his computer screen, he could see exactly what it meant. It wasn't a particularly special blouse; it was a murky dark-red colour and partially hidden by a shiny navy jacket that didn't even fit her properly. But, contrasted against it, her eyes were a deep, vivid green and, when she spoke to him, they shone.

When she spoke to the presenter, he should say. That lad beside her on the TV – who didn't deserve her.

She had extraordinary eyes. He clicked the mouse, allowed the programme to move forward for a few moments and then stopped it again. She was an extraordinary woman. So passionate. He could watch her all day. Watch how she nodded her head when she had something particularly important to say. Watch how her hands moved jerkily, thin wrists jabbing their way out of those red cuffs. Watch the half smile when she finally felt she was making progress, however slight. It was hard to know what age she was. Late twenties, maybe? She had young skin. And wise, shining eyes.

Sincere. She was so sincere. Your man on the news wasn't really listening to her. He was just doing that blank half smile they all did when you told them important things, things they didn't want to be bothered with. But she talked on regardless, words tripping over each other as she fought to make herself heard.

So sincere. A decent woman. A decent skin.

That was a phrase you didn't hear much anymore: a decent skin. It was what people used to say about his father, people who didn't know him. A decent skin: a hard-working man. A good businessman and employer too, well respected locally. Fond of his pint at the end of the day, but, sure, who wasn't? And, Stephen heard one of the teachers say one lunchtime, as he aimed his football at the wall and pretended he was enjoying playing alone, a man who didn't take root in the pub like some of the rest of them. No, you could see his father's car pull up at their house at six every evening. You could set your watch by him.

Stephen didn't wear a watch. He didn't need to then, or now. Thirty years had passed, but, no matter where he was or what he was doing, he instinctively knew when six o'clock was approaching. Felt the sky grow dim, even at the height of summer. Tasted bile at the back of his throat. Could feel his breath fluttering in his chest every time he heard a key crunch in a door. Maybe that was why he was happiest living alone.

The fear. The sound of his mother's voice, brittle in the kitchen, offering bright words about the nice bit of fish she'd bought for his daddy's tea. That gap between key-turn and greeting. The muttered hello that meant it had been a good day. The silence – or, worse, the dry, barked cough – that meant it hadn't. The acid in his stomach as the sitting-room door opened.

As neat as a new pin. That was something else they said about his father, but those who knew him best could see the signs. On the bad days, the tie would be loosened and pushed to the right, the top button of the shirt open. Ink marks on the cuffs, and a slight shake in the right hand.

Once, another boy in his class had asked him to come to his house for tea. Stephen had asked his mother for permission that evening and watched her face cloud over before she said no.

His daddy would worry about him, she said, going to a strange house on his own. And who were these people, anyway? Sure, we wouldn't know them from Adam. He was better off at home. Safe in his own place, with his own people.

But Stephen knew the real reason. Fellas went to other fellas' houses and asked them back in return. But that wasn't an option for him.

Her eyes were green – a vivid, almost emerald green, with a light shining out of them. He wasn't stupid, he knew it was the studio lights that made them look like that, but he couldn't stop staring at them, all the same. He clicked the pause button again. Elizabeth. She looked like a woman who cared about things, a woman who would listen to you. Maybe one day she would listen to him, too.

CHAPTER FIVE

'Afternoon, gentlemen!'

'Ah, howerya, Liz, love. 'Tis fresh and well you're lookin'!'

'Thanks, Richard.'

The other two silver heads didn't look up from their game of cards but Richard gave a lascivious wink as Liz poked her head into the sitting room. She offered her usual response, a wide but bland smile. Most of the men who used Tír na nÓg treated Liz either cautiously, as an authority figure, or jokily, as if she was a granddaughter they could tease. Richard, however, who lost no time in reminding anyone he met that he'd 'buried two wives' always seemed to be on the cusp of offering her the chance to apply for the role of number three. God. Liz repressed a shudder at the thought. Richard was a dapper man, to be fair to him, always well turned out in comparison to some of the others. She'd never seen him without immaculately pressed trousers and a shirt and tie, and he paid an inordinate amount of attention to the styling of his white, but still plentiful, head of hair. But he must have been, what? Sixty-eight? Seventy? Over twice her age, anyway, which hardly made her the ideal candidate to be the third Mrs . . . And there Liz drew a blank. What was Richard's second name again? Delaney, maybe? Hughes? No, it was gone.

Liz wasn't actually that great at remembering the names of everyone who visited the centre. The regular lads, sure, she remembered them alright, but the transient crowd, the fellas who only dropped in occasionally for a hot meal or a chat with Tom, didn't always make a lasting impression on her.

They all look the same to me.

She had said that to Tom once, in the early days, and he'd eaten the face off her. She hadn't meant it in a bad way, she'd explained, flustered by the strength of his reaction, and had gabbled about how much she admired the work the centre was doing and how she wanted to help the men as a group. She just didn't want to differentiate between them, that was all.

Bullshit, Tom had told her with an anger that was as fierce as it was unexpected. They are all individuals and, if you don't see that, you don't understand the place at all. They all have their own stories. *As do you*: his next, unsaid sentence. Unsaid, but she'd understood what he meant alright and ever since then had done her best to put name to face, separate grey head from bald. Focus on the eyes, not the wrinkles. It wasn't always easy. But she tried.

Ignoring the glint in Richard's eye, she walked back out into the hall and then stooped down to peel an abandoned pizza leaflet off the sole of her shoe. I really should get the Hoover out, she thought to herself, and then discarded the thought. It was impossible to get the place looking really clean, anyway.

Hundreds of muddy shoes and takeout meals had trodden a murky grey into the fibres of the once blue carpet, wallpaper peeled off the walls in cloud-shaped damp spots and the only shine in the place came from the layers of cheap gloss paint that Tom occasionally painted on to the woodwork in a vain attempt to spruce the place up. He only ever succeeded in making the rest of the house look even dingier, managing just a door or two before abandoning the project until his next, short-lived burst of enthusiasm.

In other hands, the house might have been beautiful. A two-storey red-brick on Dublin's north side, with high ceilings and much of the original cornicing still in place, Liz knew by looking at the neighbours' homes just how the building could be improved. But they didn't have the time, the money or, in Tom's case, the impetus to do anything about it. Her boss didn't seem to care how the place looked as long as the roof was secure.

'The lads mightn't feel comfortable if it was too dickied up,' he'd told her once, and she'd wondered if he was just making excuses not to do anything – had kind of admired him for it.

Leaving the sitting room behind, she kept walking down the hall and into the room Tom referred to as 'the office'. Although, even calling it a room was a bit optimistic, Liz thought. Owed a favour by the builder nephew of one of the clients, Tom had asked him to carve the house's original long dining room into two usable spaces. But the man had been called away on a paying job before he could complete the work, leaving the dividing wall rough and unfinished, with a five-centimetre gap between it and the ceiling at one end. The resulting space offered no privacy and anyone using 'the office' for a conversation or to make a phone call did so in the knowledge that they could be heard by everyone in the sitting room on the other side of the wall. Not that that mattered to Tom. He didn't like closed doors in Tír na nÓg; in fact, the only time Liz had seen him shut himself away with a client had been when a middle-aged man she'd never met before had called at the house one rainy afternoon, a letter turning to mush in his hand. Tom had ushered him into the kitchen and closed the door so gently it had sounded like a sigh. When they'd emerged twenty minutes later, they had been murmuring about flights and airfare. The man was Polish, Tom told her later. He'd lost his job and his home a few months earlier. The message about his father had taken almost a week to reach him. It was the least he could do, Tom said, to help him get home for the funeral.

That was Tom all over. Always ready to believe a sad story. That got him into trouble sometimes, of course. Most of the clients were lovely people, but that didn't mean Tír na nÓg didn't attract arseholes from time to time. Tom had installed CCTV cameras at the front door a couple of months previously, just to help them keep an eye on comings and goings, he said, but Liz wasn't sure if they'd make much of a difference. Most of the hassle happened inside the four walls, anyway. During her first week at the centre, she'd left her handbag on the kitchen counter and a man, younger and thinner than their usual clients, who'd turned up looking for a free lunch, had disappeared with the hundred quid she'd withdrawn to pay for her monthly bus ticket. Tom hadn't called the cops – told her she'd been lucky the man hadn't taken the bag as well, and that she'd have to be more careful in future. Then he offered to drive her home every day until she got the bus fare sorted.

Liz sank into one of the room's two mismatched chairs and heard an ominous creak. Falling apart, like everything else in the place. But at least the building was quiet that afternoon, and peace, rather than designer furniture, was what she needed. Coffee with Dean had been fun but the café had been too crowded and the conversation too fast, too involved. Over two years had passed since she'd restarted her life, but she still wasn't great with crowds or even normal everyday banter and her friend's chatter about 'profile' and 'reach' and 'social media' had thrown her completely. After yet another distracted 'Mm hmm', Dean had finally noticed her unease and offered to walk her back to the office afterwards, but she'd declined, craving her own company. Now, after a walk through the city centre, her iPod blocking out the world, Liz was almost back to herself and ready to work again.

And there was plenty to be done. Liz's appearance on the giant plasma screen might have impressed Dean and a few randomers in the coffee queue, but it had done nothing to tackle the teetering pile of post on her in-tray. Five of the envelopes were brown and she could see the letters V, A and T peeping out from at least two of the plastic windows. Her job title, laughably, was that of 'Communications Executive'. Tom had probably dreamed it up to satisfy whatever government department had offered to pay her a few bob as a graduate trainee. But, in reality, the role involved doing everything he didn't want to do. Paying bills, organising grants, dealing with plumbers. Being nice to the neighbours. Stuff he'd totally let slide over the past few years. It suited Liz fine. She could do the donkey work and he could get on with saving lives.

Saving lives. The words made her shiver. She had never thought of it like that before. But wasn't that what he did, when all things were considered? After all, he'd saved hers.

She had been on the boardwalk the night he'd found her, the wooden area overlooking the river in Dublin's city centre. She had been lying on the ground, her cheek pressed against the slats and remnants of Chinese food dumped there pre-, or possibly post-digestion. It made her nauseous now, just to think about it, but that night she had been too far gone to care.

'Are you alright? Can you tell me your name?'

She couldn't say it, but managed a 'Fuck off' alright, and turned her head away from him, shrugged his hand away when she felt it on her back, kept her eyes closed in the hope that he'd go away, but Tom Carthy was a persistent bastard.

'Are you ill? Is there anyone I can call for you?'

The next thing she remembered was the roughness of the car-seat fabric under her head and a smell of chips that would have made her puke if there had been anything there left to heave. Tom told her afterwards that she'd agreed to come with him and that, with his help, she'd been able to walk to the car herself. Liz believed him. Tom was a big guy, and she'd been even thinner back then, but even at three o'clock in the morning the sight of a formally dressed fifty-something man carrying an unconscious twenty-four-year-old back to his car would have surely raised some eyebrows. But she had to take his word for it because most of that night was a series of blanks interspersed with hazy memories. The car radio, playing country music at low volume. A streak of city lights against the window. The smell of vomit drying into her jeans. The radio played a song about a woman who had been gone a long, long time, and she remembered thinking that, if she was going to die, then at least she would be warm and dry.

Anyone could have taken her that night. Looking back now, from the safety of her office, her wonky chair and her teetering in-tray, Liz still shivered at the thought of it. She could have been raped, killed, thrown in the river, and no one would have missed her. She had been completely helpless and completely alone. There'd been others, earlier on that evening; they'd partied for hours, but her money had run out and, with it, their interest in her. They had left her slumped by the side of the river, completely disabled by booze and blow and a couple of tablets she didn't even know the name of. And, thanks be to whatever God had been watching out for her, Tom Carthy had found her. After the car journey, there were more gaps, but she did remember milky lukewarm tea and a musty blanket spread across a lumpy sofa – a feeling of warmth and being safe for the first time in a long time.

Months later, Tom told her he hadn't slept at all that night. Had sat on a chair outside the sitting room and berated himself for being so stupid. He should have taken her to a hospital, he'd told her, called an ambulance or the guards. He ran a men's drop-in centre; it had been stupid to bring a girl there. But he had made an impulsive decision and, in doing so, had saved her. And that's why she owed him. And that's why she was working five days a week in a job that paid her, badly, for three. That's why she had agreed to go on TV.

Tom Carthy rarely asked her for anything, so, when he did, she'd walk across hot coals to give it to him. Although, recently, she had started to wonder if that wouldn't be easier . . .

'Cup of tea, my darling?'

Liz blinked, looked up and then gave a faint smile as Richard poked his head through the open door.

'Yeah, OK. Sure.'

She pulled the chair gingerly across the floor until she was sitting at the computer. There was so much to be done; the question was which task was more important. Richard returned and pressed the cup of tea into her hand, his fingers lingering on hers for far longer than was necessary.

'That's lovely, thanks.'

Refusing to catch his eye, she waited till he'd left before raising the cup to her lips. She put it down again, the brown stain at the lip an unlovely reminder of how many had drunk from it before her. Right, that was that decision made. Tír na nÓg had a voluntary code whereby, if you drank from a cup, you washed it, but most of the lads were lazy about this at the best of times and the pathetic trickle from the kitchen tap was making them even lazier still. They needed to find a plumber urgently, and someone who wouldn't fleece them as well.

Putting the cup down on the desk beside her with a grimace – not only was it dirty, but there was scum floating on the top – Liz turned on the computer and launched the internet browser. She chose Google from the drop-down menu and then paused. What was it Dean had said? That she was trending on Twitter? Bollocks. She didn't even know what that meant. Mad stuff. Still, though, now she was here . . .

She entered the search engine, typed in her name and then gazed, open-mouthed, as the results unfolded. There were pages of them. Newspaper articles in which she was quoted. A thread on a discussion forum about an interview she had done – one poster thought she had made 'incredibly intelligent points', another felt she was 'out of her depth and talking through her arse'. A third opined that she *had* a great arse. A separate thread was devoted to her arse. Liz flushed, remembered the TV interview she'd done while standing up and the 'set-up shot', where the cameraman had filmed the back of her head while the reporter asked her questions over again. Clearly, more than her head had made it into the final edit.

Shaking her head, she remembered something else Dean had been wittering on about and ran another search, this time combining *Tír na nÓg* and *Facebook*. And there it was: the official Tír na nÓg Facebook page. Even to her untutored eye, Liz could see it was basic – no photos of Tom or any of the clients, just a blurred image of the outside of the building and a few lines of text:

Tír na nÓg is a drop-in centre for men who need to find a sense of community, some companionship or simply a cup of tea in Dublin's north inner city. All welcome.

So far so innocent, and Liz recognised the words that Tom had used in a thousand grant applications. But it was when she clicked into the comments under the photograph that her heart began to plummet.

> Hey, isn't that were that hot girl works?
>
> Does Liz Cafferky read this page? I'll donate to her any time.
>
> I'll fundraise for ya if I can get Liz Cafferky's number.
>
> Liz Cafferky shud be president for what she done for old people and the way she comes across on the TV is brilliant.
>
> Damien here from Liffey Live F.M. Anyone have a contact number for Liz?
>
> Hey, Liz, going to message you my number. Call me!
>
> I think I was in college with Liz Cafferky. Would love to reconnect. Can you get her to call me on 087 . . .

Suddenly dizzy, Liz bent double and felt the chair almost skid out from under her. She jammed her feet against the lino and fought for breath. Too much. Too soon. Not now.

Focus, Elizabeth. But the panic was coming in waves.

I think I was in college with Liz . . .

He might have been. She couldn't remember.

Blackouts. That's what they called them. But it wasn't the darkness that was the problem, more the flashes of memory that told her how bad things had been.

Evenings spent sweating in warm nightclubs, and then the rush of fresh air and cold brick against her back. Her top, hitched out of her jeans in one smooth movement. Her belt unbuckled.

'You're sure, yeah?'

'Yeah.'

Even when she didn't understand the question. Even when she didn't remember if it had been asked.

Beer breath mixing with hers. A tongue, poking. An arm burrowing. Once, her head held immobile, her cheek trapped in a large, clammy hand.

'You're sure, yeah?'

Yeah.

Because something was better than nothing at all.

The panic was sucking her under now, red heat flooding her cheeks. She pressed her fingers hard against her temples, trying to remove the memories, or bring them back. Either would be better than the grey fuzz in her mind. How many men had there been? She hadn't a clue.

She had thought she had left all that behind, had earned the right to start again. The whole TV thing had been unexpected and terrifying in many ways, but there was a sense of achievement wrapped up in there too, a validation. Tangible proof that things were better now, that she could start again, had started again. But maybe that wasn't possible, after all.

Her breath was coming in short pants and she knew that if she didn't calm down she was heading for another blackout, this time from oxygen deprivation. She hadn't had a panic attack in ages, but still recognised the signs.

Breathe. Relax. It could be nothing.

You're a terrible person.

A trickle of sweat ran down her back, her face was radiating heat and her mouth was bone dry.

You did bad things.

What was it Dean had said?

'This sort of thing probably happens all the time . . .'

They know what you've done.

She reached down and scrabbled in her pocket for her phone, found Dean's number and opened a new text message.

I need . . .

Then she deleted it and locked the phone again.

He wouldn't understand. Or maybe he would, and that would be worse still. She couldn't face telling him the whole story. He knew a small part of it; she'd had to tell him something to explain what she'd been doing in all the years since school. Tom knew more of it, but neither of them had the full picture, and that was the way she wanted it. If all the stories joined together then what had happened in her past would become real again and she couldn't live with that.

46

She put the phone back in her bag, sat straighter on the chair, forced her chest to inflate and then deflate again. Shuddered. Inhaled. Felt the oxygen hitting her blood stream. Exhaled. Don't think; be.

She turned to face the screen, forced herself to read the messages again:

> I think I was in college with Liz Cafferky. Would love to reconnect. Can you get her to call me . . . ?

Meaningless. There was no meaning to it. It wouldn't mean anything to her. Not if she didn't let it.

She slowed her breathing even further, focused on tuning out the buzzing in her ears. She thought about Tom, and what he'd say to her if he was here:

Don't mind them. It's just some oul rubbish. It's nothing to do with you, not really.

The Tom in her head was talking sense. She closed her eyes and focused on listening to him, told herself that the messages were just some shit, people flapping their gums, nothing to do with her, not really.

Then she clicked out of the Facebook page, swallowed a mouthful of lukewarm tea and stabbed the words *plumber* and *north Dublin* into the computer keys.

CHAPTER SIX

'You'll have another cup?'

Flynn opened his mouth to accept, then caught the full force of Sergeant Boyle's glare and shook his head, with some regret. He shifted his weight from one foot to another and resisted the urge to tug at his collar. Jesus, did no one on this road ever think to open a window? The smell in this sitting room was nothing compared to the stench next door, obviously, but the atmosphere was still stifling, a cloying mixture of overripe lilies, old-lady perfume and apple tart, cut through with the gassy emissions from the old-style Superser heater in the corner.

Across the room, the tall, grey-haired man who was perching awkwardly on the edge of a brown leather sofa took a sip from his own tea and sighed. His face was still a sickly grey colour, and his hands on the cup were shaking, but he seemed both awake and alert, a big improvement on how he had been just half an hour before.

As soon as he heard Boyle's muffled exclamation, Flynn had raced into James Mannion's kitchen to find her, arms out-stretched, straining to keep the tall man from collapsing on top of the victim's body. It must have taken some strength for her to do it, he mused. Although, the thought of what the tech guys would have said if they found out she'd let some bloke wander in off the street and dive on top of the corpse would undoubtedly have primed her muscles.

He'd helped her up then, and together they'd hauled the semi-conscious figure upright, before carrying him carefully across the floor and propping him in a sitting position against the wall.

'Tom Carthy,' he'd managed to mutter when they'd asked him his name, but he had refused, or hadn't been able, to say any more. Given the violence of his reaction and the fact that he clearly had a key to the murder victim's house, Flynn assumed they'd be taking him straight to Collins Street for questioning. But Boyle wasn't mad about the idea and, after following her back out into the small, narrow hall, Flynn understood why. Through the partially open front door, they could see that the usual crowd of rubberneckers had gathered on the street outside. Following a bollocking from Claire at having let Carthy in without warning, the uniform who had been posted at the crime-scene tape was doing his best, but the camera phones were out. One short, sixty-something man, his tweed jacket straining across his ample middle, was declaring to anyone who would listen that a white van full of 'dark lads' had been patrolling the area for weeks now, and that the guards had refused to take him seriously when he'd complained.

'All we feckin' need.'

Flynn understood Boyle's frustration. At least in the old

days you'd get an hour or so into an investigation before some well-connected hack ambled along to ask stupid questions. Now every eejit with a smartphone had a picture of the crime scene up online before you'd a chance to confirm the victim was dead. And if they got a shot of a man being taken away in a car for questioning, the image would be trending on Twitter before the lads in Collins Street had taken down his surname.

A sharp knock from the kitchen caused both of them to swivel round. Another uniform, the red-faced and red-haired Garda Halligan, had come to the back door and was staring in bemusement at the two bodies on the floor.

'Sorry to interrupt, sergeant, but the lady next door says she wants to make a statement. She reported the death, you see . . .'

Boyle's face had cleared. It had only taken a few moments for the three of them to raise Tom Carthy to his feet and retrace Garda Halligan's steps through the tiny backyard, out into the lane and through the wooden gate leading to the house next door. So now here they were, wedged into the neighbour's sitting room, the lady of the house smiling as calmly as if she was hosting her monthly book-club gathering. All a bit social for Flynn's liking, but at least the would-be reporters outside had no idea what they were doing.

Sergeant Boyle, who had been scribbling into her notebook, pulled herself up straighter on a wooden chair that had been pulled in from the kitchen, and cleared her throat.

'Mrs . . . um . . . ?'

'Delahunty. Margaret Delahunty. I did give all those details to that lovely young chap.'

'I know that, Mrs Delahunty. My apologies. It's very kind of you to invite us in. I'm sure Mr Carthy feels more comfortable here.'

'Are you sure you won't have a hot drop?'

'No, honestly. In fact, we really need to speak to Mr Carthy now, so . . .'

'Oh, grand, of course. I understand.'

Mrs Delahunty settled back in her own chair, patience written all over her face.

Flynn snorted – more at the expression on the sergeant's face than anything else – and then got the full side-eye treatment from his superior officer.

'I know Garda Halligan is still in the kitchen, so if you could just . . . ?'

The pause lasted one, two, three seconds, but finally the older woman got the hint.

'I suppose I should leave ye alone, so.'

'That'd be great, Mrs Delahunty. We won't be long.'

As the door finally closed, Claire pulled her chair until she was sitting directly opposite Tom Carthy and Flynn took another look around the room. Structurally, of course, it was the same as the one in which the body had been found next door, but the decor couldn't have been more different. Instead of books and bizarre dairy-based sculptures, Margaret Delahunty's walls were lined with glass-fronted cabinets and graduation photographs. She lived alone, she had told them, but her sitting room was still that of a family home.

'You're sure you feel well enough to speak to us?'

'Oh, yes.' Carthy nodded, and Flynn could see that his face, although still drawn, was starting to regain its normal colour. He was also, Flynn realised, younger than he had first thought. His grey hair was thick and wiry and the face underneath it was relatively unlined. In fact, Tom Carthy was probably only in his early fifties, and he was tall, with broad shoulders and a slim-hipped runner's body.

'I feel a bit foolish, actually.' Carthy attempted a smile. 'It's not like I haven't seen a dead body before. One of the lads from the centre passed away a couple of months ago, and there were my parents, of course. It's just . . . I'd never seen anything like that before.' He sighed, but his gaze remained steady. 'I wasn't expecting that.'

For a moment, 'that', the image of James Mannion's battered skull, hung in the still air. Boyle left it a beat then leaned forward again.

'Can you tell us when you last saw Mr Mannion?'

Carthy answered in a low but level voice. 'I suppose it would have been about two weeks ago? He wasn't one of our regulars. But we did see him at least once a fortnight, sometimes more.'

'And "we" are . . . ?'

He gave another, even fainter smile. 'I'm sorry; I should explain. I run Tír na nÓg; it's a drop-in centre for men in the parish. Our house is only a few streets away. We get a lot of visitors – all sorts, really. But it was set up with people like James in mind.'

Ah. Suddenly Flynn remembered why the name was so familiar. 'One of the lads took up a collection for you at

52

Christmas. Said he'd sent a fair few fellas over to you in his time.'

The older man's face brightened and he nodded eagerly. 'Ah, yes – Ray. Of course. He's a great supporter.'

'So you're a charity?'

Flynn, happy to let Boyle take the lead again, retreated to his spot by the window.

Carthy gave a faint smile. 'Would it help if I filled you in a bit on what we do?'

'Sure.'

Picking up on the briskness of Boyle's tone, he began to run through the story of his organisation as if he'd told it many times before.

He'd been working as a teacher in Dublin – P.E., he confirmed, and Flynn gave himself a mental pat on the back for having picked up on the athletic build – when he'd received a call to say his father needed him at home.

'One of the neighbours rang me. She sounded mortified, poor woman. My mother was only dead a couple of months and I'd say she thought he'd been on the batter. But it wasn't that simple.'

Carthy paused and stroked the side of his face, the fingers raking the patchy stubble.

'The home place is in Westmeath, just outside Athlone, so it took me nearly three hours to get down there, rush hour and that. But when I arrived at the house, Dad was still sitting out on the front step, refusing to move. Our neighbour had put a blanket around him and got a face full of abuse for her trouble,

53

poor woman. Dad told her to shag off and that he was waiting for his wife to come home.'

As Carthy shifted in his seat, Flynn thought he detected a glisten of tears, but with a blink they disappeared.

'I'll keep it short for you. Turned out he was in the early stages of Alzheimer's. Mam had been keeping it from me. Typical. Didn't want to be bothering me, apparently – I'm an only child. She thought I had my hands full.'

He smiled at Claire and shrugged, a 'you know, yourself' gesture, presumably designed to convey the martyrdom of the Irish mammy. As Flynn expected, the sergeant didn't smile back. The whole 'appeal to the feminine side' malarkey never worked on her. After a moment, Carthy continued.

'She died in her sleep – a heart attack, God rest her. Dad wasn't himself at the funeral, but I put it down to shock. He insisted I was to go back to work as soon as possible, so I did, after a couple of days. Stupid of me, not to notice what was going on, but I was upset myself, I suppose. Anyway, after that night in the garden, he was never really well again. I gave up my job, moved down home – well, it's what you do, isn't it? He went downhill quickly after that. Didn't know me at all in the end.'

'Sorry to hear that.'

Carthy gave Flynn a quick, upwards nod. 'Thanks. These things happen, sure. But look, that's how it all started, really. I've no siblings, so I inherited the house and whatever few bob there was. I'd no need for it myself, so I bought a house up here and set up Tír na nÓg. To be honest, it wouldn't take a psychologist to say I was doing it for them. For the mother, and especially for the oul fella. I just wanted there to be somewhere for oul lads like him to go, you know? Not overnight, we don't have the money, or the space to provide beds. But we cook a dinner most days, and there's a phone and the internet, so we try and get them sorted for emergency accommodation if they need it. And many of them, like James, have their own places, anyway. They're not all hard up; in fact, some of them would be quite well off, relatively speaking. But being able to pay your bills on time doesn't mean you never get lonely. They just need somewhere to go during the day. It's not much. But they seem to get a bit of ease from it.'

'You mentioned "we"?'

Carthy nodded. 'Yeah. I ran it myself for a while, but a couple of years ago we got funding for another worker. One of those government schemes. Liz is supposed to be with us three days a week, but she does way more than that, way more than she's paid to do. She'd have known James too; I can give you her number.'

'Thanks.'

Boyle made a note, but she wasn't finished with Carthy yet.

'And what can you tell us about Mr Mannion?'

'James?' Carthy paused and ran a hand over his hair. 'James Mannion was one of nature's gentlemen. One of the other lads brought him in six months ago – one of the rough sleepers. I've a feeling James might have thrown a few bob into his hat and they got into conversation. He came in around once a week, I suppose. Never arrived empty-handed. We don't allow the men to drink alcohol on the premises, but we go through buckets of tea. James would never drop in without a packet of biscuits or an apple cake or something.'

He paused, swallowed and continued.

'He even brought a chessboard one day and started teaching some of the others how to play. It's still there. We'll miss him.'

His voice finally cracked, but, as Flynn noted with interest, Boyle didn't give him time to compose himself.

'What was his interaction like with the other men? Would he have had a particular friend?'

'No, not really. James was always a little different from the others. He was an educated man – you could tell that after a couple minutes talking to him. One of the other lads said he was a retired teacher, although he never told me that himself. I'd well believe it, though; a conversation with him could be a real education in and of itself; you never knew what he'd come out with. And he loved books. Always had one sticking out of the pocket. Well – you saw that yourself today.'

Flynn repressed a shiver. The smell of the damp, under-heated house was still in his nostrils and he knew, if he closed his eyes, he could easily call the rows and rows of neatly stacked books to mind. But Carthy was still talking.

'He was a lovely man, James, but he wasn't without his problems. We could all see that. He had a few . . . habits, I suppose you'd call them. He never ate or drank at our place, not even a cup of tea. And – OK, I know this sounds weird, but he didn't like shaking hands. He'd do it if he had to, but he'd wash them straight afterwards, or clean them on his trousers, like this,'

Carthy made a brisk rubbing movement on his thighs. 'He'd do anything to avoid getting dirty. But that was just how it was, you know? A lot of the men who visit us have their own ways of doing things, detective. They are – how would I put it? – men who don't quite fit in with the rest of the world.'

Flynn got it and didn't get it at the same time. What Carthy was saying made sense given the order in the house, the almost mathematical way in which the books had been arranged, even the extraordinary pyramid. But the place had been absolutely filthy as well, which didn't fit in with the type of man being described.

Carthy smiled faintly as if reading his mind.

'I know; doesn't really make sense, does it? But, as I said, James had his problems. And in the last few months it became clear to all of us that he wasn't a well man. It wasn't just old age. I don't think James was seventy, even. But he'd started to fail in the last few months, fail badly. The weight was dropping off him – I mentioned it to him a few weeks ago, but he brushed me off. But every time he called around it was as if he had aged another year. And as well as that . . .'

He paused, squeezed his eyes shut for a moment and continued.

'Ah, the mind was starting to go, as well. He lost a few games of chess – I thought he was being kind at first, letting the other fellas win. But the truth of it was he just wasn't up to it anymore. He used to get grumpy when he lost a game – aggressive, even. That wasn't James. Jesus, he had his odd moments, but he was the kindest man you could ever meet, and the gentlest.

And the clothes – he was always neat, James. Well turned out. But the last few times I saw him, he just wore the same stained jumper, over and over again.'

'Did you ask him what was going on?'

Fascinated now, Flynn took a step away from the window as Boyle made the enquiry.

Carthy nodded, slowly. 'I did, of course. But the last thing our clients want is someone asking too many questions. James Mannion was a proud man, and a very private one. I dropped him home a few times in the last while, when it was clear he wasn't up to the walk. He gave me a key to the house – he said it was in case he ever locked himself out, but, thinking back, it should have been a clue that he wasn't feeling well, that he thought there might come a time I'd need to get in, maybe. But he never invited me past the front door.'

Sergeant Boyle closed her notebook with a snap. 'We may need to talk to you again.'

'Of course.' Tom Carthy pinched the bridge of his nose and squeezed his eyes shut wearily. 'Anything I can do. The thing is . . .'

He stood up, making Flynn jump with the suddenness of the movement. He was even taller than he had first imagined – six three, maybe – and towered over Sergeant Boyle as he addressed her directly.

'Do you think, officer . . . Do you think, maybe, it was an ease to him?'

Moving closer, Flynn could see the sergeant frown.

'I'm sorry, Mr Carthy, I'm not quite sure what you mean.'

'The sudden death – was it the best thing for him, maybe? Lookit, James wasn't a well man, we could all see that, and he wasn't a happy one, either. Maybe it was best, that he was taken so quickly?'

The sergeant shook her head, seemingly at a loss as to how anyone who had seen James Mannion's battered skull could even countenance such a thought.

As if understanding her confusion, Carthy shrugged. 'No, no it wasn't, of course. Wishful thinking on my part, I suppose. Poor James. Maybe he's at peace now, anyway. God rest his soul.'

CHAPTER SEVEN

'So that's all you got out of him?'

'For the moment, yeah.' Claire took a bite out of her lasagne, swallowed without tasting it and took another, bigger one. 'D'you make that? 'S nice.'

'No.' Matt shook his head, wearily. 'M&S. By the time I got her home and changed, it was after six, and then Tim wanted to talk to me about the new system.'

Claire took another huge bite. ''S nice, though. Grand.'

'Ah, yeah.'

Matt took a forkful of the dinner himself and chewed, slowly. There was a moment's reverential silence and then Claire's eyes flicked towards the blank television screen. After two weeks, during which Anna's first cold had caused her to produce enough mucus and other bodily fluids to remake *The Exorcist*, it sounded like she was finally, blissfully fast asleep. Fantastic. Maybe Claire could get an hour to herself. She had that Swedish series taped . . .

'So you reckon he's on the level, yeah?'

But Matt, it seemed, wanted to talk – to reconnect with his

wife over a ready meal and a glass of their finest tap water. Well, in fairness, Claire realised, he had a right to. After all, it was the first time in over a fortnight that they'd both eaten a meal in the same room without somebody screaming at them – 'somebody' being a small girl whose lung capacity was far in excess of her size. And, in the days Claire was rapidly starting to think of as 'old', even though they happened less than a year ago, she used to enjoy discussing cases with him. Not the classified stuff, obviously, but the 'big picture' information. The stuff she knew and the stuff she wanted to know and the stuff that was bugging her. She'd lay the facts out in front of him and watch as his computer programmer's mind stacked them up in ordered lines. Often, they'd find a pattern that way.

But that was then. Just now, the musty smell of James Mannion's sitting room still hanging in her nostrils, all Claire really wanted to do was nothing at all. Her brain felt like a computer with too many windows open and she would have given anything for an hour of peace, and some shite telly, to shut them all down.

Sensing the dip in her mood, Matt left the room, returning with two bottles of beer.

'Can I tempt you?'

'Ah, no, I—'

The baby monitor crackled and they both held their breath, but after a moment it fell silent again. In fact, Claire could swear she could hear a tiny baby snore. 'Calpol?'

He shook his head. 'No, Coors Light.' Then, laughing in the face of her eye-roll, he continued. 'She's drug-free. I think that tooth broke through; your mother might have been on to something, there.'

Good Jaysus. Baby teeth and Nuala Boyle. Even shop talk would be better than that. Claire took a long swig from her beer, turned her face away from the television and arranged a bright smile on her face.

'I think he told us all there is to know about Mannion, yeah. But it's not much to go on.'

Her husband's hand stroked her shoulder blade and she shifted a couple of inches away. There was too much work stuff, too much baby stuff, too much of everything stuffing up her head.

'So, let's go through it all in detail.' Matt gazed at her, soulfully.

Claire gave a weak smile. 'Well, I thought he was very interesting; I mean—'

Her husband threw back his head and roared with laughter. 'God, Boyle, you wouldn't want to take up poker, anyway. You just want me to feck off, don't you?'

'Huh?' Claire was halfway down the bottle now. 'Not at all; dying for a chat.'

'You are in your arse. You want to look at the telly and think about nothing for an hour!'

She tried to muster a face of indignation, but it collapsed in a giggle. 'Kinda, yeah.'

'Well, you go for it. I'll stick the dishwasher on.'

And that's why I married him, folks.

She raised her beer in a toast to the now-empty sitting room, sank back into the sofa and grabbed the remote. But even as she was scrolling through the recorded programmes, she realised the Swedish crime thriller had lost its appeal. She didn't think there was enough juice left in her brain to follow a complicated plot in English, let alone with subtitles thrown in. Stabbing at the remote again, she poked around the menu for a couple of moments, but nothing grabbed her. Home-improvement show? Seen it. A *Prime Time* special on the Garda commissioner? Too much like homework. Crappy romcom on RTE2? That would do.

In front of her, a pre-Oscar Matthew McConaughey tried to persuade a girl that he was more than a set of abs and a southern accent, and Claire tried to lose herself in the plot, such as it was. But her brain wouldn't stop ticking over.

Tom Carthy had waffled on in places, that was for sure, but Claire had believed his story – well, most of it, anyway. There had been a few issues she wanted to double check, but the same was true for all witnesses. In fact, it was the ones who told their stories straight, without minor inconsistencies, that you usually had to worry about.

No, Claire felt happy enough with their chat with Tom Carthy, and had learned quite a bit about the dead man, some of which was sure to prove useful. Margaret Delahunty, how-ever, was another story. She was a talker and, as Claire knew from experience, that wasn't necessarily a good thing. As soon as Carthy had left, again by the back door, and Mrs Delahunty had been released from the kitchen, she'd settled back on the overstuffed armchair and yapped for Ireland, offering several theories about what might have happened to Mannion, most of them borderline racist and none of them of any practical use. But then Flynn, fair play to him, had stepped up to the cake plate and, after ramping the bogger accent up to eleven and putting away more pie than could possibly have been good for him, had managed to get Margaret Delahunty to clarify a few things.

James Mannion had, according to his next-door neighbour, lived on Darcy Terrace for more than twenty-five years, making a living doing odd jobs – painting, gardening, cleaning guttering, that sort of thing. Jobs too small for professionals to be bothered with and that presumably saw him paid cash in hand. Mrs Delahunty had stopped at that point, looking anxiously at the guards as if she'd said too much, but Claire had more to be bothered about than the victim's tax-clearance certificate and motioned impatiently at her to continue.

'So he hadn't worked in recent years?'

'No.' Mrs Delahunty took a sip of tea and grimaced. 'No, sure, he'd be in his late sixties now. Look, this is freezing. I'll just make another ...'

But Claire had come to the end of her patience. 'Would he have had much of a routine, then? Since he retired?'

'Ah, you'd see him round and about, alright. Up and down to the library. He was very fond of his books; I suppose Tom told you that?'

'He did, yes. But he also said Mr Mannion hadn't been well this past while.'

Mrs Delahunty shook her head. 'He wasn't himself at all

these last few months, anyone could have seen that. Sure, he walked past me in the street one morning when I was on my way back from Mass; didn't even salute me. I called in to him that day, offered to bring him in here for a bit of dinner but he wouldn't hear of it. I'd a mind to ring his niece over in England, but I didn't have her number. Ye'll have it, though? Poor girl. That's desperate news to have to get over the phone.'

'Niece?'

Suddenly aware she had command of her audience, Margaret Delahunty gathered her cardigan around her self-importantly and took a forkful of pastry.

'Yes, his niece. Lovely girl. You didn't know about her, so? Lives over in Bristol, I think – or was it Birmingham? She called at his door a couple of years ago – that's when I met her. James never let her in, though, poor girl. She was banging on the door so loudly, I said to myself, "You'll wake the dead in America, child." But James didn't stir.'

Claire nodded eagerly and the woman, a crumb dangling precariously from the edge of her mouth, continued.

'"Uncle James!" That's what she was saying. "Uncle James! Uncle James, just let me in!" But he never came out to her. I knew he was in there; I saw the net curtains twitch. But he never opened the door. That wasn't a bit like him. He had his odd moments, did James, but I always found him to be a very polite man. Sure, the poor girl was freezing by the time I brought her in here, and in a terrible state. Angela, she told me her name was, and her father was James's older brother, Paul. Well, Paul had passed away suddenly – heart attack, poor man –' Mrs Delahunty blessed herself before continuing – 'and the next thing this poor Angela knew, she and her mother got a solicitor's letter from Ireland asking them what they wanted to do about the land, and whether or not Paul's brother was to be informed of his passing. Sure, they hadn't known about any land, or any brother, for that matter. It turned out Paul had a small farm – a few fields, really – that he'd rented out this past thirty years. And, seeing as he hadn't made a will, it would all go to Angela and her mother, but the brother had to be informed about it too. I was very confused, just listening to her.'

Resisting the urge to say, 'I know how you felt,' Claire gave her what she hoped was an encouraging nod.

Mrs Delahunty took another sip of tea before continuing.

'So this Angela got James's address off the solicitor and, when the funeral was over, made her way here. She just wanted to talk to her uncle, I think, find out who he was and why her father hadn't mentioned him. But she only got as far as the door. James wouldn't let her in. So, now!' Mrs Delahunty sat back with the satisfied air of one who knew she'd held her audience, and drained her tea.

Claire leaned forward in her seat and kept her voice as con-versational as possible. 'Did she tell you why the brothers were – estranged?'

'Sure, she didn't know, poor girl! Isn't that what I'm after telling you? The solicitor knew nothing and James didn't let her past the front door. She went home knowing no more than when she came.'

'OK.'

Aware that she'd probably exhausted Mrs Delahunty's supply of useful information, Claire closed her notebook and began to gather her things. But the older woman reached across and grabbed her arm.

'James was a fine man.'

'I'm sure he was, Mrs Delahunty,' Claire said, rooting around in her bag for her phone, which she'd turned off at the start of the conversation.

But Mrs Delahunty wasn't finished.

'I invited him in here all the time, you know, but he never came. Not even on Christmas Day. I'd hand him in a dinner and he'd give me the plate back – always washed, always spotless – but he never came in this door.'

'OK.'

Aware that it had been hours since she'd contacted Collins Street and that the super would be climbing the walls waiting for information, Claire stood up to leave.

But the old woman opposite her was crying now.

'I'm here all day – all bloody day looking out this window and not a stray dog goes down the street that I don't see it. And today I saw nothing!'

Claire's hand landed finally on the phone. As she pulled it out to check her missed calls, Flynn walked in front of her and pushed a tissue into the old woman's hand.

'It sounds like you were a great friend to him,' he said.

'I did my best.' Mrs Delahunty blew her nose noisily and sighed again. 'He was gay, you know.'

'OK . . . ?' Flynn's voice was gentle, but quizzical.

The elderly woman sniffed again. 'I'm sure that had nothing to do with it. But I just thought, you know . . . that maybe it was something you should know.'

Flynn continued in the same, gentle tone. 'And did he . . . Is that something Mr Mannion told you himself? Did he have a partner, or . . . ?'

The old woman flashed a sudden grin. 'Not at all. It wasn't the sort of thing that comes up in conversation. Poor James, he had nobody, God rest his soul. No, it was just something I knew. I knew it about my Robert without any of them having to tell me.'

She turned her head and smiled at the largest of the photos on the wall – a studio shot of a sallow-skinned graduate, mortar board perched precariously on top of a cloud of fuzzy nine-teen-eighties hair.

'"Gaydar" is what you call it, apparently – I read it in a magazine!'

Both Flynn and Claire smiled, the tension in the room easing.

Mrs Delahunty pulled the tissue across her eyes again. 'I knew poor James was that way inclined alright. Never bothered me. But I just thought, you know . . . that it might be of interest to you. In case it helps with anything.'

Her smile had vanished again as she realised that 'anything' in this case involved the brutal murder of her friend and neigh-bour on the other side of a very thin wall.

'All done!'

Claire started as her husband returned from the kitchen, a fresh bottle of beer in hand.

'Kitchen cleaned and bottles washed!'

She blinked and shook her head. 'Jesus, fair play to you, I was miles away.'

'I know.' He sat back down on the sofa, closer to her this time.

'I never even asked – how was your day?'

'Grand. Meeting went well, got another decent bit of the project done and herself was in better humour. So all grand.' Matt's tone was light but he placed his arm around her again, his fingers tracing gentle circles on her shoulder blades.

This time Claire didn't pull away. 'D'ya reckon she'll sleep?'

They looked towards the baby monitor.

'Ah, she will, yeah. For a few hours, anyway.'

It was the most romantic thing either of them had said in weeks.

Afterwards, as she switched the bedroom light off and nestled into him, Claire heard the familiar whimper coming from the room next door. Matt stirred sleepily but she kissed him on the forehead.

'I'll go.'

'Ah no . . .'

But he was fully asleep before he could finish the sentence. Moving quickly, Claire made it into the tiny box room she kept forgetting to call 'the nursery' before the baby worked herself up into a full cry. There was a carton of formula on the shelf and she poured it neatly into the clean bottle she'd stuck into the pocket of her dressing gown before coming to bed. There had been a time when she would have stuffed a bottle of wine and two glasses in there, but this was their reality now. Matt's books said Anna shouldn't be feeding at night anymore. Well, her little girl couldn't read yet. The baby had had a tough few weeks, having to get used to the crèche and her mother going back to work and being strapped into her car seat and handed from parent to parent on the side of the road. It would do them both good to have a cuddle. Tilting the bottle, Claire picked the baby up, then sank down on the rocking chair that had seemed like such an extravagance at the time but had actually been one of the most useful things Matt had bought in his pre-baby shopping spree.

'How's my doteen, then? How's my little girl?'

The little pink lips reached for the teat instinctively and Claire rubbed her cheek against the soft downiness of Anna's hair as she sucked, first eagerly and then more slowly, moulding her body into her mother's arms.

'That's the best baba, now.'

God, but things were good – really good – at the moment. Maternity leave had been fun. But there had been something unreal about it, all that drinking coffee and hanging around in shopping centres and parks, not to mention that one never-to-be-repeated trip to the mother-and-baby group. It had felt totally manufactured and, although you were never supposed to say such a thing, a little boring. Claire wondered if Matt had found it boring too, coming home every night to a discussion about nipple confusion and sterilising and how much the little girl had pooed.

Things were good now, though.

The bottle slipped out of Anna's lips as she drifted back to sleep and Claire picked her up and placed her gently against her shoulder. It was tiring, being back at work, trying to do everything. But nice to get her brain moving again.

And tonight with Matt – that had been good too.

Change was good.

The baby burped – a fine, fat Guinness burp – and then fell totally unconscious. Smiling, Claire laid her gently back down in the cot and pulled the fleece blanket close to her cheek, the way she liked it.

Something had changed for James Mannion too. She needed to find out what had happened, and what his niece had found out about him. Maybe those two things were completely unconnected with his death. But, at the moment, they were all she had to go on.

Anna was deeply asleep now, but Claire lingered for another moment, watching the tiny chest rise and fall. The baby would sleep till morning, as would her father. But her mother had a few things to think about first.

CHAPTER EIGHT

'One of our lads, one of the regulars, he told me once that he used to go down to the local shop and buy a paper every morning, even when he couldn't afford it, just to talk to someone. Just to prove he was alive. He said to me one day, "If I catch sight of myself on one of them cameras over the counter, then I'll know I've made it through another night." That's what he told me. Now he comes into us three times a week and drives the others mad, grabbing the paper and filling in the crossword before they get a look at it. He looks ten years younger than he did when I first met him. Ten years. So that's what we give them. A bloody newspaper, shared between ten men, and buckets of tea. And the knowledge that they are alive.'

Liz realised she was doing that weird jabbing motion with her hand again and, suddenly self-conscious, pulled it back down on to her lap. Beside her, the man with the receding hairline and the large pile of notes opened his mouth to speak, but the glamorous brunette sitting opposite them raised her own hand, smiled and shook her head.

'And that's all we have time for this lunchtime! I'd like to thank my guests, Liz Cafferky and Councillor Micheál Walsh, for joining us; fascinating stuff, I'm sure you'll agree. We'll take a break now . . .'

The clock on the wall counted down ten seconds, five, three, two, and then the sound of the news jingle filled the small studio. The presenter, Sophie, took off her headphones and smiled.

'That was fantastic, folks, great stuff. Thanks a million.'

Her voice was warm, but her eyes were already darting to the pile of scripts on the table in front of her and Liz recognised her cue to go. Grabbing her bag from the floor, she followed the politician out through the heavy studio door and into the control room. The tall man in the denim shirt who'd been watching them through the glass stood up from behind a desk-top computer and stuck out his hand.

'Thanks, Micheál; that was great.'

A mutter, a quick handshake and the politician was gone, the studio door almost catching on his heels as he made his rapid exit.

Liz looked after him, bemused, and the tall man – Ian, she thought his name was – laughed.

'I'm not surprised he didn't want to hang around!'

'Really?' Liz took a quick look around the room to see if there was a fire or something that could explain the quick getaway.

'Ah, you had him on the run there at the finish. It was a great debate; we really appreciate it. We've had loads of texts about

73

it and tonnes of comments on our Twitter feed too – look.'

He pointed back towards his computer screen but Liz shook her head.

'I don't do the Twitter thing, sorry.'

Ian smiled. He had a nice smile, Liz thought. Genuine.

'Fair play to you! I'd probably be a lot more productive if it wasn't for the technology, but – you know, yourself – we have to keep up with it. Thirty per cent of our listeners are online at this stage; there's a big push on to get them liking the Facebook page.'

'Hmm.'

Liz smiled, vaguely, and let the words wash over her. Now that the adrenaline buzz from the interview was fading, she was starting to realise just how exhausted she felt. It had been a terrible couple of days. The news of James Mannion's death had come as a shock to everyone at Tír na nÓg. But it was Tom's reaction that had upset her most. Everything had tilted the moment he gathered the men together in the sitting room and told them the news. It was only then, as tears ran down his face and his voice shook, that Liz realised how much she needed him. Needed him to be strong, constant, supportive. Needed him to be there. Hearing his voice quiver, watching him so close to losing control, made her feel, well, gutted was the word that came to mind. Hollow inside.

She'd thought about hugging him, decided against it and made tea instead. And, as she'd handed him the mug, he'd looked at her with an expression of such bleakness that she couldn't hold his gaze and turned away instead, muttering about sugar and the need to keep the kettle filled. When she looked back, he had blinked the sadness away – straightened his shoulders, swallowed some tea – turned back into the Tom she relied on. He thanked her for the drink then and opened the door to the guards who had turned up to take everybody's statements. Anyone who had spoken to James in the previous weeks had to speak to them, apparently. Tom warned the cops they would be dealing with vulnerable men, men who had to be minded. As he said that word, *vulnerable*, his eyes had met hers again and she had felt minded too. Tom was in charge and everything would be OK.

So, when he'd asked her to do the radio interview that morning, she hadn't felt able to refuse. There was a rumour, he told her, that funding to centres like theirs would be cut in the forthcoming budget. The station wanted someone to go on air and explain why that shouldn't happen. Liz had agreed, reluctantly. Then, to her absolute amazement, had found that she'd enjoyed every minute of it.

There had been something stimulating about it, so challenging. Making points and scoring points and forcing a politician thirty years her senior to agree she had a point. Feeling listened to, respected. Taken seriously. She'd been playing this part for over three months but now, for the first time, it was like she was doing it for real. There was another Liz who appeared as soon as she sat in front of a microphone. A confident, fluent woman, completely secure in herself and her abilities. A whole new person.

And it looked like this dude, Ian, really liked her.

'Thirty seconds!'

Liz hadn't noticed the technician, sitting half hidden behind the large radio desk, but Ian turned to him.

'Absolutely, be with you now. Listen, Liz –' he stuck out his hand again – 'it was fantastic meeting you; I really hope you come in again. Oh, and . . .' He paused as the sound engineer fired the sting for the news bulletin, and then turned back again. 'My sister just texted; she says to say hi!'

'Your sister?' Liz stared at him, puzzled.

'Yeah! Small world, eh? Lara Flaherty? She says you were a friend of a friend, or something; met you out a few times? Maybe four, five years ago? She said you mightn't remember her, but to say hi, anyway; she heard you on air this morning – said you did a great job!'

'I'm sorry, I don't—' Liz took back her hand.

'Just thought I'd pass it on, anyway!' And he turned away, his brain clearly racing ahead to the job in front of him.

Rattled, Liz pressed against the heavy studio door. Lara. Didn't ring any bells, but that wasn't surprising. Lara. No, nothing. Her stomach churned. That was the bit she hated most, when she looked back on everything that had happened: the blank spaces. The Fear, she heard people call it, jokingly. But there was nothing funny about it. Nothing funny about people coming up to her and saying, 'Hey, you were crazy last night!' and her laughing and backing away and trying to pretend she knew what they were talking about.

Unsettled, she pulled the door tight behind her and walked

slowly down the corridor that led to the main reception area. She hadn't had time to eat lunch; she'd grab a sandwich – that would make her feel better.

'Ah, Liz! The star of the show, huh?'

'I'm sorry? Richard?'

Away from Tír na nÓg, it took her a moment to recognise her least favourite client. Richard strode across the reception area and held out his hand.

'Bloody brilliant performance, if you don't mind me saying so! First class, first class indeed!'

Unable to avoid it, she returned a limp handshake and then cringed when his sweaty palm gripped hers for far too long.

'What are you doing here?' She was aware she sounded rude, but didn't care. This was completely out of order, his turning up here. But Richard, oblivious to her discomfort, just grinned.

'I was listening to you, you see, on the radio. And I only live down the road so I thought I'd drop in, say hi. We can walk in together, if you like? If you're going straight into work? Or I'd be happy to buy you a cup of tea?'

Was that a nervous laugh? Jesus Christ, was he asking her out? Something halfway between a giggle and a gasp caught in her throat and Liz shook her head.

'I don't think . . .' She pulled her hand away, saw disappointment in his eyes and something else – aggression, maybe? Christ almighty, just who did this guy think he was? Her first thought was how quickly she'd be able to get rid of him. Her second, how annoyed Tom would be if he knew she was thinking that way. Treat the men with kindness, treat them with respect, was his mantra. Well, feck that, Liz thought to herself. Tom didn't know what it was like to be the only woman in the centre. You needed to keep some sort of distance. Most of the clients were brilliant, total gentlemen, but every so often one or two of them came close to crossing the line, and today, by turning up at the station unannounced, Richard had stepped right over it.

'I'm actually not going back to Tír na nÓg right now; I'm meeting some friends. So I'll see you later, alright?'

Not bothering to hear his response, she strode across the reception area, pushed through the heavy double doors and walked quickly out on to the street. She took a quick look around to make sure he wasn't following close behind and then broke into a sprint, through a damp laneway and out on to the main road, not stopping until she was sure she was free.

Leaning, panting, against a garden wall, she fought the urge to laugh. Jesus, she hadn't run that fast from a fella since the fifth-year disco. Then again, maybe she'd be better off if she had run away more often – from fellas, and temptation in general. Her smile faded. Her mouth was bone dry but she'd forgotten to bring any water with her. Stupid thing to do.

The electronic sign on a nearby shelter said the next bus into town was fifteen minutes away. That would give Richard plenty of time to catch up with her, if he was so inclined. Prising herself away from the wall, Liz decided to walk home instead, and then realised she had forgotten her iPod too. More stupidity. Stupid girl.

Get a grip, Elizabeth. He's just some oul fella who thinks he's still a player. Nothing more to it than that. Don't beat yourself up. But the unplanned sprint, together with the adrenaline dip following the radio interview, had left her shaken and unsure.

Her heart was pounding now and she tried to slow her breathing down.

My sister said to say hi – really? It was probably nothing, just a coincidence, one of the thousands that happened in Dublin every day. But Liz couldn't say that for definite, because she couldn't remember anything. Had she insulted the woman one night or stolen her boyfriend? Kissed him on the dance floor where everyone could see?

A blush flooded across her cheeks. She was sweating now, and not just from the run. Who did she think she was, anyway? The bright young thing, the media star. Yeah, right. Stupid bitch. She knew nothing. Was nothing.

She needed a drink.

The thought was there all of the time, but most of the time she kept it submerged.

Don't go there.

Had she said it out loud? A businesswoman, fiftyish and fabulous in a belted trench coat and black-framed glasses, gave Liz a startled look as she rushed past. Was her misery that obvious? A drink would fix her in seconds. Or, better still, a smoke, or – oh, God, yeah – a line of blow. Liz almost groaned at the thought of it. The anticipation of the powder laid out in front of her. The tingle as she inhaled. The rush as it powered into her bloodstream and pierced her brain. The feeling of being whole again.

You're better than this.

Tom's words tumbled into her brain. Spoken the night he'd brought her home and waited outside the toilet door while she puked up the tea he'd made her, before emerging pale, tearful and desperate for something to make her feel better again.

'You're better than this.'

'You don't know me.'

'I don't have to.'

It could have been the script from some stupid romantic movie, except it was Tom, and he had meant every word of it. He promised to look after her that night, and he had kept that promise. Liz had kept hers as well, and had folded the drugs and the drink, the memory of them and the longing for them, deep inside her skin. But every so often the desire for them broke through. A little help. She wanted it so badly.

She'd walk. She'd drink coffee. She'd be OK.

But the takeaway Americano made things worse, not better. Liz's nerve endings were jangling and the caffeine frazzled them further. A smoke would calm her down. There was a pub near here, guys who'd know how to sort her out. She could be in and out in a few minutes, no one would know.

I'd know.

Fuck off, Tom. Get out of my head.

It had started to rain heavily now and she pulled the collar of her jacket up around her face. Organised people, real, functioning people, carried umbrellas with them. Most days she was lucky if she remembered to charge her phone.

'Jesus!'

Head down, she almost walked straight into a couple of lost tourists staring helplessly at a soggy map and muttering about Trinity College.

'Could you help, please?'

'No, no, I'm sorry.'

She couldn't even help herself.

The rain fell heavier and she ducked into a bookshop, but it was one of those cheap, bargain places, with shiny pastel covers and huge red signs on the wall, shrieking, *Three For Two* and, *Buy One, Get One Free*. Too much colour; too much noise; too much stimulation; too much too much. She darted back outside before the assistant could offer to help her. *Trust me, love, you can't. No one can.* A tattered pumpkin display in the next window reminded her that, with Halloween now over, she was on the downward spiral towards Christmas and New Year. The least wonderful time of the year.

Darkness fell. The figures on the streets were different now; tourists and shoppers replaced by laughing students walking three abreast, mothers with plastic-wrapped buggies, power-walking workers returning home.

'Ya stupid—'

She flinched. The yell had come from the opposite side of the street, had nothing to do with her, but she quickened her pace, anyway. *Get me home. Just get me home.* Ducking through the crowds, she banged shoulders with other pedestrians – excuse me, excuse me, can I just . . . ? – and then she stopped asking and just barged through. *I need to get home.*

An alleyway. An empty sleeping bag. Did it belong to one of their lads? Right now, she didn't care. Get me home. Her brain was aching, thoughts and regrets shadow-boxing inside her skull.

Get me home.

The one good thing that had come out of her father's death and all of the darkness: a one-bedroom apartment, her own name on the deeds, her own key. She'd never lost that key – not even during the height of the horror – had managed to stumble home to the flat every night, although not always alone.

She was almost running now, splashing through puddles, feet sliding on the wet pavement – trying not to think about how desperate she must look, or of who might be looking at her. *Just get me home.* A dart across the road, a parp of a horn and she was there.

Home. She buzzed herself in through the communal door, sprinted down the corridor till she got to her apartment. Her hands, freezing and wet, fumbled in her pocket. Crumbs and cloth; no keys. She was outside, alone, exposed. *Exposed.* Where had that word come from? There was no one chasing her. But she was truly shaken now, close to panic, her caffeinated, adrenalised heart battering against her chest, her eyes blurred from rain and tears combined.

She was so tired. But just as she was about to give up, to sink down on the grotty communal carpet and burst into tears, her fingers closed on cool metal. The keys had been in her pocket the whole time, just caught up somehow in the lining. The lock clicked open. Her alarm beeped – a friendly wink to let her know her little flat was secure, and she was safe inside it. Home. Heat from the storage system pumped through the little hall. She had left a light on in the kitchen that morning and her brain calmed immediately at the thought of the frozen dinner waiting in the fridge and the movie she'd taped the night before, ready to go in the DVR.

Home. She threw her coat on the floor, took off her sodden shoes and rested her back against the radiator for a moment. Home, and her fears had been groundless. Richard? He was just an eejit. It had meant nothing. Nor had your man Ian's sister. Nothing. It was meaningless. She was just jittery after weeks of hard work and the shock of James's death. She didn't need a drink, or anything stronger – just a bath and a cup of tea. She'd been doing too much, that was the problem. Maybe a break, later in the month? She could head west for the weekend, get a cheap B & B somewhere, go for walks on the beach. Or she could just stay here. Tape a few more movies, stay in bed. Tír na nÓg would survive without her for a few days. And she would survive without going back on her word, without betraying Tom and his trust in her.

Mind calming, heart slowing down, Liz peeled herself away from the radiator and picked up the pile of post that was lying on the floor. Three pizza leaflets, a badly typed flyer looking for old clothes, and an electricity bill. Now *that* was something to panic about. Ho ho. There was also an envelope with her address in scrawled handwriting. She opened it on her way into the kitchen and wondered why she was looking at a picture of James Mannion. Then realised it was an article on his death, torn from a paper. And a note was pinned to it.

Elizabeth. I've been watching you. You could be next. Stephen.

CHAPTER NINE

So Mr Mannion had been here, and now he was gone again. For good, this time.

Elizabeth was his only constant. On the days when he could listen to her, look at her, think about her, on those days he felt, for a while at least, that he would survive. But there were never enough of those days.

Why couldn't you have just left things alone, Mr Mannion? Why couldn't you have left me alone?

He tried to keep himself busy – cut out items from the newspaper that he thought she might be interested in, kept them safe, so they'd have something to talk about when they finally met.

If they met.

When they met.

'You should always think positively, Stephen.'

But he doubted this was what the doctor had in mind.

He kept his ideas in clear plastic folders. He'd had to go all the way into town to buy them, but it had been worth it, for her. Besides, he didn't want to buy one of those scrapbooks from the local shop, the ones kids used or those nutcases off the telly with their paranoia and their *conspiracy theories. Idiots, the lot of them. Stephen was nothing like them. He was just trying to keep in touch with a friend.*

Mr Mannion's funeral was in Dublin, not Rathoban: a Mass near his home with cremation afterwards in Glasnevin Cemetery. Stephen read the details in the paper; thought, briefly, about attending. Would it be the right thing to do? There was hardly a protocol for these things, but it would be nice to see if— No. The more he thought about it, the more the breath tightened in his chest and, by the time the morning came round, he hadn't been able to leave the bed, let alone catch the bus across the city. He had been due to start the night shift that evening, but instead called in sick to work, for the first time in fifteen years. The girl on the other end of the phone told him not to worry and to take care now and that there was something going round.

Stephen wondered what she'd say if he told her the real reason for his absence. Her voice wouldn't be so bright then, maybe.

When he'd recovered enough to leave the flat, collect his sick cert and lie to the doctor about how he was feeling, he decided to take himself out for lunch, like normal people did. Brought a newspaper with him, put his phone on the table, checked it regularly so he could look as important as everyone else. Ordered a glass of wine, smiled at the waitress as if he did this sort of thing all the time. But he could still feel them looking at him. It was always the same. Wrong shoes, wrong clothes, wrong hair. He didn't fit in anywhere.

His mother used to tell him he wouldn't go far wrong in a pair of slacks and an ironed shirt, but he hadn't gone too far right, either.

Stephen had bought himself a pair of jeans once – years back, when he was still in school. His father had given him money for a football jersey after Stephen told him he hadn't been picked for the team because he didn't have the right gear. That was bullshit, of course; he was just trying to get the oul lad off his back, but it was the best excuse he could come up with at the time, with the cigarette inches from his face and the smell of beery sweat strong enough to knock him over. Only trouble was, his father had believed him and handed over a twenty, no more questions. Just told him to get himself kitted out and that he'd turn up on the Saturday morning to see how he was getting on.

He'd made it as far as the sports shop in the village and was just about to open the door when he saw the team trainer, blurred by the glass, hanging over the counter and giving a lecture to the young fella at the till. Stephen had backed away. They probably wouldn't let him in the door, an eejit like him who tripped over his feet every time he was confronted with a ball, who ran back to his mammy when they suggested he'd be better in goal. Mightn't even sell him the damn jersey; there were maybe rules about that sort of thing. So he had turned and walked back down the main street, shoulders hunched, the twenty quid in his pocket, hand-warmed from holding, and wondered what to do.

Giving it back wasn't an option. That would have involved an explanation, and a hiding, or at the very least being called whatever name came first to his father's mind that day. He could give it to his ma, get her to spend it on herself, but, sure, that was a stupid idea as well; she'd have to account for where it had come from too.

And then Stephen had walked past the clothes shop, the new one, halfway up the main street, and seen the pair of jeans in the window. They weren't a mad posh pair; they didn't have that little red label on the arse pocket that he'd seen the other lads wearing. But they were denim, and blue, and grand. Normal. He walked in then, in a kind of a daze, and answered their questions – waist size, leg length – everything they needed to know. Turned out the sizes were the same for jeans as any other pants. He'd never known that before. And then Stephen handed over the twenty and told them he'd wear the jeans home. Maybe if they were already on him the oul lad wouldn't make too big a fuss. Maybe he'd see how well he looked in them and just let him be.

He didn't make it further than the hall. Da was having a bad day; he knew that as soon as he'd closed the door behind him. There was a strong smell of booze, and puke mixed in with it too: that was bad for only five o'clock in the evening.

'I spoke to Jim Daly at lunchtime.'

He'd felt like puking himself when he heard that. Didn't say anything, though. No point. Just let his hand trail uselessly behind him, feeling the chill of the air between him and the door. He was too far away to turn the handle and leg it; hadn't the courage, anyway.

'He said he hasn't seen you next or near the football field in weeks.'

'Da . . .'

The word came out in a high bleat – the very worst way, the way it most annoyed him. Through the closed kitchen door Stephen could hear his mother muffle a sob and his heart twisted inside him; she was trying to stay quiet, trying not to annoy his dad and bring him down on them, and there he was practically pissing himself trying to do the same thing.

It was only then that the old man noticed the jeans. He didn't say a word. Just reached out and grabbed his son by the belt buckle. Pulled him in towards him. Breathed puke and beer and fags down on to him. Jabbed him hard in the kidneys. Slapped him across the head; pucked him in the back of the knee until he fell to the floor. Muttered one word – 'Thief' – just one word and then started the kicking. Not in the head this time. Nor the arms or the hands or anywhere it would show. Just in the groin, and the kidneys. The groin and the back and the kidneys and the kidneys and the kidneys and the kidneys, until the piss ran down his legs and Stephen abandoned his silence and begged and screamed to be saved. Until the woman burst through the kitchen door and flung herself towards the mess of a child and said, 'Kick me instead! Dear Jesus, kick me instead.' His da left them alone then. One final boot, a slap to his mother and then out the door with him.

Stephen fell asleep sometime after ten. The tablets his mother had got from the doctor the last time worked well enough for the pain, and he figured he'd be safe enough now his father had vented his rage. He was wrong. Da had still been drunk the following morning and dragged him from the bed, forced him to put the damp jeans back on, threw him into the back of the car and then drove him to school, the piss-stained trousers clinging to his legs.

There was no point in making a run for it. The oul fella was going to wait in the car until he went inside. Saying no wasn't an option. So it was easier for Stephen just to make his way into the school and suffer the looks and the comments and the wrinkling of the noses from some, and the slight sympathy from others, and the confusion and then the horror on Mr Mannion's face when he finally realised where the smell was coming from. And then the questions. And the pity. And the lies.

In the end, Mr Mannion found him a spare pair of trousers and told him he'd drive him home. And after that, everything changed.

CHAPTER TEN

'I'll drive.'

Flynn opened his mouth and then closed it again just as quickly. Good man, Philip. You'll make Inspector yet with those powers of observation. Claire jammed her sunglasses on to her nose and reversed out of the parking space with a screech. It wasn't a particularly bright day but the sunglasses were a necessity, given the ache at the back of her eyes. The entente cordiale brought about by Anna's first tooth hadn't lasted long and she and Matt were back to averaging three hours' broken sleep a night, between them. The little girl just wasn't happy with life at the moment and wanted everyone to know. Her mother. Her father. The woman in the house next door who'd given them a sympathetic look on the first morning of Toothgate and had been muttering about soothers by day three. And their neighbour wasn't the only one with an Opinion.

Matt, following an hour spent buried in the baby books Claire didn't even pretend that she had time to read anymore, had diagnosed 'Separation Anxiety'. Claire's mother, who phoned with depressing regularity every Sunday evening, was of the Opinion that teeth were to blame. But, as Claire had recently found out, Nuala Boyle was happy blaming everything from nappy rash to soaring temperatures on a little bit of enamel cutting through a baby gum. In fact, Claire had a sneaking suspicion that if the teenage Anna was ever to appear in court on major charges, her grandmother would be spotted whispering into the judge's hairy ear that she hadn't meant to do it, it was just her teeth had been at her that day. And even Matt's mother – the gorgeous, ageless Eimear, who worked sixty-hour weeks as a senior partner in a law firm – had volunteered an unsolicited Opinion, looking over her fabulous gold-rimmed glasses during her monthly duty visit and proclaiming that the child needed to learn to 'settle herself', a process, she said, that 'hadn't done Matt any harm'.

Claire herself had no doubt that Anna's problem, whatever it was, would resolve itself eventually. Every other twist in the tale of babyhood had done so, from wind to colic to the nappy rash they'd finally linked to pureed veg, ensuring that those 'smears' of carrot so beloved of posh restaurants would turn her stomach forever more. All just 'phases', as her mother called them, endless when you were in them and gone in what seemed like a heartbeat when you were safely out the other side. Anna would start sleeping again, eventually. Claire was in no doubt about that. But would her sanity, and indeed her marriage, survive the wait?

Motherhood. And all that. Claire turned on the radio, flicking through the stations, trying to find something to fit her mood.

Eminem – that would do it, she thought, and turned it up, ignoring Flynn's side-eye. She just hadn't realised how different motherhood – or parenthood, she should say – would be. How intense. How never-bloody-ending. That feeling of never being off, of never having nothing on your mind, because there was always something. Being shouted at when you least needed it – at three a.m. or while trying to get ready for work in the morning – by the person you loved most.

That wasn't in doubt, thank God. Claire loved Anna alright, loved her to distraction, adored her with a ferocity she hadn't thought she was capable of before the baby arrived. But there was no denying it, the little girl was hard work at the moment and it had been with no small sense of relief that Claire had handed her over to the crèche worker that morning and watched her become Someone Else's Problem for the rest of the day.

And she'd be Matt's Problem that night. She and Flynn would be gone till early evening, maybe even later, depending on how things went. They wouldn't be back till after Anna's bedtime, anyway, that much was certain. Matt had been muttering about going for a run that evening, but it'd probably be far too late by the time she got back. Not to worry. She'd make sure he got some time to himself at the weekend.

Claire's headache was starting to lift and she nudged the sun visor upwards while making a, technically illegal, left turn out on to the quays. Beside her, Flynn winced, but remained silent. Wishing she'd thought to grab a coffee before starting the journey, Claire changed stations again, zipping through static before stopping at the loudest and bubble-gummiest pop she could find.

Flynn preferred Lyric FM. Claire knew this, and wondered how many winces she could elicit before they left the city centre. Then she shot him another look, longer this time.

'D'you do something to your hair?' she asked.

'No!'

The answer was huffed out through his nostrils but Claire was entranced to see the hint of a blush emerge. Most excellent! A bit of Flynn baiting would wake her up better than any coffee.

'You did! You got a hair style, Philip Flynn! I bet you went to a hairdresser and all. Did they put conditioner in it for you?'

'It was just a dry cut.'

He stared out the window of the car, studying the landscape as if James Mannion's killer was likely to come up and jog alongside them at any moment. Ah, it was no fun slagging him if he wasn't going to play along. Claire fell silent again and, as Taylor Swift urged her to 'Shake It Off', she guided the car smoothly through the suburbs that led to the Naas Road.

The sunny morning had brought out lots of pedestrians: mothers with buggies, kids crawling unwillingly to school, and several old women, all of whom looked to be either coming from or going to Mass. No old men. Claire hadn't given much thought to old men before. But now, with James Mannion's murder front and centre in her mind and Tom Carthy's interview transcribed on her laptop, she couldn't help wondering about them. Where did all the old men go during the day?

She pulled up sharply at a set of traffic lights outside a giant Lidl and watched a woman, who must have been in her seventies, tug a huge tartan shopping trolley behind her and then hoist it effortlessly up on to the path. There were women everywhere, shopping, chatting, stooped over in their front gardens deadheading roses. But no elderly men. Tom Carthy with his refuge, or whatever you called it, had seen a gap in the market alright. But why the hell would you want to take a man with one foot in the grave and push him fully over the side?

The phone in her lap jangled. Claire thought about answering while she drove but, casting a sideways glance at her colleague, decided it wasn't worth the lecture. Instead, she pulled into the shopping-centre car park, clicked on her hazards and rested the car lengthways across a mother-and-baby space. Sure, she'd only be a minute. The voice on the other end of the phone made her glad she'd answered the call.

'Hi, Claire.'

'Helena! Good to hear from you.'

The deputy state pathologist's voice was crisp: 'I'm emailing that P.M. report through to you now, but I thought you'd appreciate the bullet points?'

'That'd be great.'

Claire loved working with Helena Sheehy. No bullshit. No need for five minutes of 'How are the kids?' 'Isn't it a lovely day?' 'Any holiday plans?' before she came out with the information that was required. The way the other lads went on sometimes, she couldn't figure out if she was working in a police force or a hairdressers'. But Helena sounded like she was always in a hurry, which suited Claire just fine.

'James Mannion was dying.'

Claire tried to keep the smile out of her voice: 'Well, I'd nearly figured that one out myself.'

'Ho ho. No, I mean he was dying anyway. Pancreatic cancer. The technical stuff is all in the report, but it was late stage four; he hadn't a hope. Didn't look like he'd had much treatment, either; you'll have to check his medical records, but I didn't see any sign of chemo or radiotherapy. He'd painkillers in his bloodstream, alright – massive amounts of them – and alcohol. He must have been fairly out of it most of the time. But it wouldn't have made a huge amount of difference. I'd say he'd weeks left, maybe a couple of months at most.'

'You'll email me that, so?'

'Sure. Gone to you now.'

And, with a click, the pathologist's voice disappeared.

Claire put the phone back down on her knees, hauled the car out of the space and waved cheerily at an apoplectic young woman in a people carrier who had been mouthing, 'You have no children!' at her for the duration of the call.

She rolled down her window. 'I do, actually – just the one, but she's gorgeous!'

Another illegal left and they were back out on the Naas Road. For once, every green light on the dual carriageway was on their side and, within minutes, Claire – while filling Flynn in on what Helena Sheehy had told her – had navigated the Red Cow roundabout and got the journey properly underway.

'So they were right. Tom Carthy and Mrs Delahunty. James Mannion was a sick man. Dying, in fact.'

Flynn, clearly delighted that the conversation had finally turned to work matters, looked animated for the first time that day. 'Only he doesn't seem to have told anyone about it.'

'Interesting, isn't it?'

Claire drove quickly and smoothly, under- and overtaking her way along the M7. They were well out of the city now, horses and the odd sheep dotting the green fields on either side of the motorway. That was the funny thing about Dublin: how big it looked when you were in the middle of it, but then how easy it was to get away. Too easy, sometimes.

There were times Claire wished she lived in a metropolis somewhere, an urban jungle, where you'd need to get on a plane to get anywhere near a farm animal. And, although she'd never asked him straight out, she had a feeling Flynn felt the same way. She didn't actually know where he was from; he'd only ever replied, 'The far side of Athlone,' any time the topic came up in conversation. But she had a feeling his home place was somewhere similar to her own. Somewhere rural, some-where where more than two streets and a Supermac's was considered a town. Claire had legged it as far away as pos-sible from her own home as soon as she hit eighteen, and her instinct told her Flynn had done the same thing. And now it looked like they could add James Mannion to the list of people who'd come to a city to find . . . what? Salvation was too strong a word. Privacy? A sense of self? Sanctuary?

Mrs Delahunty reckoned he had been gay. No one else they

had spoken to about the victim had made that suggestion, but, if she was right, that would have given Mannion an even better reason to move to the Big Smoke. Maybe he had come to Dublin to find love – or simply somewhere to call home, somewhere where the smell of cow shite didn't linger in the nostrils. Or maybe Mannion had left home because he'd fucked up so badly he wouldn't be welcome there again.

'What's the plan today, so?'

Rolling up the window in order to hear Flynn better – besides, all that fresh air wasn't doing her headache any good – Claire outlined her plans. Following some extremely helpful and efficient contact with the police in Bristol – some of her own colleagues could do with going over there on a training course, Claire had thought, uncharitably – she'd found a phone number for James Mannion's niece, Angela Jefferies, and had spoken to her the previous day.

Mind you, she could have found her a hell of a lot quicker if she'd kept her maiden name. Drove Claire mad, that carry-on. She herself had only agreed to marry Matt once they realised they wanted a kid, and had grudgingly admitted that it would be easier for all concerned if they were legally bound before that happened. Then she'd even walked up a church aisle to keep her parents off her back. But change her name? Not a chance.

It had only taken a short conversation with Angela Jefferies to realise that that wasn't the only way in which they differed. James Mannion's niece was the scattiest person Claire had ever spoken to and so lacking in focus it was a miracle she'd made

it to Dublin, let alone Darcy Terrace. She had been able to confirm most of the details Mrs Delahunty had given them, but
had little new to offer. All she could say was that her father –
and, presumably, his late brother – had been born in a place
called Rathoban and that the solicitor who'd looked after his
affairs had been called McBride. The paperwork was back in
her mother's attic, she'd admitted, and it would take hours, if
not days, to find the right file.

What Mrs Jefferies was sure of, however, was that, after the
abortive trip to Dublin, she'd never tried to contact her uncle
again.

'He made it quite clear he didn't want to talk to me.'

She sounded very young, Claire had thought, but that could
have just been the high-pitched English accent.

'I thought it was a good idea, you know? To come over.
Thought it might help me deal with Dad's death a bit better.
But it didn't. Mum was furious when she heard what I'd done.
My dad cut all ties with Ireland – he had his reasons – I should
have left it like that. I'm sorry Uncle James is dead. But it
doesn't feel like anything to do with me, quite frankly.'

At least, thought Claire, Angela Jefferies hadn't tried to
squeeze out a tear when she heard how her uncle had died.
James Mannion's niece had merely said, flatly, 'Oh, that's a
shame,' as if she was hearing a particularly dull story at a
dinner party.

Ending with the request that the woman contact her if she
thought of anything else of importance – 'Of course, absolutely,
although I really don't think there is anything' – Claire had

ended the call none the wiser as to why James Mannion had cut off all ties with his family and died alone.

There was, of course, no reason to believe that the tensions in his family history had anything to do with his violent death. It could have been a coincidence. The attack that left him bleeding and dying on his kitchen floor could have been nothing more complicated than an aggravated burglary, but initial investigations at the house did not point in that direction. There was no evidence of money or anything else having been taken. The front door hadn't been damaged and the initial forensic examination pointed to Mannion having invited his killer in. The only struggle appeared to have happened in the living room, and even there the disturbance had been limited. Thank Christ. Claire shuddered to herself when she imagined the damage – and the smell – that could have been caused if the pyramid of milky doom had toppled over. But nothing, not one dusty book, had been disturbed. The only item out of place was the vase she had spotted under the sofa. It was a very ordinary vase, the type you buy in a tourist shop and get engraved. The legend, *Teacher of the Year, 1978,* had been etched on the side. A gap in the dust on James Mannion's mantelpiece marked the place it stood before it killed him. The line of blood leading from the sitting room to the kitchen was the only other sign of disturbance.

Flynn's phone beeped and he took it out of his pocket, muttered an apology and started to compose a text. Not to worry. The car was almost driving itself now, the road straight, and Claire was enjoying being alone with her thoughts, or the closest thing to alone she'd been in a while. Not that there was that much to untangle. Door-to-door enquiries, which had been carried out around Darcy Terrace, had, so far, yielded little. James Mannion had been seen on the morning of his murder, that much they were able to establish. A harassed au pair working in the house two doors down had confirmed to a couple of uniforms that she'd seen him sometime after eleven. But the rest of her information had been so vague as to be practically useless. Struggling to contain two toddlers, with a baby tucked under one arm, she'd barely been able to hold a conversation with the two uniformed members at the door, let alone give them any detail other than that she'd seen Mannion on the pavement outside his house, and that he'd seemed 'OK'. She'd been changing the baby's nappy, she told them. Had been gazing out the window, but then the child had wriggled dangerously and she'd had to look away again. He was a nice man, she'd told them distractedly, trying to stop her older charges from making a break for freedom. He'd always smiled at the children when they met him on the road. But how he had been that morning – or even which direction he was heading in – she just couldn't say. She was sorry to hear what happened. He was a nice man, she repeated, her accent becoming stronger as she grew more upset. She'd say a prayer.

The interviews with the other neighbours had been even less useful, most of them being at work during the day. James Mannion's house was situated right at the end of Darcy Terrace, with Mrs Delahunty's home to the right-hand side. To his left, and extending to the back of the entire terrace, was a large wild green area, once earmarked for apartments but now, judging by the cans littering the ground, used only for cider parties. The people who socialised in those places weren't usually the type to come forward to Gardaí with information, Claire knew. Mrs Delahunty hadn't returned from Mass until after one p.m. and, according to Helena Sheehy, the murder had almost certainly been committed before then. When they'd spoken to her, Margaret Delahunty had wondered out loud if the killer had known her movements and waited until she was away to commit his crime.

Claire hoped that, for her own peace of mind, she never realised how close to the truth that probably was.

'So, now.'

Flynn put away his phone ostentatiously and cracked his knuckles, just falling short of sticking a *Ready for Action* sign on the dashboard. Claire sighed. His enthusiasm was touching. Her own wasn't far behind. But the fact was, they knew shag all. A probable murder weapon; a possible time of death. Was the gay thing relevant? She didn't think so. Even if Mrs D had been correct, nothing they'd learned about James suggested he was the type to bring some young fella back with him. No, they had nothing, really – nothing of any use, anyway. Hence the day trip to the Mannion family solicitors in Rathoban, to see if they had anything they could tell them. Mannion's niece had claimed he had lost all contact with the place thirty years before. For the sake of the investigation, Claire was hoping that this simply wasn't true.

CHAPTER ELEVEN

Five streets, a church, two sweet shops, twenty-seven pubs and an incomprehensible one-way system. If you Googled 'Small Irish Town', you'd probably come up with a picture of Rathoban, Claire thought as she abandoned her search for on-street parking and manoeuvred her car through the gates of St Anthony's. She pulled in beside a sign that warned her she'd be clamped if she was using the facilities for anything other than Catholic worship, and scowled at Flynn to pre-empt his objection. Police business was next to godliness and, anyway, the local cops would surely give her a dig-out if anyone had a problem with her use of the facility in her time of need.

Grabbing her briefcase from the back seat, she exited the car and told her colleague to get a move on. There was no need to rush, really. The journey out of Dublin had taken less than two hours and their appointment with Gavin McBride wasn't for another fifteen minutes. But the day was nice, the air was fresh and Claire felt like moving at speed. It was one of the things she had missed while on maternity leave, that lovely crisp sense of urgency, the adrenaline rush, the ability to gallop ahead without checking to see if she had snacks in her bag and a muslin cloth thrown over her shoulder. Just one thing, though: she turned and took a quick look at her reflection in the car window. Her short dark hair, newly cut and coloured thanks to the joy of baby-free lunch breaks, looked pretty good. Her second-best navy jacket went well with the new black Marks & Spencer's trousers and, most importantly, everything fitted. Excellent. Her body was back, and so was she.

Flynn unfolded himself from the passenger seat, gave a stretch as if to say he was his own man who wouldn't be hurried, and then hurried after her. They hadn't bothered getting directions to McBride's office but, just as Claire had anticipated, they spotted it the minute they left the car park. The firm of solicitors was located halfway down Rathoban main street, sandwiched between a sweet shop and one of the twenty-seven pubs. The buildings looked like they'd been built in the nineteen-fifties and had had minimal redecoration since then. A plastic ice-cream cone hung outside the shop and, as they approached, Claire could see ads for long-discontinued chocolate bars fading in the window.

'Jesus, I hate this place. The state of it.'

Flynn looked at her, surprised at her tone. 'What, Rathoban? I thought you said you'd never been here?'

'This place, these places, these types of places. Small towns. God, I feel smothered just standing here. I couldn't stick living here, could you? Everyone knowing your business. I'm surprised there wasn't a brass band brought in to announce that we were in town.'

'I suppose.' Flynn shrugged. 'Some people like living in places like this. This McBride guy; sure, he's probably well set up. Nice business, nice few bob in it, as well, doing wills for farmers and handling farm sales. There's worse ways of earning a living.'

Maybe. But Claire couldn't think of any, and she was still scowling as she halted in front of the building that housed McBride and Son. It wasn't quite as scruffy as the others on the street; in fact, it looked like it had been done up in the recent past, which, in Rathoban, clearly meant around nineteen ninety-nine. The firm's name was fixed to the outside on a large blue-and-white sign and the front of the red-brick building featured large white u.P.V.C. windows through which an expanse of laminate flooring and a large airy waiting area could be seen. You wouldn't, thought Claire, want to be trying to manage your affairs in private.

A handwritten note on the entry keypad announced that it was out of order, but the big windows had rendered it unnecessary anyway and, before Claire could rap on the glass, the door buzzed and the receptionist inside signalled at her to push it open. Typical, Claire huffed to herself. She had probably been watching them from halfway down the street.

Aged anywhere between fifty and sixty, the woman had hair that matched the ash-blond wooden floors, while her designer nails must have made operating the computer keyboard in front of her something of a challenge. Phone clutched to her ear, she continued talking while beckoning Claire and Flynn to come forward.

'Yeah, yeah, I know, yeah. 'Tis indeed. I know. You're right. I will. I know. C'mere, there's someone here for himself. I do. I do, indeed. I know. Leave it with me, so. Leave it with me. Mm hmm. I know. I will, indeed. I will, indeed, Sheila! Take care, now!'

Replacing the phone with a flourish, she bestowed upon them a bright, utterly welcoming and utterly fake smile.

'Now! Ye're here to see Gavin.'

It wasn't a question, and Claire nodded rather than replying, feeling even more sympathy for anyone who thought they'd be able to get discretion in this place. Her own father travelled into Galway on the odd occasion he had to do legal work associated with their farm, rather than use what he described as 'the local crowd', and she was beginning to see why. Still, she was hoping the open-plan atmosphere in the office would extend to Gavin McBride's willingness to talk about the Mannion family.

The receptionist directed them towards a set of three steel chairs.

'Take a seat there, now; he'll be with you in a minute. Ye'll have coffee?'

Claire nodded again. But before the red talons could become engaged in a tussle with the stack of gold Nespresso discs to the left of her computer terminal, an inner door opened and the smile broadened even further.

'Sure, there he is, now! Ye can go on through; I'll bring the coffees in. Milk, was it?'

'Yes, thanks.' Only Flynn managed a mutter and a half smile

as they were steered past the reception desk and through the open door.

'It was my father's practice.'

Gavin McBride, like the decor, looked like he had been styled around fifteen years ago, and his black pin-stripe suit had clearly been bought when he was a thinner man. The crumpled jacket hung off the back of his large leather chair and his gleaming white shirt strained at the middle, while an expensive-looking gold tie wasn't quite able to hide what looked like a tomato sauce stain near the third button. There wasn't a rib of grey in his close-cropped red hair, but Claire reckoned that the wrinkles at the corners of his eyes and the weight he was carrying put him in his early forties. A dulled wedding ring and a gold-framed photo of a wife and three equally red-headed munchkins told her everything else she needed to know. Poor fecker. Probably made it as far as Dublin to study before Daddy kicked the bucket and he was hauled back to Rathoban to take over the family firm. Stuck here now with three kids in the house he grew up in. Gawd. Claire could almost feel the suffocation of it, like living in slowly drying cement. She thanked God every day she'd had the cop on to join the guards and avoid a similar fate.

Pushing the large square glasses up on to his nose – they had probably looked great on the model, but succeeded only in making his freckled face even fatter – McBride shuffled some papers around his desk before finally giving his visitors what looked like a genuine smile.

'So, the Mannion family: what exactly do ye need to know?'

Shifting uncomfortably on yet another metal chair, Claire outlined what little information they'd gathered already. The solicitor nodded, looked down at the papers again and sucked his top lip before replying.

'Well, ye have the most of it there, to be honest with ye. Mr Mannion senior, Timothy, had a small farm just a few miles outside the town, here, in Rathoban. His wife died when his children were young and he brought up the two lads, James and Paul. 'Twas my father drew up Mr Mannion's will; he was the only solicitor in town at that stage. I have the records here; I looked them up when I heard ye were coming down. It's a bit unusual, actually.'

He reached across the desk and pulled a cardboard folder towards him.

'Mr Mannion senior drew up his first will in nineteen seventy-two, which must have been just after his wife died. It's straightforward, divides the farm between the two lads. It was a fine farm, plenty there for the two of them. James went into teaching; ye probably know that? He taught in the school, here, locally, for a while. Anyway . . .'

He paused, let his hand rest on the yellowed paper for a moment and then picked up another page from underneath.

'Here – this is more interesting.'

He passed the paper across the desk.

'The father drew up another will in nineteen eighty-five. Left everything to Paul; nothing to James, this time, not so much as a blade of grass. That would be unusual, now, that you'd have such a significant change of mind.'

Claire nodded. She had an instinct that the information was important, but wasn't sure, as yet, in what way. She'd find out, though, she was sure of it.

McBride closed the folder.

'That was the last will. Timothy died a couple of years after that – heart attack, I think. Something sudden, anyway. I remember it well, actually; I was down from college for the weekend and I remember my mother saying James hadn't come home for the funeral. That wouldn't have been normal at all, for those times. It stuck in my head, I suppose. Mam said they were all talking about it at Mass – I hadn't gone; sure, there was a row about that too!'

He laughed and shook his head.

'Anyway. Paul had no interest in farming; he set the land out, as ye know, and headed to England. So.'

The solicitor removed his glasses again and polished them with the end of his tie.

'Where are we? Well, Dad was gone by the time Paul died and I'd taken over here, so I wrote to James to tell him what was going on. My father had his address on record, thankfully; otherwise, I don't think the poor man would have known he'd lost his brother at all. I did expect him to turn up at that stage, to be honest with you. God knows, land was making great money around here in those days. But not a word. You know the rest, I think? Paul's widow and daughter went ahead and sold the place; they did well out of it too. And James never appeared. God rest him.'

He looked at Flynn briefly and then dropped his gaze.

'I read about it in the paper. Jesus, that was an awful way to go.'

Flynn nodded, waited a beat and asked the obvious question:

'Have you any idea what it was? What happened to cause the rift, I mean? It must have been fairly serious if James – if Mr Mannion – didn't turn up for his own father's funeral.'

The solicitor put his glasses back on and blinked at them.

'Well, there was some scandal beyond at the school, as far as I know, anyway. I was only a child myself when it happened; I heard my parents talking about it alright, but it wasn't meant for my tender ears. I knew about the farm; I would have gone through all that sort of thing when Dad handed over the reins here. But we never discussed James Mannion and, to be honest, I never felt I could ask.'

Claire rearranged her features into a suitably sympathetic expression. 'And when did your own father pass away?'

'Pass away? Oh, Jesus!' A sudden burst of laughter made the man look younger than she'd first estimated. 'God, I'm sorry if I gave you that impression. No, no, Dad's flying. He took early retirement a few years ago, but he's having a ball, other than the golf handicap. He's up at the house now, if you want to talk to him. You're lucky that he's around, actually; himself and Mam have a place over in Florida and they'll be heading out next month for the winter. We'll be going ourselves at Christmas. Have you ever been? No? Jaysus, it's a fine place.

There's a swimming pool and all in their apartment complex. Dead? Ah, that'll give him a great laugh.'

He sat back in the chair and beamed at them.

'The house is only a mile or so out the road; I'll give you directions. Dad was a county councillor too, you know, for nearly thirty years. Mayor, at one stage. There's nothing that happens within a ten-mile radius of Rathoban he wouldn't have the inside track on. I'd be surprised if he couldn't tell you what you need. Just head out the road there, straight through the crossroads; it's the second turn on the left when you pass the garage; you can't miss it. Ah, that's cheered me up, now. Me poor oul Da!'

He folded his arms across his stomach, giggling gently.

Kicking herself for her assumption about his father – it was a small thing, but she hated being wrong – Claire forced a smile. 'You've been very helpful. I appreciate it.'

She moved towards the door, but her colleague didn't follow her. Instead, Flynn nodded towards the desk and the gold frame.

'You're bringing your family up around here, so?'

'Indeed I am.'

Gavin McBride gave the photo a possessive pat.

'Studied up in Dublin; you know, yourself. But I couldn't wait to get back down here and, when the oul lad retired, I was in like Flynn. Sheila's from Dublin, but she wanted to move back here too. Sure, you couldn't beat it. We built the house for half nothing on the folks' bit of land and the commute is ten minutes door to door. Sheila's running an aromatherapy clinic from the house and the kids love it too. Jesus, no, I wouldn't move back to the city now if you paid me.'

Flynn opened his mouth as if to continue the conversation, but Claire glared at him and shepherded him back into reception. They had an interview to conduct. He'd made his point; she had completely misjudged Gavin McBride. Feck it. She didn't have to be right all the time. But hopefully, for the rest of this investigation, at least, she'd be right most of the time.

CHAPTER TWELVE

'And that one there, that was taken just off the Galapagos Islands – a cruise for our fortieth wedding anniversary. God, it's beautiful there. Have ye ever been? Just beautiful.'

'No, I can't say I have, now,' Flynn managed to mutter.

Claire was too distracted to answer him. Distracted by the way the man was bringing them on a tour of his home, as if they were valued guests instead of two out-of-town guards investigating a murder. Distracted by the house itself, which had clearly been built when *Dallas* was at its zenith, and differed from Southfork only in its lack of a pool. Distracted, most of all, by former-councillor Richie McBride's hair, which rose majestically from his high forehead in soft rippling waves. She thought back to his son's carroty crop. This couldn't possibly be the man's natural colour, could it? But, as he continued his sweep around what he called, without even a glimmer of modesty, his 'wall of fame', she found herself mesmerised by it, a golden, gravity-defying bouffant, which, according to the photographs on the wall, had looked the same for the last thirty years.

'I think, Sergeant Boyle, if we could . . .' Flynn coughed and kicked her softly on the ankle.

'Oh yes, of course.'

Claire blinked, told herself to stop focusing on the man, his hair and the bizarre way he pronounced 'Galapa-goes', and straightened her shoulders.

'We really don't want to take up too much of your time, Mr McBride. I know you're a busy man.'

'Of course.'

The smile was half grimace, half smirk. Almost half of the photographs on the wall had shown McBride in a mayoral chain and it was a smile that, Claire assumed, had opened a hundred supermarkets. But they weren't here to reflect on McBride's magnificent career in public life. McBride's son seemed to think his father knew everything that had moved in Rathoban over the past thirty years and she badly needed some of that expertise. Plastering a smile on her own face, she turned to the man and gestured towards a set of long comfortable-looking sofas at the opposite end of the vast sitting room.

'So, if we could just . . . ?'

'We'll sit over here, shall we?' McBride turned his back on the sofa, and the huge picture window that made the far end of the room so inviting, and led the two guards instead to an imposing lacquered dining table. 'I'm not sure if I'll be able to help you at all, but, of course, anything I can do, just ask!'

Curse him, anyway, thought Claire as she accepted the uncomfortable dining chair her host indicated. She had badly wanted him to choose the sofa. She knew from experience that the more comfortable the interviewee got, the more likely he was to forget he was in the presence of guards and tell them something they actually needed to know. But McBride, it seemed, was the type of man who needed to be in control. As he took his place at the head of the table, she had to work hard to rid herself of the impression that he was still chair of the local council and she a newbie councillor who'd turned up late for her first meeting.

Resting lightly on the edge of his own seat, the older man settled his features in an approximation of a helpful smile. 'Always delighted to cooperate with An Garda Síochána, of course, but I haven't seen James Mannion in over thirty years.'

Yes, Claire thought to herself, you said – once, when you opened the door with a lack of surprise that indicated the Rathoban bush telegraph had announced our presence without the need for a 3G connection, and again when you insisted on the bloody grand tour. She pulled her notebook out of her bag, enjoying the wince he failed to hide as she slid it roughly across the surface of the table.

'Terrible, to hear of a man dying at such a young age.' McBride touched the bouffant lightly, grinned at Claire and continued: 'What was he? Late sixties? It's no age at all, these days. Tell us, anyway, what happened to him?'

The voice was mildly inquisitive, no more, as if he was enquiring about the result of a football match he'd only a passing interest in.

'I mean, I read some rubbish in the paper about him having

been killed, or something, but I assume that was all made up, was it? Sure, those buffoons in the press would write anything to make a few bob. What happened to him? Heart attack, was it? Fell and hit his head? Savage, the way a man can be taken so quickly.' He shook his head sorrowfully.

Claire frowned. 'I'm sorry?'

McBride, she decided, was either being deliberately obtuse or genuinely stupid. Despite what politicians loved to think, newspapers, as a rule, didn't actually make up details of murder cases, and the reporting of James Mannion's death had been straightforward and, in the main, accurate. There had been no need for embellishment, anyway. The man had been bashed on the head and left bleeding to death in his own kitchen. The facts of the case were lurid enough on their own.

'Mr McBride – this is a murder investigation. We've come down from Dublin to talk to you about James Mannion's murder – we did explain this?'

'Ah, yes, but –' McBride gave a bland smile and offered his hands to her, palms up in a weird, almost supplicating gesture – 'I assumed it was all exaggerated in some way.'

Claire shook her head. 'No, Mr McBride. This is a murder investigation. And Mr Mannion led a –' she fought for the word – 'a quiet life in Dublin, so we've come down here to find out what else there is to know about him. Your son tells me you know everyone in Rathoban. What can you tell me, for example, about why he left so suddenly? What was it – thirty years ago?'

McBride's smile didn't waver.

'Thirty years at least. Lot of water under the bridge since then.'

Claire remained silent. Sometimes it was best to leave a gap that could be filled in. But McBride was a seasoned public performer and stared at her unblinkingly until she spoke again.

'Your son said there was some sort of family disagreement? That James's father changed his will? Cut Mr Mannion out of it?'

'Sure, now, what's the point of dragging up any of that oul talk? It's a long time ago. Long before your time, anyway.'

The smile broadened into what could only be described as a leer and Claire found her dislike for the man growing by the second.

'There's nothing I can tell you that would be any use to you.'

Claire was sick of the bullshit. 'Mr McBride, we'll be the judge of that. I need you to tell us, please, why Mr Mannion left Rathoban. As much detail as you can.'

She left 'now' off the end of the sentence, but it hung there in the stuffy air and, beside her, she felt Flynn's silent approval.

The older man sat back, giving a long, put-upon sigh.

'Ah, there was trouble over at the school. You know, yourself.'

'No, Mr McBride, I don't. That's why I'm hoping you'll tell us.'

McBride reached up as if to run his fingers through his hair and then patted it down instead. 'There was trouble. Trouble with a young fella. Abuse, I suppose you'd call it these days. We hadn't a name for it then.' He shook his head in a gesture of regret. 'And maybe that was half the problem!'

'OK'. Claire nodded, slowly. Finally, some information. She had figured that it must have been something like that, although she needed to hear more.

McBride fell silent again, studying his reflection in the polished wooden table.

'What exactly happened?' Flynn's voice was level, but Claire could hear impatience in it, mirroring her own.

'Stephen Millar was the lad's name.'

McBride folded his arms across his chest and tipped his head back, directing his words to the ceiling.

'He would have been – what? Fourteen, fifteen at the time? Apparently it was going on a while before anyone noticed. Poor young fella didn't say anything; sure, kids didn't, back in those days. They didn't have the courage, I suppose. Anyway. Stephen used to stay late at the school the odd time to do a bit of homework and that. He was a quiet fella; nice lad, but quiet. James gave him a lift home a few times. They lived out the same direction; sure, nobody saw anything unusual in it. It wasn't like today. You can't have one child and a teacher alone together in a car now, but it was different back then. And then one day the poor lad arrived home in an awful state. Said Mannion had tried to . . . Well. I don't need to go into details.'

The colour rose in his cheeks, but Claire leaned forward in her seat, forcing him to meet her gaze.

'I'd very much appreciate it if you did, Mr McBride. We're guards; we've heard it all before, trust me.'

'Well, he said he tried to . . . you know . . . touch him, and that. Said that his hands were . . . Anyway.'

The man was totally flustered now and Claire watched, fascinated, as one strand of hair broke away from the rest and waved lazily across at her.

'The main thing is, anyway, he told his father straight away. Thank God. There's many a lad that didn't, back in those days, and, sure, that led to bigger problems. And his father marched back down to the school the next day and demanded James be sacked. No messing around, he just wanted him gone. The next I knew, James was walking out the front gate, no questions asked. I'm not sure if he even handed in his resignation. He just left. He left town the same night too, so I was told, anyway. Never appeared around here again.'

He patted the strand of hair firmly back into place and looked from Flynn to Claire.

'I was only thankful it resolved itself before anyone else got hurt.'

Flynn frowned. 'And did anyone go to the guards?'

McBride shook his head. 'No. People would have thought there was no need to, I suppose. James was gone; the matter was over. That's how things were dealt with in those days – you know that as well as I do. People moved on. I never saw or heard from James Mannion again, anyway. No one did, around here.'

'And the boy? Stephen?'

McBride shrugged. His colour had returned to normal now, his composure all but restored. 'I'm not sure. The family moved away a short time later. His father opened a business in England, I think. Sold the land. There's a housing estate on it now;

you can see it out the road. Lovely job they made of it too. So, now!'

The retired councillor sat back again, a faint smile on his face.

'I don't know if that was any use to you at all.'

It was the smile that finally shattered her composure. The former mayor was clearly a man who was used to steering conversations. Well, Claire wasn't going to let him steer this one.

Reaching down into her briefcase, she pulled out a handful of photographs and slid them across the table. The lacquered surface lent them speed and they made it all the way to McBride, coming to a rest gently at his elbow. He looked down and paled so quickly she suddenly wondered if she'd done the right thing.

'Oh my God.'

The older man tried to turn his head away, but his gaze was pulled inexorably back towards the photos. They were in black and white, but the damage done to James Mannion's skull didn't need to be in colour to have a full impact.

'Jesus!'

McBride reached out and touched the top picture tentatively. It was the response, the human response, that Claire had been looking for. Technically, she wasn't supposed to show crime-scene photos to witnesses, especially not people – like Richie McBride – who were on the periphery of the investigation. But McBride and his hair and his Galapag*oes* had pissed her off and she needed to get through to him.

Stretching out her finger, she poked the edge of one photo and kept her voice level.

'You see, Mr McBride? It wasn't a heart attack. Mr Mannion was brutally attacked – murdered. And we need to find out why.'

Leaning forward, Claire could see more clearly the red veins that had broken out across the bridge of his nose, how he had missed several spots when shaving that morning. How his hair was indeed dyed.

The three of them stared at each other for a moment in silence. McBride seemed to be asking himself a question. Then he looked down at the table, almost embarrassed, and muttered.

'I know nothing more than I've told you.'

And Councillor McBride was back chairing the meeting.

They sat in silence for another moment, but it was clear the man had nothing else to say. Claire and Flynn gathered their notes, their bags and their coats and went through the usual routine – the handing over of the cards, the exchanging of numbers.

'If you think of anything else—'

'Sure, sure.'

The older man pocketed the cards without looking at them. Claire's head ached, and it wasn't just from the smell of the furniture polish in the stuffy room. She and Flynn had come down to learn more about James Mannion but were leaving with more questions – questions that clearly wouldn't get answered today. She was knackered and frustrated and so many things were bugging her she didn't know where to start. She wanted Anna, and Matt, and a cup of tea in her own tiny house. She wanted to get away from this overly polished museum with Kim Jong McBride sitting under photographs of his former glory.

She wanted to go home.

CHAPTER THIRTEEN

'Seven-letter score! Championay, Championay!'

Touched by Felim's enthusiasm, Liz attempted a smile but stopped when even that slight movement caused unbearable pressure in her temples.

'I haven't lost it, have I? Eh?'

A tall, broad-shouldered man with sharp, handsome features, Felim leaned back from the table and looked triumphantly around the room. Across from him, his opponent, a new client called Eugene, rifled through the dictionary but his frown indicated he was unable to come up with anything that would call the winning word into question. He settled for muttering to himself instead, turning and warming his hands against the radiator on the wall. A musty, cattish smell rose from his damp trousers and Liz shuddered. Watching the game had been mildly diverting but her hangover was still at DEFCON 2 and she was nauseous as hell.

'Not feeling the best, pet?'

Oh, no. Lost in misery, Liz hadn't noticed Richard come into the room and, clearly unabashed by her abandonment a couple of days previously, he grabbed an empty chair and wedged himself in beside her.

'Anything I can do?'

'No.'

She searched her sodden, aching brain for a more comprehensive retort but couldn't find one. Richard leaned closer, the sharp scent of his cheap aftershave cutting through the mugginess of the under-ventilated room. Liz's eyes sought out Tom's but, although he too was sitting at the table, it was clear he might as well not have been in the room at all. Gazing into the middle distance, he looked as shell-shocked as Liz herself felt.

'How about a shoulder rub?'

Minty mouthwash was added to the aftershave, and, underneath, the fetid tang of rotten breath. Liz failed to repress a shudder as Richard breathed into her ear.

'I haven't had many complaints.'

Every one of her nerve endings screamed at her to push him away, but the fog of her hangover, coupled with the knowledge that Tom would notice if she was rude, kept her pinned to her chair.

'Let me in there, now, till we have a look . . .'

Richard scraped his chair back a fraction until he was sitting directly behind her, flexed his fingers ostentatiously and then began to knead at her shoulder blades. Liz twisted in her seat, trying to evade his touch, but her chair was trapped by his. She was even more nauseous now, dizzily claustrophobic, but no one else in the room seemed to notice, or care what was going on.

'Another game? Best of three, maybe?'

Across the table, Eugene gathered the tiles towards him and put them back in their cloth bag. But Felim merely smiled, stood up and wandered away. Eugene's face fell. They were seated at what had once been a family's dining table, rescued years ago from a skip by Tom and given pride of place in the sitting room at Tír na nÓg. Covered with scratches, the remnants of someone else's family life, it made Eugene look like a dejected grandfather trying to get the kids to hang on after Christmas dinner while they just wanted to get their hands on their electronic games.

'Ah, go on – one of yiz will.'

Sensing an escape route, Liz made another attempt to wriggle away from the poking, probing fingers and managed to twist her head around.

'Why don't you have a go, Richard?'

But the silver-haired man behind her shrugged and smiled.

'Not for me. I prefer my games a little more dangerous, if you know what I mean.'

Ugh. Richard's fingers found a particularly tender spot just below her ear and Liz moaned in pain, before realising, correctly, that he'd take the sound as an instruction to continue.

'I don't think—'

'Ah, relax, now; sure, we all need a bit of looking after.'

Dear Lord, why was the place so packed today? It was a Tuesday, an ordinary Tuesday morning. Usually there'd be four or five men in around now, reading the paper or drinking tea. But today there was over twice that number, driven inside by the biting wind and threatened rain. Who were they, anyway? These men with nowhere to go? Had they failed in some way, to end up here? And, when it came down to it, hadn't she failed in the same way?

'Enough!' Gathering all of her strength, she shoved her chair back from the table, narrowly avoiding Richard's toes, and stood up.

The noise seemed to wake Tom, who blinked and then looked across at Eugene.

'Sure, I'll give you a game, so.' He shook the bag of letter tiles and drew it towards him.

Liz turned away. 'Sorry – bit of a headache . . .'

Hurt and anger flickered across Richard's face as she pushed past him and, after a moment, he stood up too and moved quickly towards the door. She crossed the room to where an ancient grey sofa was wedged between fireplace and wall. It was the same sofa she had slept on the first night Tom had brought her here. Or passed out on, or whatever you wanted to call it. That wouldn't be the worst idea right now, she thought, wanly, just to lie down and stick a cushion over her head and hope sleep could make the events of the past few days go away.

Bloody Tom, insisting she come here. Then again, it wasn't like she had had anywhere else to go. Her boss had turned up on her doorstep that morning, after she'd failed to come to work for the second day in a row, and, when she hadn't answered the intercom, had let himself in, anyway.

'Leave me alone.'

She had a vague sense that she could accuse him of tres-
passing, or something, but her brain couldn't locate the word.
The shorter sentence got her message across just as well,
anyway, and, before her legs gave out, she collapsed on to the
sofa directly across from him and repeated it.

'Leave me. The fuck. Alone.'

'I didn't break in, you know. You gave me a key, ages ago.'

'Well, use it to get out again.'

That didn't really make sense, she realised dully, but it was
the best she could come up with under pressure. She grabbed
the TV remote control and turned the set up as loud as she could
in the hope it would force him to leave, but after a moment
she realised the noise was doing her far more damage than it
was him and she turned it off and stared at him, sullenly.

'What do you want?'

'You didn't show up for work yesterday, or this morning.'

'Worried, were you?' The snarl in her voice felt good, relieved
some of the tension, and she intensified it. 'Afraid you wouldn't
get your money's worth out of me? Tight bastard.'

She watched him wince and that felt good too, but even as she
spat out the words she was already doubting what he had said.
Yesterday? Had two whole days passed, then, since she'd opened
that envelope, read that note? She couldn't be sure. OK, there had
been the first evening, when she'd prised herself away from the
flat long enough to find a pub and some people who could get her
what she wanted. After that, though, it was harder to remember
the sequence of things. Had she stayed out for long? Had a few
drinks, a bit of a party? That was ringing a bell. Possibly. But what

had happened then? And how had she got home? Oh, Christ; who the fuck cared? Maybe it had been two days. Maybe it had been a month. What difference did it make, anyway?

'I was worried about you.'

She lifted her head, squinted at Tom, noticed how tense he was looking and then felt the skin on her scalp contract, the need rising in her. 'Do you have any money?'

He sat down heavily on the sofa. 'I was worried about you. You haven't been answering your phone.'

'Well, maybe that was because I didn't want to talk to you.'

The roughness in her voice hurt him – she could see that even through her own misery – and he turned away. 'I'll make coffee.'

Then a great wave of need and cold and shame and desperation had washed over her; she gave a huge rolling shiver as her skin crawled.

'Can you lend me twenty quid? Please, Tom, I'm in the horrors, here.'

'I don't have any money on me.'

'Please . . .'

Then she was crying free-flowing, helpless tears. Tom walked over to her, grabbed her by the shoulders and, for a moment, held her tightly. Then he pushed her away again and told her they had to leave.

He brought her straight to Tír na nÓg, asking her on the way, almost in a whisper, what had happened 'to set her off', as he put it. He'd nodded patiently when she said she couldn't tell him. Not yet. To admit it would be to make it real.

A flash of memory. A cigarette. Hands shaking, paper catching fire. She tossed the burning letter into the sink and watched black ashes float for a moment, then swirl away.

'I can't say.'

Couldn't, wouldn't. Didn't understand it. Couldn't face thinking about it. Just wanted the words not to exist at all.

You could be next.

'Here, get this down you.'

Without her noticing, Felim had come back into the room and was pressing a can of Coke in her hand.

'I saw you looked a bit rough earlier. I got you crisps as well.'

She looked at the bag he had handed her. They were the dear, hand-cut kind, which must have cost him a couple of euro. The thought of eating them made her want to throw up again, but she appreciated his kindness and attempted a smile.

'Ah, you're very good, but I can't—'

'Head at you? Stomach as well? Listen to me, now; this is your only man.' He took the can from her, pulled back the strip tab and pressed it into her hand again, steering her elbow upwards, gently moving the drink towards her lips. 'It'll do you good.'

He sounded so like a father, this kindly grey-haired man in his ancient brown suit jacket, that she smiled at him and took a sip. The bubbly liquid fizzed over her tongue and ran down her throat into her poor, tortured stomach. It seemed to soothe it, a little. She took another gulp and burped. And smiled.

Felim grinned back at her, and opened the crisps.

'Careful, now. You don't want it coming back up on you. Here – have one of these.'

Salt and vinegar. The mixture shouldn't have worked, but the strong chemical salty tang mixed with the cola was the most wonderful thing she could imagine. She hadn't, she realised suddenly, eaten for two days.

'It was the only thing that ever sorted me out, back in the day.'

'Right. Of course.'

Liz hadn't known Felim had a drink problem, or used to have, but it didn't surprise her. Many of the men who used Tír na nÓg's services battled with addiction, or depression, or a mixture of the two. Tom didn't allow alcohol on the premises, but he had been known to let some of them sleep it off if they were drunk but calm when they arrived. And she herself was hardly going to criticise them for that.

She shivered, and felt her mind reawaken as the sugar entered her bloodstream. Too soon. The drink was making her body feel better, but her head was still in the horrors.

Better to talk, not think.

She turned back to Felim, smiled again. 'Are you off it long yourself?'

'Fifteen years.'

His eyes were, she noticed, a startling shade of blue, and the whites were clear.

'Not worth it, is it?'

'No.'

Their heads were close together now, knees almost touching

on the sagging sofa. The room had emptied a little, three of the men having left to go outside for a smoke, and Liz could feel herself starting to relax. In one corner, Michael was reading the paper and muttering to himself about chancers in the Dáil. At the table, Tom and Eugene were still engrossed in the game of Scrabble. Life was going on as normal, or as normal as it got in Tír na nÓg.

'You're only a young one, though; you don't want to throw your life away.'

Felim sounded so sincere that Liz gave a genuine smile.

'Do you want to tell me what's wrong?'

She shook her head, about to say no, and then looked at him. She hadn't been able to tell Tom what had happened, couldn't bear the thought of it. He had put so much work into fixing her, she hadn't had the heart to tell him how little it had taken to mess it all up again. A couple of stupid anonymous notes, destroying everything they both had worked so hard for. But there was something about Felim that made her feel like she could tell him anything – confess to him, without the need for an act of contrition afterwards.

'I got a couple of letters. From this guy called Stephen. Weird stuff, mentioning James and that. They've just freaked me out, that's all.'

He nodded, calmly. Felim was a man, she figured, who didn't get freaked out often. Maybe he had seen it all before.

'And have you gone to the guards?'

She took another sip of Coke.

'No. My friend, Dean – he says this sort of stuff happens all the time. You know, because I've been on the TV and stuff. Anyway, I did something stupid. I threw the first one away, and I got pissed and burned the other one. So I've no proof. And I'm afraid they'll laugh if I tell them that.'

Felim raised his hand as if to pat hers, and then took it away again. His respecting of her boundaries, after Richard's earlier advances, made her so grateful Liz almost burst into tears.

Felim gave a shy grin. 'They're not all bad, the Gardaí. You might find a decent fella, someone who'll listen to you.'

Liz shook her head. The guards hadn't been on her side, back in the day. She had no reason to believe things would be different now.

As if he knew what she was thinking, Felim smiled again. 'You're a good girl, Elizabeth. I can call you a girl, can't I? You're only a young one. I don't care what you do or what you did outside of here. In here, in this place, you're a hero. You do great work. You shouldn't let this type of thing drag you down.'

He looked across the room to where Tom was now locked in a debate over a triple-word score.

'Everyone in here thinks a lot of you, and that lad over there is very fond of you. You've a good friend there. But do you know something? He can't fix you.'

It was funny, she realised, how they had both used the exact same word without knowing it.

'He can't fix whatever happened. Whatever happened to you in the past and whatever happened this week to set you back, he can't make it better. It's you that has to tackle it, face up to it. Lookit, anything would be better than this, wouldn't it?'

The sweep of his arm encompassed the Scrabble players, the dingy room, their lives.

'I'm just an oul fella, seeing out my days. You've fifty years of life ahead of you to enjoy, if you want to.'

This time he did pat her hand, squeezing it awkwardly before pulling away again. Liz sat back on the sofa, drained, but, for the first time that day, somewhat at peace. Eugene laughed, a surprisingly high-pitched squeal, and in an instant the room seemed to have shifted back on its axis again. The furniture was homely, not scruffy. The men friendly, not strange.

Not home, but something like it. Somewhere safe.

CHAPTER FOURTEEN

It was three o'clock in the morning when Stephen realised that writing to her would never be enough. He needed to see her, speak to her. Needed to tell her everything.

Memories of Mr Mannion had kept him from sleeping. Always 'Mr Mannion'. Never 'James'. Gone now, but still with him – the memories too. Hot breath on his neck, spittle in his face.

Hurt in the places the marks don't show.

He drifted into an unsettled sleep then and woke again at noon, foggy headed, shaken, less certain. Why her? Why now?

Why not?

A pain, deep beneath his kidneys. The body remembers. Stephen heaved himself out of bed and stood for a moment, dizzy, as the blood sank from his head. Maybe it would be best to lie down again, wait for it all to go away.

But maybe it never would.

He would tell her, and then everything would be OK.

He was too anxious to eat, but spent a long time in the shower, using scented shampoo that had been left in there by one of the other tenants. Then he ironed three shirts before deciding which one to wear, pulled *on socks without holes in them and polished his shoes. By the time he was ready to leave, it was the middle of the afternoon, but the delay would have been worth it, if he got to meet her. If she noticed the effort he had made. Elizabeth.*

She would understand. He could make her understand.

My Elizabeth.

Stop right there.

It wasn't a long journey and Stephen considered walking, but didn't want to sweat inside his shirt so caught a bus instead. Then, almost immediately regretted the decision. The vehicle was packed, clammy and airless and, after inching his way to the only available seat, he found himself pinned against the unopened window, hemmed in by a bearded tourist whose backpack made him look like a large upended beetle. An old man on a disabled seat stared at him as if he knew exactly where he was going, and what he was going to do.

But how could he, when Stephen wasn't sure himself? Well, not really.

Lost in misery and self-doubt, he almost missed his stop and had to scramble past the beetle, two laughing women and a large baby buggy to get to the door. His heart was racing now, his fingers slipping on the plastic pole and they missed the button that would get the bus to STOP and let him out of there and then the baby was crying and the women were still laughing and they didn't see him trying to MOVE past them and GET OFF HE NEEDED TO GET OFF. 'Excuse me please I think I . . .'

The driver noticed him, in the end, and slid open the doors while they were stopped at a set of traffic lights. They weren't supposed to do that, but something about the panic on the face of the man in the sticky shirt made her not want him on her bus for longer than she could help it.

Stephen stumbled down the steps, accepted abuse from a passing cyclist and clambered, shaking, on to the footpath. Nearly there. It had been a bad decision, to get the bus. But when had he ever made a good one?

Maybe today.

He started to walk, slowly. No point in rushing. Better to collect his thoughts, to know what he wanted to say.

To do.

To say.

Would she understand him? Would she appreciate how stupid he felt, walking along, shoulders hunched under the sweaty shirt, thoughts jumbled up in his head like tangled twine, looking for someone to find the end and pull the rope taut again?

Would she see how much he needed her? How far he was willing to go to be with her? What he was willing to do?

In many ways, he wasn't a man at all. In his head, he was still fifteen. They said that happened sometimes, after trauma – that you stay that age forever. He read it in a newspaper; cut it out, put it in his scrapbook. Maybe he'd show it to her.

The closer he got to her, the more he thought about going home. But he had come so far. So he kept walking; took out his phone as if he was checking directions, but he didn't need to. The address of the centre was the only solid, anchored thing in his head. That, and the thoughts of her.

He would know what to say when he got there. Wouldn't he?

He licked his top lip, tasted salt, worried about it, sweated some more. Worried some more. The closer he got to her, the sicker he felt.

He leaned against a wall for a moment, bent his arm around and failed to reach the muscle in the small of his back that was twanging in pain. He imagined for a moment what it would be like to have someone *rub it for him; felt a need warm and glow and grow inside him at the thought of it.*

To have someone touch him there.

To have someone touch him anywhere.

Take it slowly, now.

You need to live your life again.

She'll fix me.

Another road, a side street and, too quickly, he had arrived.

He paused at the gate. There were beads of sweat on his forehead, running down his neck. He hadn't thought he'd get here so soon. He needed to plan what he was going to say. Somehow, at three o'clock in the morning, he had imagined the words would come easily to him, but now his thoughts were scrambled.

There is only one way to do this and that is by doing it. Advice someone had given him a long time ago. It hadn't made sense then and it didn't make sense now, but the rhythm of it was comforting and he turned and felt his back contract and the pain rise and subside as he walked his feet forward, through the gate, up the path and as far as the door. Only one way to do it, by doing it. Only one way to do it, by doing it. He lifted his eyes from his shoes and felt his breath flutter in his throat.

He knocked at the door.

You'll know what to say.

'I want to speak to Elizabeth.'

'I'm sorry, pal. She's not here.'

The man was easily thirty years older than him, his clothes even shabbier than his own, but there was an air of contentment about him. Belly full of food, happy smile on his face.

'Tom's right here – will I get him for you?'

Stephen was not prepared for this. No words came.

The man moved closer, a question in his eyes. 'Are you alright, boy? You don't look the best, if you don't mind me saying so . . .'

His throat dry, Stephen scraped words from somewhere.

'No, thanks. I'm grand.'

He forced himself to meet the man's eyes, saw confusion there.

'Sure, come in for a minute, anyway, and catch your breath.'

A shadow moved in the hall and Stephen felt the sweat dry cold on his skin.

He knew he was taking a risk, coming here. But he hadn't realised just how dangerous it would be.

Wordlessly, Stephen turned and strode back down the path but the man walked after him, reached out his hand and grabbed him on the shoulder.

'Hey – what's your name?'

'It's OK; it's fine,' he muttered, stumbling, shaking, trying to escape. But the big man did not want to let him go.

'No, c'mere a minute.'

The man moved closer – his eyes searching Stephen's face, his expression suddenly hostile. 'Here, did my brother send you looking for me, is that it?'

And other questions Stephen didn't understand.

He stumbled his way back down the garden, out on to the footpath and crashed straight into a woman, sending the contents of her bag spilling out on to the road.

'Here – you! I suppose a sorry is out of the question? Fuck's sake.'

But the big man was chasing him now too, hurling questions. Stephen tried to answer him but everything he said made things worse. In the end, he just ran, the woman's voice drifting after him.

'Fucking eejit!'

Yeah, he thought to himself as he stumbled towards the bus stop. That's me.

CHAPTER FIFTEEN

'A bottle of Coors Light, please. No, actually, make it a pint. Lovely. Thanks.'

Claire slurped the foam off the top of her drink and walked slowly back to the centre of the pub, where the rest of the lads were standing in a circle, yelling at each other. It was pointless, really, drinking those fecky little bottles. She'd spend the night going up and down to the bar, if she stuck to them. She hadn't planned on coming out this evening but, seeing as she'd gone to the trouble, she might as well make the most of it.

Taking another reviving swallow, she elbowed her way into a space between Rory Deegan and Sean Caulfield, catching the end of what sounded like a far-fetched story about a crustie, a five spot and a missing evidence bag. Deegan was hyper, hands darting, beer splashing everywhere as he gave the anecdote socks, and, although she didn't fully understand the punch line, Claire laughed along with the rest of them, anyway. It was great, being back in a gang like this. Matt had been right to make her go.

She slid her phone out of her jeans pocket and checked the screen. Nothing. Good man, Mattie. Anna must be fast asleep, so – or at least happy to spend Friday night without her mother. Nice one. She took another gulp of her beer and had to stop herself doing a comedy exhalation – *ahhhh!* – as the bubbly liquid slid down her throat. Typical Matt, to know exactly what she needed.

The invite to Dave Rourke's retirement do had been stuck to the fridge for weeks, but when she'd stomped in from the office earlier that evening, tired, sticky and frustrated by her lack of progress in the Mannion investigation, Claire hadn't had a notion of attending. But her husband had insisted she go. She hadn't been out in ages, he'd reminded her, and she'd enjoy it when she got there. The following day was Saturday. She could let her hair down.

There had been a funny expression on Matt's face when he was saying it, though, like he'd been trying to say something else at the same time, and it had bothered her, a little. She'd smiled down at the child, who was playing happily in her bouncer, and then leaned against the fridge and narrowed her eyes.

'What is it to you, whether I go or not?'

She realised the words sounded confrontational as soon as she'd said them, but something about the look on his face continued to provoke her, so she didn't take them back, just folded her arms and waited for his reply.

'We haven't been out in ages – either of us.'

'Oh, here we go again.' She sighed, and picked up Anna's

soother, which had fallen on the floor. 'You don't want to come with me, do you?'

'Christ, no!'

His look of horror took some of the tension out of the conversation, and she smiled, despite her bad mood.

'What, drink warm beer and listen to cop talk all night? Absolutely not. I just think we should get out more, both of us, and if we can't do it together, then we might as well do it separately. You, on a Friday; me, on a Saturday. Or whatever. Let's just make time for it, yeah? Then maybe we'll take your mum up on her offer of babysitting. In a week or so.'

'God.'

Claire shuddered. She knew Matt was right; Anna was nearly seven months old and they hadn't been out on their own since she had been born. But Matt's mother wasn't the type to relish the prospect of spit-up on her jacket, and her own parents, even though they were dying to get their hands on their only grandchild, would have to travel up from Galway and stay overnight, which, quite frankly, made a few drinks in the local sound like more hassle than they were worth. They could ask one of the girls from the crèche to do a nixer but that would add forty quid to the night's bill, easy. So they'd just got out of the habit of it, she supposed. Nights out had turned into nights in with box-sets and bottles of wine. And that was fun, it its own way. At least, that's how she looked at it, and she had thought Matt felt the same.

'I'm perfectly happy staying in with you.'

Curse him, he always could read her mind.

But her husband hadn't finished speaking and, reaching over, brushed a strand of hair away from her cheek.

'But I think it's important we do other stuff too. It doesn't have to be a big deal. I want to get back running again; I miss it. There's a half-marathon next year I'd really like to train for. And other stuff, you know – see a match on a proper screen, have a few pints with the lads, that sort of thing. I just think it would be nice if we could set aside an evening a week to do whatever we want to do. No questions. Just one night each. And we'll work on finding a babysitter for the weekend if you don't want to get the grannies involved.'

'Ah, come on.' She laughed at him then, rolled her eyes. 'Tuesday can be my yoga night and Thursday can be your night with the boys? Jesus, Matt, we laugh at those kind of people!'

He'd smiled at her then, and waggled his fingers at the baby. 'Hon, we are those kind of people now.'

Depressing thought. Still, he'd been right about tonight, though. Claire drained her glass and winked at Dave Keegan, who was heading to the bar.

'Go on, then; if you insist.'

She stole a crisp from Michael Harris and felt the tension melt from her shoulders. They were a great bunch and it had been, what, nearly a year and a half since she'd been out with them? Out properly, that was. She'd tagged along, the odd night, when she was expecting Anna, but it just hadn't been the same. Sitting around, nursing a fizzy water while the conversation grew rowdy; trying to join in with the crack but always being half a beat behind. Not worth the trouble. But tonight, tonight she felt she was right in there.

Keegan came back and Claire shrugged her jacket off her shoulders and threw it on a nearby bar stool before accepting the new pint with a smile. Even the heat of the bar felt good against her skin. She sank into it, the smell of the place, a welcome mixture of beer, aftershave and damp fleece jackets. None of the lads were in uniform, but they didn't need to be. Everyone else in the pub could see exactly who they were and were giving them a wide berth – which, Claire thought to herself, was exactly as it should be. They deserved a night out, the same as the next crowd. And there was no gang like them when they were on form.

Keegan shouted something at her but she smiled vaguely and waved him away, unable to hear and unwilling to put much effort in. She was happy just to stand back, sip her fresh drink and let the conversation ebb and flow around her. It was nice, just being able to think back over the day, without Anna to mind or – good and all, as he was – Matt to include in the conversation. Standing here, surrounded by half-cut cops, Claire felt as alone as she had been in a long time, and far more peaceful.

The case conference that morning had been short and bitter. Superintendent Quigley had allowed her to present what they knew so far, which, to be honest, was fuck all. She and Flynn had pieced together a few more facts about the victim, but nothing particularly interesting. James Mannion hadn't worked as a teacher since leaving Rathoban. In fact, officially, although he'd still been in his mid thirties when he arrived in Dublin, he'd never worked again. He had drawn the dole for a while, and supplemented it with nixers, mostly as a painter and decorator. The house on Darcy Terrace wasn't his, but he'd secured a long-term lease decades ago and his landlord, a man of a similar age who owned multiple properties around the city, had been happy to let him stay there. And that was hardly a selfless act of charity, Claire realised. The place hadn't had so much as a lick of paint since Mannion moved in and the kitchen was a health hazard, even before the tenant crawled in there to die. There had been practically nothing of value in the place, either, just an ancient radio, Mannion's books and, of course, the milk cartons. Claire still didn't know what to think about them. Were they evidence that Mannion was a hoarder, maybe? That he'd feared being trapped in his house, running low of supplies? She would never know. The dead man's GP hadn't been much use to them either, telling them merely that Mannion had been an infrequent visitor to the surgery. Dr Coughlan, a busy, freckled man in his early fifties, had confirmed that Mannion had complained of stomach pain in recent months and that he'd referred him to the hospital where a cancer diagnosis had been made. He was a nice man, he'd mumbled, looking up from his notes for a moment, a little eccentric but sure that was hardly a crime, was it?

He hadn't looked particularly upset at the news of Mannion's passing, but that was doctors for you, Claire supposed. They had to get used to their patients dying in the end – occupational hazard. In fact, as far as Claire knew, Tom Carthy's were the only tears that had been shed at James Mannion's death. Siobhán O'Doheny, who had been sent with Flynn to Tír na nÓg in the aftermath of the killing, had told her that none of the clients from whom they took statements had seemed particularly upset. They hadn't been particularly chatty either, just came out with the usual guff about how Mannion had been a *nice man who had minded his own business*. Oh there had been head-nods alright, O'Doheny told Claire. Downward glances and sighs, and here and there a 'God rest him' or a 'Poor oul James'. But no tears. And the assistant Tom Carthy had spoken about, a young woman called Liz, hadn't been much use to them either. O'Doheny swore she had seen her on TV a couple of times, although Claire had to admit the name wasn't familiar to her. So, that's all they had. Shag all. And what was worse was the papers were starting to question the investigation too, and the phone-in radio shows, with one programme devoting an entire hour to the discussion, 'Why aren't our elderly safe in their homes?' One caller had even suggested a vigil be held in the city centre to show solidarity, she said, with old people who live alone, although what good that would do, Claire couldn't imagine.

Maybe another pint would give her inspiration. She leaned towards Keegan, ready to admit it was her round and head up to the bar – and then noticed that he and the rest of the lads were staring past her left shoulder.

She turned, followed their gaze and realised she'd have to actually turn herself into a pint of Guinness to win back their attention. Most of the lads had made some sort of effort that evening – showered, shaved, run the iron over the best shirt, or got someone else to do it for them. She herself had thrown on a new top for the occasion, and jeans that were Weetabix-free. But Garda Siobhán O'Doheny looked like she was attending a different function entirely. As she paused in the pub doorway and took a slow look around the room, Claire knew she wasn't the only cop there dying to wolf-whistle; except, the others would have been deadly serious. O'Doheny's long blond hair looked fuller than usual – she must have been to the hairdresser's – and her white sleeveless top showed off arms that would make Michelle Obama jealous. As she turned around in a further effort to find her friends, Claire noticed an arse that could only be described as peachy.

Peachy. Claire snorted. She must be a bit pissed. Well, a lot pissed. Fuck it, it was Saturday tomorrow; she'd handle the hangover.

Finally spotting the rest of the cops, O'Doheny glided through the doorway and an even better-looking specimen, male this time, walked in close behind her.

'Whoa! I'd fancy that, meself.'

Keegan nudged Claire and she grinned back at him.

'Well matched, aren't they?'

Claire took a slug from her pint and then stopped, glass halfway from her lips, when she realised Philip Flynn was standing at the other side of the bar, eyes out on stalks. Poor fucker. There'd been a funny atmosphere between himself and O'Doheny ever since the night of the Miriam Twohy verdict. Claire didn't know what had happened; Anna had been just six weeks old and she'd only hung around for an hour, anxious to celebrate the victory but knackered and, she admitted to herself, missing her new little girl. But it looked like, whatever had transpired after she left, Flynn had yet to get over it. Feeling suddenly protective, she walked over to where he was standing and edged in beside him.

'Having a good night?'

He tore his eyes away from O'Doheny and the boyfriend and gave her a weak smile. 'Yeah, grand. You?'

'Great!'

He was looking well, Flynn; a decent black shirt on him and the new haircut was a huge improvement. She'd noticed him yapping to a few of the others earlier, as well; it looked like he was finally making friends. Jesus. She caught sight of herself in the mirror behind the bar and grimaced. What was she, his mother? Still, though, if he was going to have his heart broken, she might as well keep him company. But before she could steer the conversation towards something more neutral, the crowd of guards parted and O'Doheny glided over to join them, her fella a few paces behind. Hands were shaken, names exchanged. 'Diarmaid, lovely to meet you.' 'Likewise.' Blah, blah. Flynn, not the chattiest at the best of times, appeared to have been struck dumb, so Claire decided to give him a hand and smiled at the newcomer.

'So, how long have you known Siobhán, then?'

Diarmaid looked at her, and grinned. 'Nearly thirty years?'

Several pints into the night, it took Claire a minute to cop on to why the others were laughing.

'He's my brother,' O'Doheny explained, her eyes wide.

Ah. Feeling the effects of the beer at last, Claire smiled foolishly – then realised she might be in a position to do Flynn a favour, after all. Resisting the urge to do a comedy nudge, she edged towards the lovely Diarmaid, leaving her colleague and O'Doheny wedged together at the bar. Right, Black Beauty, I've led you to water, now sup away.

In fairness, though, engaging O'Doheny's brother in conversation was no great hardship. He was a lovely bloke, Claire realised after a few minutes; no side to him at all, happy to yap away about most things – movies, books, TV. Some of the stuff he mentioned, she only had half a notion about – plays he'd seen and that sort of thing – but he had a lovely way about him, a way of making you feel that whatever you had to say had merit in it. After a while, Siobhán and Flynn joined them and the four of them had the crack. Flynn was looking more at ease as the conversation, and the beer, flowed.

'Two, three, four!'

Ah, feck it – 'The Fields of Athenry'. And it was only – Claire checked her watch – twenty past twelve. Later than she thought, actually. Late enough, anyway, for some of the lads to have lapsed into rowdiness. The barman, ostentatiously polishing glasses, gave them a look as if to say, *Yiz might be guards, but don't push me.*

Across from her, Siobhán stretched, showing off those sculpted arms to full advantage. 'I think it's time for a bit of a bop; who's coming with me?'

'Not me.' Claire's yawn almost split her face in two and she stumbled a little as she moved away from the bar.

'Careful!' Diarmaid grabbed her by the elbow and steadied her. 'Can I give you a lift home?'

She peered at him, confused, and then remembered he'd been on the mineral water all evening.

'Ah, no, I'm grand.'

'Honestly – Shiv's going on with the rest of them; I've room in the car. I can drop you home too, if you like?' He looked across at Flynn, who nodded.

'That'd be great, thanks', he said draining his pint.

'I'll leave ye to it, so!' beamed Siobhán, who looked as sober as the moment she'd walked into the bar. She kissed her brother on the cheek then strode away from them and straight into the centre of a group who were debating the merits of Copper Face Jacks versus Vanilla. Looking at them, faces glowing with drink and excitement, the prospect of a late night and a quiet house in which to sleep it off shimmering before them, Claire felt suddenly old and worn. Part of her wanted to nudge Flynn, to point in O'Doheny's direction and tell him to enjoy the rest of the evening, but mostly her feet hurt and she wanted to sit down. And if this nice young man wanted to save her the hassle of a taxi queue, what harm?

Minutes later, she found herself in the back of a very large and very clean Audi, Flynn buckling himself in in front. Flynn? That didn't make sense; sure, he lived over the other side of the city. Maybe he had come to chaperone her, Claire thought, and giggled. Chance would be a fine thing. Nice, though, if he thought she was in danger from Diarmaid, the out-and-out ride. Misguided, but nice. The engine started with a well-tuned purr and she leaned her head back against the seat, suddenly exhausted. Letting someone else take charge for a change – that was lovely, too. Sound man, Diarmaid. Nice voice; she could hear it rising and falling, Flynn replying, the two of them laughing and then it rising again, washing over her as her eyes drooped . . .

'Claire? We're here.'

She opened her eyes with a jerk. Jesus, she'd dropped right off. Oh, Gawd, she hoped she hadn't snored. She wiped her chin, but there was no evidence of drool. It was a good thing Flynn knew her address. Good Lord, she'd been out for the count; that was the downside of having a small baby. She could sleep on a clothes line now, whether she wanted to or not. Her head felt a little clearer, though, and she tapped Diarmaid-the-ride on the shoulder.

'Thanks a million for the lift.'

'Not at all! Lovely meeting you. Siobhán's a big admirer, if you don't mind me saying.'

Claire grabbed her bag, peeled herself off the seat, considered pecking her chauffeur on the cheek and then shook his outstretched hand instead. She punched Flynn on the shoulder and told him she'd see him Monday. After struggling out of the car, she slammed the door shut and then gave it a quick tap on the roof for good luck before watching it pull away. She scrabbled in her bag for her keys and then cursed loudly when she realised she'd forgotten her jacket. Feck it, it was a nice one too. She turned, and realised with relief that the car hadn't gone any distance at all; in fact, it had pulled in just a short distance down the street and . . .

Oh.

The street light shining through the window lit up the car. The kiss, when it began, was hesitant, and then, after a moment, not hesitant at all.

Claire kept looking until it dawned on her fuzzy brain that it was rude to stare. But neither Flynn nor Diarmaid were in any position to notice.

CHAPTER SIXTEEN

Eugene only really made up his mind when he saw the safe. Up until then, he'd had no real intention of ripping them off. They were sound enough, the crowd at Tír na nÓg. Eejits, obviously, but harmless with it. And they made a decent cup of tea. So, no, he'd no real notion of stealing from them or of doing anything to them, really, until he'd looked into the makey-uppy room they called 'the office' and seen the glint of tin in the top drawer. He'd slid it out for a quick look and, sure, it practically leaped up into his arms at that stage. A tin box, for fuck's sake. You wouldn't store your communion money in it. It was like they were asking to be robbed.

It was all . . . What was that word the sister's young fella kept using? *Random.* It was all totally random, anyway. He shouldn't even have been in Dublin that week, let alone hanging around their poxy little charity. But he'd got himself into a bit of trouble down home, with the brother and that, and it was a case of either hang around and risk getting his head kicked in, or get the fuck out of Dodge for a while. So Eugene had hopped on the first bus leaving out of Cork and ended up, four hours later, standing on O'Connell Street in the pissings of rain with barely enough money in his pocket for a cup of tea. Hoor of a place, Dublin; he had never liked it, but it was far from home and no fucker was looking for him there, that was the main thing. So it would have to do, for a week or two. Just until things died down.

The first few days, he'd stayed quiet enough, kept his head down, nicked a wallet off a tourist that gave him enough money for a few dinners and a bed in a B & B, and kept to himself the rest of the time. But when that few bob ran out, Eugene hadn't been sure what to do next. He didn't know the city well enough to chance too much dipping and, besides, if the cops lifted him, they might find out what had happened at home and that would lead him to a path he definitely didn't want to go down. So he spent a night in a doorway, and then a second one, and by day three he was sick of it all, tired of being hungry, filthy and bored stupid, and cursing himself for getting into trouble in the first place. In fact, Eugene was actually beginning to think he would have to take his chances back in Cork when this oul one crossed the street and bent down in front of him. He held out his cup to her, hopefully, but, instead of throwing in a few coins, she shoved her face into his.

'Have you nowhere to go, love?'

Yeah, he wanted to say, it's just the cleaners are in my penthouse apartment and I wanted to give them a clear run at it.

But he couldn't be arsed taking the piss and, besides, he

was fairly sure the sarcasm would be wasted on her, so he just waggled the cup in front of her face in the hope she'd throw in a few bob or at least get the fuck out of his light.

But she wasn't going anywhere.

'There's no need to be sitting here in the damp; you'll catch your death. You should head along to that Tír na nÓg place – they'll sort you out.'

'Where's that, then?' He hadn't meant to talk to her but it had been three days since he'd said anything to another human being, other than, 'I'll have a Coke with that,' and he was interested, despite himself. 'What is it?'

'Oh, it's a marvellous place.'

She raised herself slowly back up to a standing position, and Eugene squinted up at her. She was the same age as himself, if not older, he realised, and, judging by the cheap plastic raincoat and laddered tights, not much better off, either. She was mad for the chat too, that was obvious, and he began to regret ever having caught her eye. But there was no stopping her now; she was yammering away about what a wonderful resource this Tír na nÓg place was and how it was – how did she put it? – fulfilling a vital role, and wasn't there this wonderful girl working there who went on the television talking about it and, sure, she should be running the country, not the crowd who got in the last time.

Eugene had to lift his hand in the end to stem the flow. He gave the best approximation he could of a smile and explained that, although it sounded wonderful, he wasn't long in Dublin himself and hadn't a clue how to get there.

'Well, it's about a forty-five-minute walk from here; you go straight down this road and take a left . . .'

But when she saw his eyes glaze over, she smiled and took an envelope out of her pocket.

'I'll write it down for you, love.'

She scribbled something, then tore off a corner of the bit of paper and handed it to him.

'Now. May you be warm and dry, anyway.'

With another smile, and a 'God Bless, now,' she shuffled off, her scuffed shoes making a slapping, squelching sound on the wet pavement. Didn't give him a cent, just the bit of paper. Eugene thought about chucking it, but then he felt a drip on his head and realised he was minutes away from another soaking. Feck it. He looked down, squinted, read what she'd written. *Tír na nÓg*. The old girl had written a bus number as well. Right so. It wasn't like he'd anything better to do. He could phone home, try and patch things up, but he'd be better off waiting till he got a few bob together to pay Anthony back. It had been his brother's own fault, really, leaving the money under the mattress like that, and how was Eugene to know his usual supplier had passed his order on to a far less reputable source? But Anthony was funny about that sort of thing, so it was best all round to leave going home until he'd got the cash together. In the meantime, this Tír na nÓg place would have to do.

Less than an hour later, he'd found himself sitting on a scuffed but clean chair and drinking the first of several free cups of tea. Tír na nÓg: the magical, mystical land of Youth.

There was no sign of Niamh or a white horse, though, and the whole 'Óg' thing was a pile of shite too, because there were only two people in the place under the age of sixty: some bloke called Tom, who seemed to run the place and had that 'trying to be everyone's friend' thing going on, and a young one who made a big show of shaking his hand when he got there and then wrinkled her nose when she thought he wasn't looking. Cheek of her. Fair enough – Eugene was aware he reeked to high heaven; three days of sleeping in doorways wasn't exactly conducive to good personal hygiene. But she didn't have to let on she'd noticed.

Liz, her name was, and Eugene couldn't figure out why she was there at all, or what was in it for her. Spending her days sitting in a manky office and drinking tea with oul lads like himself. He could only assume she was riding Mr Friendly Tom, or wanted to ride him, or got a kick out of him wanting to ride her, or something. There had to be some excuse. One of the lads, Richard, clearly fancied his chances, and another one of them swore blind to him that she was a hero, a saint of a girleen who had devoted her life to the place and the men and went on television and everything to try to get money for them. But Eugene knew there were few saints in this world.

Poor eejit, though – Felim, that fella's name was – if it cheered him up to believe in living saints then Eugene wasn't going to disappoint him. He wasn't one of the worst ones, anyway; at least you could have a chat with him or play a game of cards. Some of the other oul fellas were half mad, gone loo-lah after years spent living on what the ponces on the telly called the 'margins of society'. But, what matter? At the end of the day, the centre was warm and dry, and there was usually tea in the pot and a pack of cards on the go. It would do. In fact, as far as hideaways went, Tír na nÓg had a lot going for it.

So, no, Eugene had no intention of ripping them off – not initially, anyway. But he'd had a really shitty day. He'd been too late for a hostel bed the night before and had ended up dossing down in a shop doorway where he'd slept fitfully until some junkie skanger had turned up at three a.m. and insisted it was his spot. Eugene had considered arguing the point with him – the fella might have been younger than him, but he was thin and fierce unhealthy looking – but then decided against it. You couldn't take your chances with druggies, in case they were carrying needles. So he'd sloped off instead and walked around the town until Tír na nÓg opened. A crap way to spend a night, no matter how you looked at it.

The lack of sleep had put him into a bad mood for the day, and then there had been that whole business with the weirdo at the door. Eugene had only answered the bell because he'd been sitting on his hole all day and was bored, and, when your man asked him if 'Elizabeth' was in, he'd been polite, just told him truthfully that he hadn't seen her around.

But then your man had looked up at him like he'd seen a ghost or something and legged it back down the garden. It was so weird and unexpected that Eugene had followed him, just to find out what was going on. Got a bit worried, actually – worried that maybe the brother had sent someone up to put the frighteners on him. So he'd followed him out on to the road.

Your man was practically running by the time he got to the gate and ran straight into a woman carrying a load of shopping bags. Her stuff went flying but it was like he didn't even notice, just stood there, winded, with this kind of frightened look on his face. Eugene grabbed him by the arm then, asked him if the brother had sent him, but your man just kept muttering under his breath about Elizabeth and how he needed to speak to her, and other shite too, stuff that didn't make sense at all. The whole thing was really fucking unsettling and made Eugene's mind up for him. It was time to go home – leave Tír na bleedin' nÓg and head back to where he belonged. He'd a few bob put by, not everything he owed the brother, not by a long shot, but hopefully it would be enough. He could catch the last bus, turn up at the flat with a ten spot and a few cans and persuade Anthony there were no hard feelings. He'd been gone long enough; surely things would have calmed down by now.

And that's when he saw the box. Tom was in the sitting room playing cards with Felim, so when Eugene asked him to lend him a bus timetable he told him to go into the office and help himself. They might as well have stuck a sign on the door: *Money In Here*. Eugene was well sick of being a good client at that stage, so he shoved the tin box down his trousers and walked out the door. Thanks, Tom, and goodnight from me.

He even knew how much was likely to be in it. That's how much of a feckin' tool your man, Tom, was. Eugene had overheard him, two days previously, talking to Lady Liz about a donation that had been slipped in through the door.

'Five hundred euro!'

The two of them had been in the office, but the dodgy dividing wall meant Eugene, in the sitting room, could hear every word.

'An anonymous donation! You see, Liz, I told you it would be worthwhile doing all those interviews! That's the heating bill looked after till well into the new year.'

And then the rattle of the box as it was locked and put in the drawer. Anyone that thick deserved to be stolen from.

Eugene usually left the centre via the main road, but this time his head was down, all his energy concentrated on keeping the tin box tucked inside his pants, so he took a left instead of a right and ended up in a little cul-de-sac of red-brick houses he'd never seen before. Next to them was a brick wall and a door and, walking through it, Eugene found himself on the bank of the Royal Canal. Just the job. He checked his watch: three hours to kill before the Cork bus left. That would give him plenty of time to check out the contents of the box and then walk into town. Nice one. There'd surely be enough in there to pay his brother back, and keep a few bob for himself too, even. All in all, a very good day.

The grass was damp under his feet and, as Eugene walked along the canal, he realised he only had an angry-looking swan and a couple of ducks for company. That was perfect too. By day, this place got pretty busy – you'd get the odd jogger, young ones pushing buggies, or office workers carrying poncy cups of coffee and thinking they lived in New York or somewhere. But come night-time, the only drinks consumed around here tended to be out of brown paper bags. This evening, however, it looked like walkers and boozers alike had all been scared away by the bad weather – which suited Eugene just fine. Great weather for ducks. And fellas looking for a bit of privacy.

Turning his collar up, Eugene quickened his pace and walked briskly until he came to a large patch of shrubbery about thirty feet away from the door in the wall. In front of him, the water glistened blackly and, across the canal, a high stone wall divided the waterway from a seldom-used railway line. Eugene took the box out of his pants, hitched up his trousers and dropped to his hunkers. He reached out, grabbed a sharp pebble and gave the lock a quick tap. Just as he'd anticipated, it sprang open immediately. Jesus, the innocence of it; they couldn't have made it any easier for him. And then he took a proper look inside.

'What in the . . . ?'

A fiver. One tattered five-euro note, anchored to the bottom of the box by a few coppers. But that didn't make any sense. It was only yesterday Tom had been blathering on about how many donations they were after getting and how he'd have to do a bank run . . .

The tip of the blade skimmed over his collar and stopped at the nape of his neck.

'Shuffle forwards on your arse. Don't turn around. Don't make a fucking sound.'

There was something familiar about the voice. Instinctively, Eugene tried to turn his head but immediately the knife poked deeper and he could feel a trickle of warm blood mix with the rain on his skin.

'I said, don't fucking move.'

It's only a fiver, he wanted to say. *Five quid. You can have it, if you like.* But as he felt himself being pressed forward, feet scrabbling for purchase on the wet grass, he realised this wasn't about the money. He was on his knees now, gravel drawing blood from the palms of his hands as he found himself being steered towards a thicker clump of bushes, the knife pressing ever closer, hot breath mixing with the blood that was soaking into his collar.

I'll give it back, was what he wanted to say, but the words dried in his mouth as he felt his shoulders being pushed roughly downwards. He was sitting by the side of the water now, hidden from the road by the bushes, and the knife was tickling away at him, but surely that was the wrong word – it was being lifted and then pressed against him. Pressed and then pushed and then there was a jabbing motion and it was in, it was all the way in and he could feel it, the heat of it, the hot tearing pain of it, and he could feel the blade ripping its way across his throat and the blood spurting and the pain and the red and the hot and the pain. And it was only a fiver. Nothing more.

CHAPTER SEVENTEEN

I'll be there in ten.

Claire sent the text without further embellishment. It was ten past six in the morning; she was freezing, grumpy and more than a little hungover. She'd dragged herself from her bed when Flynn had called. He'd have to live without politeness.

'Early start, love?'

'Umph.'

There should be penalty points, Claire decided, for taxi drivers who tried to engage their customers in conversation at this horrendous hour of the morning, and anyone who called her 'love' deserved to be put off the road altogether. Replacing her phone in her pocket, she turned her head in a deliberate movement and stared out of the window. The taxi driver shrugged and pumped up the volume on the radio, sending a nasal whine out into the pine-scented fug. Fantastic, thought his passenger. A phone-in show. What was the topic this time? 'Cops, and how useless they are.' Oldie but goodie. Old men were being murdered in their beds and nothing was being done about it, apparently. The guards hadn't a clue what was going on. Claire sighed. James Mannion had died in his kitchen, rather than his bed, but, other than that, she couldn't actually disagree with the caller, this time. At least the radio show was occupying the taxi driver and stopping him from talking to her. Talking would have been far too much to take.

The night before, heart warmed by the unexpected romance she'd accidently spied on through the rear windscreen, Claire had treated herself to a nightcap once she'd got her key in the door and couldn't quite remember what time she'd eventually fallen into bed. She had a vague memory of hearing the baby crying at some stage and Matt's groans as he went out to settle her. And an even more vague memory of plunging back into sleep again. But what she could remember, very clearly, was the sound of the phone as it rang at six a.m. and the rounded hunch of her husband's shoulder as Flynn's voice knocked on her fuzzy brain.

'I'll only be an hour – two, at most.'

Matt hadn't bothered to respond, which was a good thing, because she knew she was probably lying. The truth was she didn't know how long she'd be gone, and Matt's day off, his quid pro quo for her night with the boys, would have to be postponed. But, hangover banging in her temples, Claire hadn't the energy to go into that sort of laborious explanation, and just muttered, 'Work – will give you a shout when I know the story,' and tiptoed out of the house as quietly as she could. Not quietly enough, unfortunately. Just before she pulled the door tight behind her, Claire could hear the little bleating noise that meant Anna was minutes away from rising for the day. Poor Matt. She'd try to give him the evening off. Hopefully. Or a few hours the next day.

The taxi driver rounded a corner, too quickly, and Claire tried to give a warning cough, but her tongue was glued to the roof of her mouth and the sound came out more like a burp. *Bleaurgh*. God, she'd murder a can of Diet Coke, or, better still, a cup of tea – with two sugars, served in bed. That's where she should be right now, she told herself: tucked up in bed with a cup of tea by her side and the promise of a full Irish in about an hour's time. Maybe she'd make it home in time for lunch – that would be something.

The car drew up at a set of traffic lights and, beside her, another taxi's engine idled, its back seat crammed with a gang of girls who looked like they had yet to make it home after their night out. By the side of the road, an older woman stood forlornly at a bus stop, stuck on an early shift on this cold and miserable November morning, but other than that Dublin's streets were deserted. The lights turned green again and, as the car began its climb up Dorset Street, Claire saw a blue light flash, a beacon indicating where she needed to go. These streets wouldn't stay quiet for long.

Her phone buzzed and she checked the caller I.D. – Dean Evans. That was quick. The young journalist had first interviewed her almost two years ago, during the guards' annual Christmas drink-driving campaign, when Quigley had insisted a woman be found to go in front of the TV cameras. Claire had been shitting herself at the thought of being interviewed, but your man, Evans, had been sound enough to deal with and, at the end of the interview, she'd found herself giving him her personal mobile number in case he had any follow-up queries. In fairness to him, he hadn't abused the privilege, just called her a couple of times a year when he had a question the press office couldn't, or wouldn't, answer for him, and he'd never dragged her name into it when quoting 'sources' in his reports. He'd done her a couple of favours too since he'd started working for Ireland 24, including running a 'Gardaí seeking information' story about an elderly woman who'd gone missing, when none of the other hacks wanted to bother. Nice enough fella, really. A chancer, but, sure, they all were. The driver was fiddling with his radio now and they were still a few minutes from the crime scene, so she pressed the green button.

'Morning, detective; you're up early.'

'Ah, you know me, Dean; I'm mad for work – you can't keep me away from it. How about yourself? Sure, you're probably only on your way to bed!'

She heard a weary chuckle on the other end. That was the game you played; Claire was used to it by now. You kept the banter going, made out like you were two people shooting the breeze – she, a workaholic cop and he, the feckless young journo, coming home from a night on the tiles. Not a hungover mother who was desperate to get back to bed and a freelance hack who was gagging for a lead that would guarantee him a decent story and employment for another day.

Obligatory banter over, she waited for his question.

'I'm on an early shift with Ireland 24 today. We got a call about a body?'

'Did you, now?' Claire liked Evans, but she wasn't going to give in that easily. 'What sort of body?'

'Down by the canal? Dorset Street end?'

'Mm hm.'

'So, um –' Evans knew it was time to chance it – 'can you confirm anything?'

'All the details will be provided by the press office, Dean, you know that.'

From the other end of the phone, a deep sigh. 'I already rang them and they said they don't know anything. Just tell me, detective, please – is it worth my while leaving my cosy office and heading down there?'

Claire hesitated, and then decided to take pity on him. North Dublin was starting to wake up and someone was going to notice the white tent soon and tweet a picture of it, or some such nonsense. She might as well give a jump to someone she knew.

'Yeah. You're not hearing it from me, but yes. A body was discovered by a member of the public.'

'Was it an accident? Or—?'

'Obviously it's too early to say.'

'You wouldn't be up at this hour if it was.'

Claire saw the taxi driver's shoulders twitch and lowered her voice.

'Put it this way, I don't think you'd be wasting your time if you came down, OK?'

'Cheers, detective. Appreciate it.'

He hung up without another word. Claire appreciated the brevity. Appreciated the use of her title too. One of the local radio hacks had tried calling her Claire once, in a painful 'all girls together' type greeting. She hadn't tried it again. It wasn't that Claire liked pulling rank, not really, but it was best to keep things on a formal footing. Best for everyone.

'Just in here is grand, please.'

The taxi pulled up outside a locked and shuttered garage and Claire took out her purse.

'Receipt?'

The driver had, she noticed, dispensed with the 'love'. Which possibly meant he had copped on to who she was and where she was going.

'No, thanks, I'm grand.'

Claire heaved herself out of the back seat and stood in the drizzle as he dug around in an ancient Man United wallet for change. She wasn't going to claim this one back on expenses. Most people she knew would – in fact, many would have driven themselves in the first place, despite all the warnings about leaving 'one hour per unit' since the last drink the previous night. But Claire hadn't felt like taking the risk, and she hadn't rung Collins Street looking for a lift, either, not wanting to remind everyone that she'd been on the batter the night before. She had no time for the 'how's the head?' merchants who could be found still gossiping about Friday night on Tuesday after-noon, turning perfectly innocent fun into something vaguely seedy. She'd take the hit on the taxi instead. The price of the rare night out was worth it.

She scooped the pile of fifty-cent pieces the driver finally offered her into her pocket and gave the cab a bang on the roof in lieu of a tip as he drove away. Then she pulled the neck of her coat tight around her. The taxi had been too warm, the smell of air freshener combined with the driver's takeaway Americano almost nauseating. But here, by the side of the canal, Claire understood why he'd had the heater up to the max. The morning was freezing, a breeze sending needles of cold air through her layers and raising goosebumps on her skin. She shivered, a large rolling shiver like a dog drying itself after a swim, then rubbed her eyes hard and told herself to get over herself. A quick march across the bridge that led to the Royal Canal would get her blood flowing again.

The Royal Canal: a location linked in every Irish person's mind with the nearby Mountjoy Prison, the very mention of it enough to prompt a chorus of 'The Auld Triangle'. By day, the area looked fine – attractively urban, even. Claire had brought Anna for a walk here a couple of times while she was on maternity leave. But, at five to seven on a miserable, wet Saturday morning, she could think of few places in Dublin that were less inviting. Crossing from the tarmac on to the grass, she felt something squelch underfoot and suppressed a moan. It was still too dark to see what she'd stood on. Probably just as well.

Across the black water she could see the tent clearly now, and Flynn, standing outside it, gave her a brief wave. Claire shivered again, then gathered her long coat tightly around her and climbed gingerly on to the lock bridge that offered the only access to the far bank. She clung to the handrail as her shoes slid on the rain-spattered wood, and then clambered down, ungracefully but gratefully, on to the other side.

All Flynn had managed to tell her during the course of the hurried early-morning phone call was that the body had been found by a Polish man, caught short on his way home from the pub. Poor bloke had a keener sense of modesty than most of the males of his adopted nation and had left the main road and wandered right down to the canal bank to take a slash. He'd been about to turn away again when he'd seen the body, half in and half out of the water. His first thought had been that some poor unfortunate, on a mission similar to his own, maybe, had fallen in, and he'd reached down and started to drag him out. But then he'd realised the man's head wasn't going to come neatly along with the rest of his body. He was still here, the Polish witness, sitting on the grass, waiting for Flynn or someone else to tell him he could go. Claire glanced across at him. Poor bastard. That'd be some tale to tell the mammy in Gdańsk on the next phone call home.

Flynn gave her a brief nod and poked his head inside the tent again. Claire frowned. He looked great, the fecker – far healthier than she did, even though he'd been out just as late. Later, probably. And the rest. He hadn't sounded a bit embarrassed on the phone. And why would he? She dug her hands in her pockets and gave herself a silent reprimand. He had nothing to be ashamed of. He'd had a night out and a snog at the end of it – or more, or less, or whatever. It was no big deal.

He was single; Diarmaid too, as far as she knew. There was no reason she should pass any heed on any of it.

All she did know was she looked and felt like the back end of a bus after her evening on the tear, and her colleague was glowing as if he had just completed a spa treatment. That was enough to put her into a bad mood for the rest of the day.

But the look on his face as he left the tent and walked towards her drove all other thoughts from her mind.

'Morning, detective. The body is that of a man; looks to be in his early sixties, maybe. We found this in his pocket.'

He handed two plastic evidence bags to her without a word and she moved under a street light to get a proper look. The first contained a social-welfare card, belonging to Eugene Cannon. But it was the second item that drove all other thoughts from her mind.

'Jesus.'

'Yeah.'

Flynn was unable to keep the excitement off his face and now Claire understood why he'd been so insistent she visit the scene.

'Elderly man?'

'Yeah. Well, over sixty, anyway, by the looks of him. So, yeah, similar. It fits. Could fit.'

'OK.'

She looked down at the plastic bag again.

'And this was where?'

'In his pocket. Inside pocket. Clean and dry.'

That fitted too, that it was an older person, or at least that the paper belonged to an older person – someone who wasn't a slave to text or electronic reminders; someone who still wrote down important information.

She peered through the plastic. The handwriting was old too, spidery.

Tom Carthy. Tír na nÓg. Bus no 44.

Christ.

She looked at Flynn again and he nodded. There was no need to say what they were thinking, because they were both thinking the same thing. Two murders; one centre for old people. Two men; both linked. This had just got interesting.

And another thought: Sorry Matt. You're not going to get your day off for a while.

CHAPTER EIGHTEEN

'Why in the name of Jaysus didn't you tell somebody?'

Claire saw Flynn wince, but decided to ignore him. OK, so it wasn't the type of language they encouraged in the Garda training college, but to hell with it. Any chance of seeing her family this side of bedtime had all but disappeared and now this young one, this pale-faced, save-the-world young one, had apparently been failing to pass on vital information pertinent to a murder investigation. The time for patience had passed, and Claire raised her voice again.

'I'm just not getting it, Miss Cafferky. Someone wrote to you, sent you a newspaper clipping about a murder and told you that you would be next, and it took you, what, nearly a week to come to us? You do know this is an ongoing investigation, don't you? A murder investigation? Both James Mannion and Eugene Cannon were clients of yours – doesn't that mean anything?'

Liz Cafferky looked up at her briefly, then ducked her head again. 'Yeah. I mean, I don't know. It does, of course it does. Look, I'm sorry, OK?'

'So, do you feel ready to tell us exactly what happened, now?' Flynn's voice was gentle and Claire shot him an irritated look. There was absolutely no point in going easy on this kid; she knew it just by looking at her. Even behind the unwashed hair and miserable expression, you could see that she was extraordinarily pretty, but the young woman also looked fathoms deep in misery and completely unaware of just how much trouble she was in. In fact, it was highly likely she wouldn't have come to the station at all if her boss hadn't driven her to the door and all but carried her in.

Anxious to confirm the dead man's identity and the link to Tír na nÓg as soon as possible, Claire had called Tom Carthy on his mobile shortly before seven a.m. on Saturday morning, only to find that he was already at the centre. He liked to 'spruce the place up' before the clients got there, he told Claire and Flynn when they arrived less than half an hour later. Claire couldn't see evidence of much sprucing, but she welcomed the opportunity to see Carthy alone.

'Another death?'

She was even more thankful for the privacy when she witnessed his reaction to their news. Carthy's stance, mouth gaping, coffee mug paused halfway to his lips, would have been comical in another situation, Claire thought. And then she saw how quickly the colour drained from his face. They were standing in a dusty, unkempt hall and she nodded in the direction of the sitting room.

'Perhaps if we could sit down?'

Moments later, perched on the edge of a knackered grey

sofa, Carthy placed his mug on the floor and looked at her, anxiously. 'So there's no doubt? That he's one of ours, I mean.'

Quickly, she filled him in on the identification they'd found on the body.

'So, if you have any records of his family . . . ?'

Carthy shook his head slowly, and then paused. 'Eugene is . . . was from Cork, I think? Yes, I'm almost sure I heard him mention that. I don't know if that will help but—'

'Anything at all you can tell us now would be useful.'

'OK.' He dropped his head again.

Flynn stole a quick look at Claire and then offered further information: 'There was a metal box lying beside him? Like a cash box? It had been broken open; we're not sure if . . .'

But the sudden flush of colour on Carthy's cheeks told them he knew exactly what they were talking about. As Claire and Flynn looked on, the man swallowed nervously and then seemed to deflate, folding in on himself until he was almost lost in the shabby grey material of the couch.

'That . . . that sounds like it could be ours, alright.'

Moving slowly, Carthy hauled himself up off the sofa and lurched out of the room. Claire hit Flynn with an eyebrow raise. Overreact much? The twist at the corner of her colleague's mouth indicated he was thinking the same way. When Carthy reappeared moments later, empty-handed, he was walking like a much older man. He lowered himself slowly down on to the sofa and Claire could see that his hands were shaking.

'It's . . . I mean, yes. That must have been ours. Our cash box, the one we keep in the office, it's gone, alright.'

'There was a fiver in it, Mr Carthy, and a few bits of change. Would that be accurate? We didn't find any more cash on his body.'

Carthy looked at them again. 'That's – I don't – I'm not sure—'

A shuddering intake of breath and then, as Claire and Flynn watched him, Carthy unfolded his arms. With what looked to them like a supreme effort of will, he straightened his shoulders, inhaled, shook his head gently from side to side and unfurled his spine. He took another long, slow breath and blinked, focusing on her.

Get a hold of yourself. Claire's mother used to use the phrase; she hadn't heard it or thought of it in years but it seemed like the only one that fit. Tom Carthy had grabbed courage from somewhere and straightened himself out. Taller now, and in full command of the room, he sat back on the sofa and offered Claire a faint smile.

'I'll have a think about the money situation, but, no, that sounds about right. We haven't had a lot of donations recently. Anyway, I'm coming across as a bit distracted. This ... this news has come as a shock to me, that's all. Dreadful business. So, is there anything else I can help you with?'

There would be, Claire decided. Two deaths linked to Tír na nÓg within a two-week period meant she wanted to have a much longer conversation with Tom Carthy. Not straight away – there was too much immediate work to be done first to get a murder investigation underway – but soon.

What she hadn't expected, however, was that he'd drive

himself to Collins Street, first thing on Monday morning, a reluctant Liz Cafferky by his side.

'I knew there was something going on with her. But she wouldn't tell me anything ...' His young employee staring miserably out of the window, Carthy had muttered in Claire's ear, 'She's been in bad form for days, but she wouldn't tell me what was behind it. Then, when I told her about Eugene ... Oh, look, she'll fill you in herself. But go easy on her, OK?'

And then he'd left the young woman with a pat on the shoulder and the instruction to ring him when she was finished.

Claire had felt railroaded and didn't appreciate it. Her mood darkened further when Liz Cafferky told her about the mysterious letter and newspaper clipping she'd received. Who did that? Who got nasty mail, really terrifying stuff, and then clapped their hands over their ears and sang 'la la la' for the best part of a week? Claire was determined to find out, even if it took her all day. Especially if it took her all day.

In the pocket of her jacket, her phone buzzed. Oops. Claire had made a big show of telling Saint Liz to turn hers off when they'd started the interview but had forgotten to do the same. She'd ignore it, though; it couldn't be anything important. Matt knew not to call her at work, especially not on a day like today. She'd zapped him a quick text before they started the interview to let him know that she couldn't be disturbed and that she'd pick up milk when she was finally able to make it home, whenever that might be. So, no, it couldn't be anything important. She waited for the buzzing to stop and then looked at the young woman again.

'How about you describe this note to me, so? Handwritten? Printed? Where is it, anyway? We'll have to have it tested, although I presume you've put fingerprints all over it—'

'I can't really remember.'

The girl stared at the table and Claire didn't bother to disguise a sigh.

'You're going to have to start talking, you know. We can sit here all day, if you like.'

Liz's face appeared green under the fluorescent lights, and she gave a quick, violent shiver.

'I . . . Just give me a second, OK? I need to think this through.'

We don't have a fucking second, Claire wanted to say, but she reckoned Flynn would blow a head gasket if she used another expletive. It was true, though: they really needed some new information. If the death of James Mannion had led them to a cul-de-sac, then throwing Eugene Cannon's murder into the mix had blocked their exit altogether.

If only the Cannon killing had happened in isolation, then Claire would have known exactly where to start. Carthy had been able to tell them Cannon was from Cork, hadn't been in Dublin more than a few weeks, and a quick call to the guards in the southern capital had confirmed he had a string of previous offences the length of his arm and a history of violence. Given that he and his equally charming brother had had a very public fall-out almost a month previously, under normal circumstances his death would have prompted them to simply haul the brother in for questioning and start digging through the long list of people who wanted to cause him harm.

But the Tír na nÓg link had blown that nice easy solution right out of the water, and now she had this Liz person, someone else connected with Tír na nÓg, claiming she'd received a threatening letter several days ago but hadn't bothered to tell anyone until today. It was, Claire thought gloomily, about as far from simple as you could imagine.

Her colleague cleared his throat, and leaned forward slightly on his chair. 'I know this must be frightening for you. But I'm sure you understand that anything you can tell us could be very important indeed.'

Claire resisted rolling her eyes. Alright, Flynn, try it your way. But, as she suspected, the good-cop routine didn't work either. The girl just raked her fingers through her greasy hair and continued to stare down at the table. Liz Cafferky: online, Claire had seen her described as one of Ireland's 'hottest intellectuals' – Flynn wasn't the only one who knew how to use Google – but she wouldn't make any top-ten list today, except perhaps Ireland's most shell-shocked. It was amazing, Claire thought to herself, the damage a bad night's sleep could do to a person. And worry. And fear.

Right, it was time to try spoon-feeding. And, as the mother of a seven-month-old, she was good at that. Hell, she'd make aeroplane noises, if that was what it took. Forcing a smile, Claire took her irritation down a notch. 'So, you got this letter in the post, when? Three, four days ago?'

The girl made eye contact for a moment and then dipped her head again. 'Yes – four. Well, it was a piece of paper, really;

I mean, a bit clipped out of the paper. A bit about James, with a note attached to it.'

'And it came to your home address?'

The girl nodded. 'Yeah. That . . . that freaked me out more than anything.'

'And it was signed *Stephen*?'

Another nod. 'Yeah.'

'So where is that paper now? We'll need to get it tested.'

Liz dropped her head into her hands, muffling the answer.

'I'm sorry?'

'I said, I burned it.'

'I don't believe—' To hell with level tones. 'You are taking the piss.'

'I'm sorry, I'm sorry! I know it was a stupid thing to do. I was afraid, that was all!'

And then the eighth-hottest babe in Ireland (intellectual category) was weeping, great gasps of air interfering with anything else she wanted to say.

Flynn took a look at his superior officer and gave what she hoped was a sympathetic eyebrow raise. 'I'll get some tea.'

It took them nearly two hours to get all of the details out of her. It wasn't an easy story to listen to, but Claire believed Liz Cafferky was telling the truth, mostly because she couldn't imagine why anyone would manufacture such a tale.

'Can I go back to the beginning? It's just . . . Well, it might make more sense that way.' She shot Claire and Flynn a quick, nervous look.

Claire nodded and took a sip from her Styrofoam cup of

tea. Liz Cafferky looked like someone standing on a high-dive board, terrified of jumping, but aware there was only one way down. She was just going to have to hold her nose, and go for it.

The young woman took a large gulp of her own drink, a muddy-looking black coffee, and then nibbled delicately at the edge of the cup. That must have burned on the way down, Claire thought, and wondered why she cared. There was just something fragile about the girl, she realised, a sense of aloneness that made you want to look after her. No matter how irritating she was being.

'I had a pretty shit time in secondary school.'

Oh God, how far back did they have to go? But, following a glance from Flynn, Claire repressed the sigh. OK, she'd see where she was going with this.

'It started when I was about fourteen. I can remember the day, actually. I was in religion class and the teacher – you know, one of those ones who think they're, like, totally cool and down with the kids? You know the type? Anyway, she was giving us this talk on bullying and shyness and how some people around our age find it hard to speak in crowds, and that they might get embarrassed or even blush or something, and that we should just ignore it? Or support them. And, just like that, I could feel myself getting red – like, this massive flush rising up from inside me; I was on fire. It was horrific.'

She looked at them and Claire could see livid patches of colour on her neck.

'Yeah, I still get it sometimes.'

The young woman – although Claire was increasingly

thinking of her as a girl – waved her hand in front of her face and then shrugged resignedly.

'All the time. Anyway. Everything was pretty shit from then on. I just got totally self-conscious. I couldn't speak in class – I tried to, one day, and I could hear this giggle from across the room – "Hey, Elizabeth, what colour is red?" – and I nearly died. And it just got worse and worse.'

Fair enough. Claire had no idea where the conversation was going but sometimes you needed to leave things alone, let the information flow, and pick out the nuggets afterwards.

'And then my dad stepped in. And he was amazing. I'm an only child and we had, like, this bond?'

Liz was crunching the cup in her hand now and some of the murky brown liquid splashed on to her skin. Flynn reached over and passed her a tissue, which she accepted with a half smile.

'I mean, I got on fine with my mum, but Dad and I were mates, you know? Eventually, he found out I was skipping school and I cracked and told him everything – how shit everything was. And he was amazing. Brought me to the library and got me books and stuff. Took me to the G.P., even. Told me loads of people got nervous, or shy, or whatever, at my age. It really helped just talking about it. Things weren't perfect; I mean, I wasn't about to go on the debating team, you know? But I was able to answer questions in class, pass my exams, that sort of thing. I was getting by; things were fine. And then my dad died.'

Her tone was conversational, her eyes dry, but she had

abandoned the cup now and began to tear small pieces off the tissue, depositing them neatly in a pile on the table.

'Cancer. Diagnosed in June, dead by Christmas. A year later, my mum got married again. That was . . . That was tough too.'

She looked up at Claire.

'It was really shit, actually.'

'I can imagine.'

'Can you?'

The pile of paper snowflakes on the table was growing quickly.

'Brian, her husband, he's a nice guy. Safe, you know? An accountant, of all things. He's OK; he's not, like, nasty or anything. But he's not my dad. So I moved out. My dad left me this apartment he owned in town, and enough money to go to college. So I had a home, at least. Mum and Brian moved away themselves, soon afterwards, to the States. Mum had another baby. We speak on the phone the odd time; I don't go over much. She seems happy.'

Slowly, deliberately, she extended an index finger and poked a hole in the centre of the snowy pile.

'That sounds tough, alright.'

It was exactly the right thing to say and Claire glanced over at Flynn, impressed. But her colleague didn't notice. Instead, he just caught the young woman's gaze, and held it. Claire was reminded of a farmer who had lived down the road from them when she was small. He had had a reputation for catching stray animals – horses, dogs, even a sheep once. He could look them in the eye and tempt them towards him, gain their trust somehow before penning them in again. He used to have the same expression on his face as Flynn had now, Claire remembered. Gentleness, compassion in his eyes. And there was a watchfulness about him too, a sense he knew exactly where he wanted things to go from here.

'And what age were you, when all this happened? Seventeen?'

'Yeah. Well, nineteen by the time I'd sorted my things and gone.'

'That's young to be left on your own.'

Flynn's words echoed Claire's own thoughts and the girl shrugged.

'It doesn't seem so at the time, though, does it? You know, you're nineteen, you're out of school – you're, like, the queen of the world. You can tackle everything. Except, I couldn't. I couldn't, and I ended up fucking up really badly.'

'How do you mean?' Claire was interested now, not just in where the story was going but in the girl herself – how she had got from there to here.

'I got a place in Trinity, to study arts, and I went for a few months. But my head wasn't in the right place for any of it. The shyness, the anxiety – whatever you call it – came back, worse than ever. I was completely terrified of going to lectures, couldn't stand the thought of having to get up and speak in front of people. And it got worse. The more afraid I was of making a fool of myself, the more I hid away. I didn't even want to eat in the canteen in case someone asked me to join them. Then one night I forced myself to go to a social, the smallest one I could find. I was climbing the walls of the apartment,

I was so lonely. So I went along to the Games Society, of all things – just to get out of the house. And there was free beer. And I had a pint. And . . .'

She looked at them, a faint smile appearing.

'I was happy for the first time in years – at peace in my own skin. I hadn't really drunk alcohol before. My dad had asked me not to and I pretty much did everything he told me, back then. But this feeling was amazing. I could stand and yap away to people and I didn't go red and I didn't stutter. It was the best night of my life, to be honest with you. I felt like shit the next morning, obviously. All the usual nerves, and worse. Did I say too much? And were they all laughing at me? But there was a simple solution to that, wasn't there?'

She smiled again, bitterly this time.

'Just grab another beer.'

Claire nodded. She wouldn't be the first student to go a bit doolally, first time away from home. But, in this case, there seemed to be more to it. Liz was still talking.

'I ended up dropping out. The rest of them seemed like kids, running home at the weekends to get their washing done. I had literally nothing in common with them. I had plenty of money – my dad left me pretty well off – so I started going out in town at the weekends and hanging around with a different crowd. An older crowd. They didn't care who I was or what I did, as long as I got my round in. I didn't bother going back to college after Christmas, and after a few phone calls they stopped chasing me. It can be quite easy, actually. To disappear.'

SINÉAD CROWLEY

She gathered the torn tissue in one cupped hand, divided it, made another pile.

'There were a lot of guys too. Happy to hang around with me. Not surprisingly, really; I always stood my round.'

For the first time, her voice faltered and Claire saw in her face the shadow of the nineteen-year-old she had been. And then she blinked, the teenager disappeared and there was aggression in her voice when she next spoke.

'You need to hear all this, do you?' She sounded accusing, as if they were steering the conversation and not the other way around.

They said nothing and, after a moment, she sighed.

'Yeah, well, whatever. I was a piss head. That's the short version. So, yeah.'

The nineteen-year-old was back again, confused and embarrassed, and Claire was surprised to find herself wanting to reach out and touch her hand.

I know what it's like, she wanted to say. To feel alone, and desperate. To wake up one morning to find the only person who understands you is gone and everyone else is driving you mad. I was lucky; I got out in time. But not everyone finds an escape route, or the right one.

She didn't say any of it, but the girl seemed to sense Claire's empathy.

'There are whole piles of it I don't remember – blanks, gaps, whatever you want to call it. When I look back, it's like it all happened to a different person.'

She looked at Flynn this time.

'It's been over two years since I got my shit together, properly got away from it all, but sometimes I'll be in town, or in a shop, or something, and someone will come up to me and say, "Hey, how are you? Haven't seen you in a while!" Or, "Hey, that was a great night we had that time; bet the head wasn't the best the next morning." And half the time, I don't even know who they are. It's pretty terrifying, actually, especially if it's a guy.'

Her cheeks were flushed again, her breathing shallow.

'Sometimes I'll meet someone and he'll be, like, "Hey, remember me? Remember that night?" And, a lot of the time, I can't remember anything. So that's why I didn't come to you, why I didn't want to tell you about the letters. Because I knew you'd be all, "Is there anyone you can think of who might wish you harm?" And I'd have to say I hadn't a clue. I was just fucking mortified, thinking about it. And terrified I'd have to start thinking about it again.'

Her hands were clasped now, fingers intertwined as she kneaded the palms together.

'There's something else too. I've never actually told anyone this before. Anyway. There were a few nights when the stuff we were doing wasn't, you know, legal. Drugs, and that. We were in this pub one night – a lock-in – not the type of place I usually went to. I was dating this guy and he knew someone, you know the way it is.'

She paused and then named a pub, notorious for its connection with the Dublin criminal underworld. Claire frowned. Not the type of place she could imagine a gang of over-privileged students getting their jollies. Liz looked up briefly and then ducked her head again.

'Yeah. You've heard of it. So, around three in the morning, the place was raided. The guy I was with was shitting himself. He had . . . He didn't want to be searched, put it that way. So he dragged me out through the kitchen; there was a back door – he said we could get out that way. This other girl followed us out. I don't even remember her name. She was someone else's girlfriend, but she was totally wasted. This guy I was with, he kinda hooshed us over the bins at the back of the yard and then climbed out after us, and we started running down this dark lane. It was a miserable night, lashing rain. Then I heard this thud behind me and the girl had tripped over something, or fallen, I'm not sure which, and she didn't get up.

The words slowed and she dipped her head again.

She was just lying there on her face and her legs were at a kind of a funny angle. And she didn't move. The guy . . . The guy I was with told me I had to leave her there. He was yelling at me; he said he was on probation, or something, and it would be this big deal if he was found with anything dodgy on him. He said I had to move, now, otherwise he'd leave me behind too. I was totally freaked out – there were guards everywhere, you could see blue lights flashing over the roofs of the houses. So I followed him. And I left her there.'

She pressed her fingers against her eyes as if she could rub out the memory.

'I left her there, and afterwards I couldn't get her out of my head. Anything could have happened to her. I was afraid to turn on the TV or listen to the radio for weeks after, in case I heard that a body had been found, or something. I was in bits – so fucking scared. I was totally paranoid that she was dead and there'd be this murder enquiry and that they – you – would be after me. I just kept heading out every evening, drinking and trying not to think about it. It was horrific. And then Tom saved me.'

She looked up and saw the question unformed on Claire's lips.

'Yeah, Tom. Tom, and running out of money, and wanting it all to stop, I suppose. But it was mostly Tom. He turned up at the right time. Picked me out of the gutter, literally, helped me through the whole withdrawal thing, found me the right people to talk to. And he gave me a job. That was almost two years ago. I never found out what happened to her. I don't even know her name. I'll never forgive myself but . . . Well, in a way, I suppose working at Tír na nÓg felt like I was making amends. Putting something back. Helping other people, because I didn't help her.'

Flynn looked puzzled. 'I see where you're coming from, but what I don't understand is why you did all those interviews, then? All that TV stuff? I mean, I can understand why someone with your . . . your background, shall we say, would want to work in Tír na nÓg and help others. But why chose to put yourself out there like that?'

'Because Tom asked me to do it.'

The nineteen-year-old was gone again and the woman opposite Claire looked older than she was.

'I owed him. When he asked me to come to work for Tír na nÓg, it made sense. He helped me, so I could help others. And I thought it could be, like, a fresh start, in a place where no one knew me. Then I met this guy I knew from school, Dean Evans, he's a journalist now and he asked me to do the interview for the news."

Interesting, thought Claire, how Mr Evans had popped into the story, and she filed the information away for future use. The young woman was still talking:

'So Tom was all, "Oh, that's a great idea." I just felt I couldn't refuse. And every time I went on TV or on the radio, people started sending money to the centre and I was kind of locked into it. Tom looked so happy; he kept talking about how we could improve things with all the donations we were getting. So I felt I hadn't a choice, really. And then, the weird thing was, I actually started to enjoy it.'

She looked straight at Flynn for the first time.

'Sorry if this sounds all "me, me, me", but the whole media thing has been really good for me. Like a real sign, you know, that I was getting my shit together. Then the first letter came and I was totally freaked out by it. Even though it looked harmless. So I chucked it away. And when the second one came, I was too afraid to tell the guards, because I was too embarrassed and ashamed to say that there are whole fucking months of my life that I can't remember.'

It was a lot of information. But one point leaped out at Claire. 'The first one?'

Liz sighed. 'Yeah. There was another letter, maybe two weeks ago, only this one came to Tír na nÓg. Same guy again, Stephen, saying he was keeping an eye on me and that he'd like to meet me sometime. And there was another clipping from the paper – a bit about me, this time. Dean said it was nothing to worry about, that that sort of shit happens all the time to people on TV, so I threw it away. I assumed he knew what he was talking about. And he was right; I mean, loads of people have been trying to get in touch with me since I started going on TV. I don't really do social media, but I've had a look a few times. So I believed Dean when he said it was normal. But then I got the second letter . . .'

Her voice trailed off and she shivered before speaking again.

'I'm really sorry. I thought I could, you know, start again? But everything I touch just turns to shit.'

'Well. It sounds like you've been through a tough time. But you shouldn't have destroyed those letters, you know.'

'I panicked. I'm sorry. That's not much use to you, but I am.'

Claire shrugged. She had a lot of sympathy for the girl, really she did, but there was work to be done. 'Stephen was the signature on both letters?'

Liz nodded again, miserably. 'Yeah.'

'OK.'

Claire closed her notebook with a decisive thud. It wasn't an unusual name, but there had been a Stephen somewhere in James Mannion's story; it rang a bell alright. So at least it was something to go on.

She gave the girl a half smile. 'I think that's all, for the moment. I do appreciate you being so honest with us. It goes without saying, of course, that if you get any other communication like the last one, you have to tell us.'

Liz rubbed her eyes wearily. 'Of course. Certainly.'

'So is there anything else you need to tell us?'

She shook her head and made a faint attempt at a smile. 'That's enough, isn't it? My life and times. I hope you can make some sense of it. Because I sure as hell can't.'

Flynn gathered his own notes. 'Is there someone coming to get you? Mr Carthy?'

Liz shook her head. 'No. I need to be alone for a while.' She looked from one to the other in turn. 'I'm OK, aren't I? To go home?'

Claire thought for a moment. 'I'm not mad about the idea, to be honest. Not since the second letter came to your home address. Is there anywhere else you can go?'

The girl nodded. 'Yeah. I guess. I don't think I'd feel safe at home, anyway. I'll find someone.'

Claire stood up. 'You sure? I mean – I understand family isn't an option.'

Liz stood too, and forced her shoulders back. 'I'll be fine. Feel a bit better, actually, having said all that. Hope it helped.'

'You can be sure it did.' Flynn reached across and shook her hand. 'I'll give you a lift. Wherever you decide to go.'

The girl looked up at him, the dark smudges under her eyes distinct against her pale skin. 'Thanks. I'll go to Tír na nÓg.'

CHAPTER NINETEEN

Second body linked to Tír na nÓg charity.
Protect our elderly! #prayforJames

Fantastic. Claire clicked out of Twitter and threw her phone down on to her desk. The second murder was still prominent on all of the main news sites. It had taken the Guards in Cork some time to track down Eugene Cannon's brother and bring him to Dublin for the formal identification of the body, but several of the better informed hacks – chief among them Dean Evans, she noted – had already named him in their stories and were reporting a link with Tír na nÓg. And several tweeters, or twitterers, or whatever you wanted to call them, were echoing calls made earlier on a radio station for a vigil to be held for the dead men, to highlight, as one tweet put it, the need for 'extra resources' to help others like them. Well, they were perfectly entitled to do that, Claire mused. But she couldn't help bristling at the implication that the Gardaí weren't acting fast enough to protect the city's elderly. And she also worried that any sort of public event might do more harm than good. If the murderer got off on getting attention – and many of them did – she couldn't think of a better way of giving it to him.

'Lots to think about there, so?'

Flynn, who had driven Liz Cafferky back to Tír na nÓg, walked into the room and took his seat across the desk from her.

'That didn't take long.'

'No.' Flynn frowned. 'I believed her, did you? I mean, it was a sad story, but it sounded accurate enough. It's not easy, being nineteen, even without that sort of shit happening.'

'You can say that again.'

Claire had been thinking a lot about being nineteen, since Liz Cafferky's interview had ended. It was at about that age, maybe a little younger, that she herself had lost her boyfriend and her relationship with her parents over the course of one black weekend. The fact of the matter was, without support and good advice from a local guard, she might not have ended up in the Garda training college at all, but someplace else entirely. And, who could say? Her story mightn't have been dissimilar to Liz's.

'It's a tough age for any sort of big change.'

Flynn was probably speaking from experience too, Claire mused. Well, no 'probably' about it. He was clearly cool with his sexuality now, but it can't have been easy, growing up in Ballygowherever. She wondered when he had told his parents. Had he told them now, even? It was none of her business, but the question intrigued her. She hadn't ever thought of Flynn as having a personal life before. Now it seemed it may well be full of drama.

The buzz of her phone interrupted her thoughts. Matt, again. She'd barely spoken to him in days, other than to exchange information about Anna. She'd been so wrecked on Saturday night she'd fallen into bed at the same time as the baby, and he'd gone for a run on Sunday before shutting himself into the sitting room to work on a business proposal of some sort. Her mind almost totally occupied by Eugene Cannon, Claire hadn't listened to the details. Anyway, she'd answer him in a minute. She'd a few notes to write up first.

Flynn cleared his throat. 'Did you call McBride?'

'Yeah.'

Claire rolled her eyes. Flynn had been gone less than forty minutes, but the conversation with the former mayor of Rathoban hadn't taken even a fraction of that time. Yes, Richie McBride had confirmed cautiously, Stephen had been the name of the pupil at the centre of James Mannion's dismissal, or resignation, or whatever you wanted to call it. Stephen Millar. But, no, he had no idea where he was now. England, possibly; at least, that's where the family had moved to when they left Rathoban. No, he didn't have an address for him. No, there were no relatives back in Rathoban as far as he knew. Sorry, detective, I'd love to help you, but it was all so long ago.

Claire had run the name through Pulse, the Garda database, of course, but hadn't come up with anything. Not to worry. She'd track down Stephen Millar. But it was going to take time.

And those letters, the ones Liz said she received, were bugging her. OK, it had only taken her five minutes to confirm that Liz was listed in the phone book and had mentioned the fact that she lived close to Tír na nÓg in several interviews. So there was no huge mystery about how this Stephen guy had got her address. It could all be just someone messing, some eejit, living with his ma, with funny ideas about how to pick up girls; some freak, and there were plenty of them out there, deciding to capitalise on what had happened at Tír na nÓg. Or there might be more to it. After all, who stalked people with handwritten notes these days, when there were many more electronic ways to make a nuisance of yourself?

Claire was just about ready to hit the road. She'd better return the call to Matt first though. He had probably just been checking to make sure she was on her way.

But her husband's voice, when he answered, didn't sound friendly.

'Hello, yes?'

'Hi there. Sorry I missed your call. Hell of a day; I was locked in an interview room. Did you get milk?'

'I called you five times.'

'Did you? Sorry, I had my phone on silent.'

'I really needed to talk to you.'

Claire's heart jumped.

'Oh, shit – is Anna OK?'

'She is now.'

He sounded angry, yes, but Claire suddenly realised that her husband also sounded utterly exhausted.

'The crèche called. She woke up from her nap with a temperature of a hundred and two.'

'A hundred and two? Shit.'

Claire thought back to the book on childhood illnesses her mother had sent her and that she'd thumbed through in the bath one evening when she'd forgotten a magazine.

'That's really bad, isn't it?'

Her husband sighed. 'Well, it's not great. I brought her home and it came down after bath and some paracetamol. And after she puked all over me.'

'Well, thank Christ for that. Not for the puke, obviously, but—'

'Claire.'

Her husband's voice had an edge to it that broke through his weariness.

'My meeting with O'Neill was today. For the website contract?'

'Oh, shit; yeah. Did you manage to go, or—?'

'No, I had to cancel.'

He was speaking slowly, emphasising each word.

'I cancelled at very short notice. And, after I'd calmed Anna down, I called to rearrange but they'd already spoken to someone else at that stage. They are probably going to go with him, too. They called me an hour ago, thought it was only fair to let me know.'

'Shit. I'm so sorry.'

'Are you?'

Claire bristled at the hostility in his tone. 'Well, yeah, I am sorry that it happened. But there's nothing I could have done.'

'You could have answered your phone. You could have looked after your sick child.'

'Are you pissed off with me?'

'I'm pissed off, Claire. That contract was important, for all of us. I could have done a lot of the work from home; it would have saved us from precisely what happened today.'

'Yeah, but I was in an interview!' She could feel a pulse beating in her temple. 'This is a murder investigation, for God's sake. You can't just walk out in the middle and . . .'

Suddenly aware that her voice had risen and that Flynn had stopped typing on the other side of the desk, she climbed out of her chair and walked into the corridor, still talking.

'I was in an interview! I can't even keep my phone turned on in there, the lawyers would—'

'Yeah, yeah, lawyers.'

'Yeah, lawyers!'

Claire's temper was at boiling point now. Everything was just so bloody hard – the case, the long day, the guilt she was feeling about not being around when Anna was sick, guilt about feeling guilty when she'd only been doing her job. And there was only one person to whom she could complain, so she gave him both barrels.

'This is a murder investigation. I am a detective. I'm sorry, Matt, I know your meeting was important and I will make it up to you but, not trying to be funny, here, but this is literally life and death, you know?'

'The guy's already a corpse, he's not going to mind waiting around a few hours anymore.'

Dead silence. And then they both burst out laughing.

'I can't believe you said that.'

Matt groaned. 'Me, neither. I'm having such a shitty day.'

'Tell me about it.' She leaned her forehead against the wall, not caring who passed by. 'Look, I'm leaving now. I'll get milk, OK? And pizza. And I'll wash the puke out of your shirt.'

'Make sure you do, woman.'

'Promise.'

She glanced down at her watch. Nearly five p.m. She'd a mountain of paperwork to do and needed quiet time too, to think about what Liz Cafferky had said, let it sink in. There had been a time when she'd just drive around on an evening like this, stick on some music, anything, hum along, maybe, and let her brain turn things over. She'd had some of her best ideas doing just that.

But not tonight. Her baby needed her. It sounded like Matt did too.

CHAPTER TWENTY

The square-ish but goodlooking-ish cop gave her a lift, but Liz insisted he let her out before they got to Tír na nÓg, peddled him some bullshit about how the sight of a cop car might freak out the clients, but the truth was she just needed a few minutes to herself. To stop, and think, to breathe in some cold air before the fustiness of the cop shop was replaced by the aroma of stale food and neediness that permeated her workplace. So she thanked him, even managed a smile, and then climbed out of the car at the top of the road and watched while he drove away.

And that's when they jumped out at her.

'Liz!'

There were at least three of them, maybe more; she fumbled in her handbag for her keys.

'It is her; I told you she'd turn up here.'

'Liz! Over here, please!'

The flash dazzled her and she took a step backwards, out into the street, a cyclist narrowly avoiding her and swearing as he raced past.

'Liz, can I ask you your reaction to the latest killing?'

They were sticking things in her face now – a microphone, a mobile phone.

'How well did you know Eugene Cannon?'

'Are you worried for other people at Tír na nÓg?'

'Elizabeth? Are you worried for your own safety?'

'I don't . . . I can't . . .'

Shaking her head, she turned right and then left as question after question slapped against her face. It was hard to tell how many of them there were now. She stumbled, stepped on a man's foot and heard him swear.

'I'm sorry.'

'Liz! Ian Flaherty, here; we met the other morning! If I could just have a quick word . . . ?'

Liz met his eyes and gave an instinctive smile of recognition. Then realised his microphone was closest of all.

'I don't think—'

'Can you at least confirm Ireland 24's story? That Eugene Cannon was a client of yours? That's two deaths linked to Tír na nÓg, Liz; have you anything to say about it?' It was a woman asking, this time, her face familiar from a thousand television bulletins. Liz had admired her once, thought her calm and authoritative. Now all she could see was how hassled the woman looked as she tried to get her microphone in even closer than the others.

'Liz, just a quick word.'

'Will you miss Eugene?'

'Of course, I . . .'

She tried to find a gap, to spot a way through to the front gate of the centre, but there were more of them now and she was completely hemmed in, the panic rising as she wondered just how excited they would be and how high up their news bulletins they'd carry it if she fainted right in front of them.

Suddenly, she felt a hand on her elbow and a hiss in her ear.

'Come on; the car's around the corner.'

For a moment, she thought about resisting. Then she realised that whatever he had in mind for her couldn't be any worse than this. Liz kept her head down as he tugged her through the crowd and into his car. She stayed silent until they stopped at the next traffic lights, then she looked down, made sure the handbrake was on, reached out and slapped him on the face.

'The fuck?' Dean's hand reached up and he massaged his cheek. 'I'm on your side! Jesus' sake, Liz, I got you out of there.'

'You got me into it, you mean.'

If the lights hadn't changed at that precise moment, she'd have hit him again, but instead she settled back into her seat and glared at him.

'They were all shouting about some Ireland 24 story. Was it yours? Did you tell them that Eugene was a client of ours?'

Dean's grip on the steering wheel tightened. 'I was just doing my job.'

'That's the excuse, is it? Your job? Well, that's alright, then. I hope you enjoy your job. I hope they make you the presenter of the main freaking evening news. I hope you make millions out of us—'

'Ah, Jaysus, Liz, calm down, will you?'

Dean slowed the car at a *Yield* sign and glanced over at her before speeding up again.

'It's called news, Liz – having an exclusive. It was going to come out in a few hours, anyway; I didn't do anything wrong; the family were all informed.'

'Give me your phone.'

There was no point in hiding from it, not at this stage.

'What?'

'Your phone. Give it to me. I want to see what they're saying.'

He hesitated for a moment, then shrugged, pulling his phone from his pocket before tossing it into her lap.

'Look away. I didn't make anything up; it's all true.'

She tapped into the home screen and Googled her name, then shuddered as page after page of news unfolded in front of her.

Terror at Tír na nÓg.

Lovely Liz linked to double murder.

Grim discovery of man's body linked to prominent charity.

A Dean Evans exclusive.

There were images too, pages of them: a photograph of Tom standing at the front door of Tír na nÓg, hand raised in front of him as he greeted, or maybe tried to get rid of, someone just outside the frame; a photo of Eugene that looked to be at least twenty years old; the front of the building, lifted from the Facebook page; and Liz herself, pictured just minutes previously on the footpath, looking distracted, exhausted and completely freaked out.

'How do they even get this on there so quickly?'

Dean, glancing over, rolled his eyes. 'One of the hacks would have tweeted it. There – look.'

The car swerved dangerously as he pointed out a tiny black name written under the photo.

'And whoever is on the paper's rolling blog lifted it. It's pretty standard, I'm afraid.'

But she wasn't listening anymore. Not caring whether or not he crashed, and maybe hoping he would, Liz flung the phone back into Dean's lap and rested her head back against the car seat, her eyes gritty and dry.

A Dean Evans exclusive.

Who was he, anyway, this Dean Evans that she considered a friend? She hadn't even known his phone number until six months ago, might have walked past him in the street if he hadn't called her name. Now here he was, giving her lifts and writing *exclusives* about her.

'It's not as bad as you think.'

Dean slowed the car and then stopped in a long line of traffic, using the opportunity to try and grab her hand. But Liz jerked it away. What was it her father would have said? *To hell with you and the horse you rode in on.* God almighty, how had she even ended up here, anyway? The job at Tír na nÓg was supposed to be a halfway house, a place to rest, regroup and reconsider until she could leave Back Then behind her and make her way to some place better. And now things were worse than before.

'Paper?'

'Good JESUS!'

The man's face was pressed against the car window, his bright orange jacket lighting up the side of her face.

Liz's heart hammered in her chest.

Dean looked over, concern written on his face. 'It's OK, hon; it's just a lad selling the *Herald*; tell him to feck off.'

'No.' The word came out louder than she intended and, fingers trembling, Liz lowered the window down. 'I might as well see what they're saying.'

She handed him a euro and the man slid a paper through the window.

Liz looked at her picture on the front page.

TERROR AT TÍR NA NÓG

She shoved the paper at Dean, wordlessly, and he shrugged. 'I'm sorry. Look, let me make it up to you. Buy you a drink?'

'Sure.' She nodded and then looked down at the paper again. 'Actually, no. A coffee. I need to think.'

CHAPTER TWENTY-ONE

He pulled the covers up over his head and, in the darkness, swooped backwards in time.

'I'm thinking of building a playground.'

It had been such an unusual thing for his father to say, so unexpected, that neither he nor his mother answered straight away. For a moment, the scrape of her fork against the plate was the only sound in the room. Her mouth twisted and Stephen knew she was holding the food in her mouth, seeking an excuse not to reply. Saying nothing was better than saying the wrong thing. Always.

'There's nowhere around here for the kids to go – so Richie McBride told me, anyway.'

His mother patted her mouth nervously with a tissue.

'Sure, that's a lovely idea,' she ventured, finally, the fork now shaking slightly in her hand.

Stephen had hidden behind her words and stayed silent, concentrating on the soggy lumps of turnip, sucking them down so they didn't touch the sides because the taste made him feel ill but there were children starving in Africa and you were an ungrateful pup if you turned your nose up at good food.

Now, years later, lying in his lumpy bed, the sheets balled up and uncomfortably warm beneath him, he knew what had prompted his father's sudden interest in the welfare of the local children. There had been talk around the town of low wages at the factory, of the men joining a union. The playground had been his father's way of making himself the big man again – throwing up a few discounted swings and making sure a grand big plaque with his name on it was put on display. Nobody said Lar Millar wasn't a smart man.

Just not a very nice one.

Back then, though, his son had seen it as just another source of worry. His father bought him new clothes for the opening ceremony: grey trousers, a yellow shirt and brown shoes that pinched his feet as they walked across the tarmac to where Mayor Richie McBride was waiting to cut the ribbon.

The children had all been tentative at first, Stephen remembered. Even after the speeches were made and the gates to the playground opened, they had all just wandered around, reaching out to touch the new equipment, not wanting to be the first to have a go. Eventually, they'd all gathered at a large contraption in the corner – a cone-shaped metal climbing frame which soared into the bright blue spring sky. And, as the children and their parents nudged each other in silence, the tips of Stephen's da's ears had turned red. A stage whisper came from the back of the crowd.

'It doesn't look safe, does it? I heard they didn't want to build it, but Millar insisted it was the latest thing.'

The dig of a fist into the small of his back made Stephen stumble forward.

'This lad here will show you how it's done, won't you, son?'

Neutral words, but their meaning clear. Climb the fuck up there and don't make me look like an eejit. Look like you're enjoying it, or there'll be trouble later.

It was like a spider's web, Stephen thought, a terrifying, metallic spider's web that stretched up so far you could barely see the top of it. He reached out, felt the metal cold under his fingers, hauled himself up the first rung and climbed up another one. Looking around then, he realised, for the first time in a long time, that he was doing everything right. Faces in the crowd looked impressed, supportive. He climbed another rung, and another. And then his foot slid from under him, the new shoes completely unsuitable for this task. Another rung and his hands had grown sweaty, their grip unstable. There was no fun in this now and his trousers were too tight; what if they tore? What if they tore right across the arse? And half the town standing underneath him. Stephen climbed up another rung and then even that image disappeared, replaced by the bigger fear of falling and plunging on to the tarmac below.

Another rung. He looked down again and then wished he hadn't. Below, the men drew on fags and feigned nonchalance while not taking their eyes off his retreating rear end, and the women vied with each other to see who could tut the loudest. A couple of fellas from his class were nudging each other in excitement. His father caught his eye. *Make it look like fun, you little scut. Make it look like fun or there's no need to bother coming back down again.*

It was that last glance that broke Stephen's concentration altogether and, as he reached for the next rung, his foot slid again and the handrail slipped from his grasp. He swung out into the blue, dangling on one arm. The crowd gasped and, from the centre, his mother screamed.

'Oh, Jesus, Stephen, come down! You'll kill yourself, son. Come down to me.'

A beat. And then, from the back of the crowd, Francie Daly, the biggest boy in the school, guffawed. 'Mind yourself, now, Stephen, or your mammy will have to climb up there and get you.'

The laughter was much louder than the gasp had been.

Francie's mate, Colm, leaped forward and started swinging his way up like a monkey, his scuffed runners clinging to each rung. His swift movements made the rest of the climbing frame sway, and Stephen clung tighter. Within seconds, Colm had climbed as high as him and then higher, and then they all flooded forward, all of the boys and some of the girls as well, swarming up the rungs, up as far as Stephen and then past him, some of them hanging one-handed, showing off to the parents below. Still Stephen clung. He knew he'd made a fool of himself, again. It was only a kid's climbing frame; look, there were toddlers now messing around the bottom rungs. But he was too shaken to finish the climb and join the rest of the lads at the top; too afraid, when he saw the look on his father's face, to go back down.

He had been right to be afraid, Stephen thought, as he shifted miserably in the bed and listened to the wind rattle the ill-fitting windows of the flat. He pushed his face into the pillow, wondering, if he wished for it hard enough, whether sleep would come. But his body wouldn't let him lie still. There was too much pressure, too much anger, too much shame; he could feel it in the twitching of his nerve endings and the pounding of the blood in his temples.

'It's all your fault, you know.' His father's words. Or his, maybe.

It would be easier not to think if he was on the move. So he got out of bed and pulled on yesterday's clothes, letting his feet lead him on the usual route. He thanked the Chinese girl when she sold him the paper, even though she was on her phone again and didn't even look up this time. He found himself, for one wild moment, tempted to show her the front page – the picture of the tent and the canal and the little blurry insert of the man whose name he now knew was Eugene – and say, 'I did that. That was all my fault.' He wanted to point at it and say, 'Isn't it a dreadful world?' And to hear her agree. But she wasn't even looking at him. It was a dreadful world. But no one else seemed to notice.

CARING LIZ'S TEARS FOR EUGENE

He opened the paper as he walked, and there she was, on page two, face half covered by her hand as she ran past the camera. He hadn't been expecting that. He'd anticipated the picture of the man, the tent, the police. But not his Elizabeth, not here. How frightened she looked!

Oh, Elizabeth. I'm so sorry.

He sat on the small wall outside the shop, smoothed the pages. Touched her face gently with his finger. Was she crying? It was hard to tell. But the paper said she had been, that caring Liz, twenty-six, had been seen at Tír na nÓg weeping following the killing of a second client. And that shattered Liz had said she feared for the lives of the rest of the residents. And her own?

Oh, Elizabeth. Stephen rocked back and forwards on his small wall, closed his eyes and summoned her face. Those green eyes. She was right to be worried.

Oh, my sweet Elizabeth. My girl.

CHAPTER TWENTY-TWO

'They like it when you wear the cap, sir.'

'Huh?'

Quigley was fiddling with his tie and Claire realised, with no little amusement, that he was nervous.

'Your cap. They like it when you wear it. The press office, I mean.'

'Ah, yes. The press office.'

Quigley sighed deeply and then tugged at his tie again, looking over at Claire as if considering asking for her help and then deciding against it.

'Remind me whose idea this was again?'

'Yours, sir.'

'Yes. Hmm.'

Giving him a moment, she walked over to the window and peered out through the dusty blinds. Quigley's office was at the front of Collins Street Garda Station and, out on the street, she could see that two TV news vans had been added to the unruly line of parked cars on the far side of the road. As she watched, a familiar-looking female journalist climbed out of a taxi and headed through the front gate.

'Many of them out there?'

'There's a fair few down in reception, yeah.'

'Hmm.'

Quigley gave the tie a final yank and sat down at his desk again, the slim file on Eugene Cannon's murder investigation open in front of him. It was its very slenderness that had made him decide to hold the press conference in the first place – that and the previous day's case conference, when he'd overheard one of the sergeants describe the amount of information they'd gathered as being somewhere between slim and fuck all.

With few witnesses to speak to and victims about whom very little was known, Claire had thought it was an excellent idea. But she hadn't realised just how much her boss would dread the whole procedure. She turned back from the window to where Quigley was now staring, dejectedly, at the front of the file.

'Have you, um, thought about what you want to say, sir?'

'Huh?' Quigley said again and Claire found herself in the unusual position of losing patience with her boss.

'What you want to say? The information you want to get across?'

'Ah, the usual; you know, yourself.' Quigley looked mildly confused. 'That anyone with information should give us a shout, I'll read out the phone number, that sort of thing. The usual stuff. Yeah.'

He looked down at the file again, but Claire wasn't going to let him get away that easily.

'And if they ask you about the Tír na nÓg link?'

'Well, I'll . . .' Quigley frowned.

A ray of sun, filtering through the blinds, found the top of his head and, for a moment, Claire thought she could see pink scalp showing through. Hardly, though. Probably just the way he'd combed it.

'Sure, I won't say anything about that, just that it's part of the ongoing investigation and that we can't . . . Sure . . . they mightn't ask that at all.'

Claire walked back to the desk and sat down in front of him. 'I'd be fairly sure they'll ask about that, sir.'

Quigley glared at her. 'So I suppose you've a better idea?'

'Well . . .'

She paused, unsure of how far to push it. She and Quigley had a good relationship; she'd been on his team for years and he'd always had her back. He'd even been, she suspected, instrumental in minimising the repercussions after what she'd heard him describe as her 'unorthodox' method of solving the Miriam Twohy case. Unorthodox. She'd wanted to shake his hand when she heard that. A lot of other supers would have had her disciplined, if not worse, given what she'd done, despite the positive outcome. She had even considered sending him a thank-you text one evening when she'd had her first glass of wine after Anna was born. Hadn't done it in the end, of course; had seen sense before she'd pressed the *send* button. But, yeah, she owed him one. And that was why she wasn't going to let him make a tit of himself today. She'd have to be subtle about it, though.

'Well . . .'

She paused, as if thinking hard of a strategy. In actual fact, Claire had been dying to take part in a high-profile press conference ever since Collins Street had sent her on that day course in media relations the previous year. But she knew Quigley, knew how these things worked. Best let him think she was just coming up with suggestions.

'Well, sir, you know, yourself, what has to be said. I mean, you're right, of course you are – about the need for people to come forward, and that, and give us any information they have. Absolutely. But, I suppose . . . I suppose what we really want is for anyone who noticed anything unusual to really listen to you? To understand how important it is for them to call us? And – I don't know, sir – people just have the news on in the background, a lot of the time. So I think you'll have to give them something. Something a bit personal. You have to give these journalists something to go on, something other than a phone number they could get off a press release.'

'OK.'

Quigley's face was perfectly still, but he wasn't trying to interrupt her, which Claire took as an instruction to continue.

'So what is it you want to know?'

Quigley looked at her. 'Are you serious?'

Claire nodded, and Quigley narrowed his eyes.

'We want to know who the fuck killed these two and if it was the same fucker that did the both of them.'

Claire grinned. 'Well, that would certainly get you on the news, anyway, sir.'

'Bit too blunt?'

'Little bit.'

His face softened into a smile for a moment, and then he raised his eyebrows again, an unspoken invitation for her to keep talking.

'Well, we've spoken to everyone who knew the men; at least, everyone who we know knew them, if you get me. So it's more the others, isn't it? People we don't know, people who might have known them or seen them, even, on the day they died. I mean, we know where James Mannion was killed, and roughly when, but we know very little about this Cannon chap. We know he left Tír na nÓg before it closed – around five thirty, Tom Carthy said – and his body was found at the canal before six the following morning. And we've nothing else. So we need a timeline, I suppose.'

'Uh huh.'

'So . . .' Claire inhaled, suddenly realising she was veering dangerously close to giving advice to a superior – far superior – officer. 'Well, sir, if it was me – and this is only a suggestion, now – but, if it was me, I'd tell the press that the deaths were brutal, you know the sort of thing. Make it sound like you give a— Like you really care about the victims. Which you do, obviously. But, you know, like you were shocked by it. Something to make what you say stand out.'

Quigley nodded, impatiently. 'And?'

He was dying to write it down, she realised, but that would have crossed a whole motorway full of white lines.

'So I suppose what I'm saying is, I'd make it a bit personal, sir. Like you're, I don't know, a bit upset or something.'

The eyebrows disappeared into his hairline. 'Ah, now, come on; I mean, do you expect me to burst into tears or—'

She shook her head vigorously. 'No, no, God, no. Sorry. I just mean a bit of, you know, something a bit human-interesty, I suppose.'

A bit human-interesty. Brilliant, Claire. Prepare the uniform; those stripes are only hours away. She wished, for a moment, that she could level with him. Tell him the truth – that Matt had a mate who worked in P.R. and had given her the stats over dinner one evening. There'd be fifteen stories on the news that night, and most of the people watching would only be half listening, anyway – drinking tea, or having their dinner, or giving out to their children at the same time. And chances were the person who knew something – the person who didn't even know they knew something, maybe – would be one of them, sitting there, supervising homework, or looking for a missing sock, or arguing over whose turn it was to walk the dog and thinking they were listening to the news but not taking it in, not really.

Truth of the matter was, Quigley needed to put a serious bit of effort in or else this whole press-conference thing would be a waste of time. He needed his words to stand out, to make someone remember something they hadn't even known was important at the time. If all he did was recite a phone number then there wasn't a hope of that happening. The public was pissed off, the deaths of the two men had come too close together and there was talk of a public protest now, a rally in the city centre. The organisers were saying on social media that they just wanted to keep the men's deaths in the public eye, to encourage people to 'keep an eye on their elderly neighbours', that sort of thing. But she'd no doubt that the usual hotheads would be out too, slagging off the guards and anyone else they considered to be Them to their Us.

But the best advice she could come up with was, 'a bit human-interesty, I suppose.' God, was this baby brain? No, Claire decided, she couldn't even blame Anna this time. She'd always been a bit incoherent in front of Quigley – that was the truth of it. She'd just have to trust he got the message.

Quigley pursed his lips and then nodded briskly.

'Well, appreciate the advice, Boyle. What time did we ask them to be here, anyway? Noon?'

'Yeah. It's just gone that now, sir. They'll be trying to catch the one o'clock news, I suppose.'

'Grand, so.'

He strode past her and down the corridor, looked backwards as if to say something, and then caught sight of his reflection in the window instead and straightened his cap. Then he turned to face her.

'So, are you coming?'

'Down with you?'

'Yeah. I thought you might . . .' Quigley paused, allowed a half smile to creep across his features and then folded it away again. 'I thought you might like to see how it's done, Boyle.'

'Absolutely.'

Straightening her own jacket, Claire strode after him, surprised at how pleased she was at the invitation. She was also surprised to find herself wondering what the cap would look like on her.

So, while Boyle had got the glamour gig – and her mug on the TV news, no less, – he, Flynn, was doing the donkey work.

Thanks be to God.

He took a sip from his bottle of water and thought back to the scrum he'd just witnessed down in the front office. Journalists, cameramen, all that crowd, dressed to the nines and trying their hardest to look bored, as if they had much better things to be doing than hanging around a suburban Garda station in the early afternoon. All fake nonchalance and occasional pokes at their phones to indicate there was much more exciting news happening elsewhere.

Then Boyle had walked in and told them the super would talk to them outside, and you could practically see their antennae quivering. They were elbowing each other out of the way as they tried to get their microphones up the nose of the big man, their cameras right in his face. And the questions? Mother of mercy, the stupid questions:

'Do you have a suspect for this crime?'

'Is there a link between this latest death and the death of James Mannion?'

'What details can you give us of Eugene Cannon's final movements?'

Sure, if they knew that, Flynn thought to himself giddily, there'd be no need for the press conference at all. In fairness to the super, though, he'd handled it well. Even got a bit, well, emotional was the wrong word. But he said a few strong things towards the end, stuff about how both killings had been brutal and horrific and how he was sure someone out there knew something and that it was important, even if they thought it was small or insignificant, that they call the guards, anyway.

Even if they thought it was small or insignificant. Quigley had said that bit twice and glanced into the camera a couple of times. It had worked too; they'd been playing the clip all afternoon on Ireland 24, and near the top of the bulletin, not halfway down like they usually did. Flynn had also seen the clip a couple of times on Twitter, attached to the #vigilforJames hashtag, and it seemed to have softened the online opinion of the guards, and their role in the case, as well. The lads on the desk said they'd had several calls offering information, even at this early stage, and that some of it sounded quite useful. Fair play to Quigley. Truth be told, Flynn hadn't thought he had it in him.

He wondered briefly if Boyle had enjoyed herself. You could see her quite clearly on the TV, standing beside Quigley, all intense head-nodding and grimly efficient stares. Well, let her at it. It wasn't for him, all that TV stuff. Well, not being on it, anyway. He looked at the tiny grey screen in front of him. Watching it, that was more his line. This wasn't exactly Netflix, though.

He opened the Tupperware container that held his lunch, took a mouthful of couscous and chewed, thoughtfully. Dinner and a movie, what? Chuckling at his own joke, he picked a bit of fresh mint from between his two front teeth. The CCTV footage from outside Tír na nÓg wouldn't win any Oscars, but, if he did his job right, it might end up being something far more important than that.

On the screen in front of him, a grey shape wobbled, twitched and then revealed itself to be a cat. Or a dog. Tom Carthy had bought the cheapest security system on the market, which made it hard to be sure. Flynn squinted. A larger figure, definitely a man this time, shimmered his way up the garden path. Flynn leaned forward and paused the picture. It wasn't Eugene Cannon, anyway; this fella was a lot shorter, for one, and his hair looked white and bushy, not dark and close cropped, like the victim's. He reached over, grabbed a still image and then noted the date and time in his notebook. The footage he was watching was dated the day before Cannon's body was discovered. So everything was important. Well, it might be.

Could all be shite, of course. But at least it was something to do, genuine graft, something to get his teeth into. Like this roast salmon, he chuckled to himself again. Well, you wouldn't be fit enough for promotion if you lived on canteen food. And Boyle wasn't the only one round here with ambition. But he wanted to make his way through real policing, not dealing with the press and all that jazz. Asking the right questions and making the right connections, that was the sort of thing he liked. He took another drink of water and focused on the screen again. He was looking at footage from two o'clock in the afternoon, or so the little clock in the corner of the screen informed him. But it might as well be two a.m. for all that activity that was going on. Still, though, he'd plough on. He'd nothing better to do, anyway.

As if it had read his mind, a text pinged into his phone. Flynn picked it up, read it and nearly spluttered salad dressing (home-made, two parts oil to one vinegar) all over the TV screen. Ah, here. That was a bit cheeky, now. But, despite himself, he was grinning and he chose his words carefully before texting back.

Not tonight, sorry. Long day tomorrow. Another time?

That should do it; keen but not desperate. Flynn read the text again and smiled. It was mad, really, how the whole Diarmaid thing had come about. After the worst of beginnings, too. Flynn still cringed every time he thought of the night in the pub, after the Miriam Twohy result, when Siobhán O'Doheny, fuelled by victory and the guts of a bottle of Pinot Grigio, had ambled over to him and dropped a heavy hint that they head off somewhere to celebrate, alone. Flynn had almost choked on his pint when she suggested it, and his muttered revela-tion that that particular scenario could never be a runner had had a similar effect on O'Doheny. But, in fairness to her, she'd recovered quickly and even made some comment about how she had a brother she could introduce him to, before heading off to try her luck elsewhere. Flynn, thinking she was just trying to save face by proving how cool she was with the whole gay thing, had forgotten about the offer almost instantly. But, who would have guessed it? It turned out she'd meant every word.

His phone pinged again and Flynn's grin widened as he read Diarmaid's riff on the word *long*. Chancer.

Then he thought for a moment and texted back.

Ah, go on, then. Only the one, mind you.

This time the response was even faster. Flynn read it, coloured and put the phone down on the desk.

And picked it up again almost immediately. Sure, what the hell.

X

Well, Diarmaid had said it first. It seemed only polite to respond. Only the one, mind you.

Then he turned off the phone and addressed himself to the monitor again.

Twenty-nine calls. Not bad at all. Most of them would almost certainly be useless, but it was a respectable haul. More than the usual amount, anyway, and they'd come in faster than usual too. A very decent result for a half-hour's work, and she knew the super agreed. You'd swear, grinned Claire to herself, that he'd put a bit of extra effort into the press conference. Or something.

'Anything leap out at you?'

'A couple are worth chasing. Few loo-lahs in there as well.'

'Ah, sure, that goes without saying.'

Garda Gerry Whyte was a quiet young fella, but Claire trusted his judgement and she took the sheaves of paper he handed her without further comment. She settled herself at her desk and began to read, dismissing most of the information without a second glance.

Wrong month. Wrong county. Believed Eugene Cannon to be her ex-husband. Wished Superintendent Quigley could be her current husband.

Oh, here was one. A man thought he'd sat next to Eugene Cannon on a bus going to Dun Laoghaire the week before he was killed. Claire put that to one side and then marvelled at people who remembered stuff like that. She herself would be pushed to remember what she'd had for dinner two nights ago. Work stuff, fine – that was pretty much always buzzing around in the corner of her brain – but not other stuff. You had to have a bit of a weird streak, she reckoned, to keep your eyes open all the time, to remember random strangers who walked past you, car drivers behaving strangely on the road. Fact of the matter was, it was the people her mother referred to as 'nosy parkers' who made the best witnesses. And the guards would be lost without them.

Stifling a yawn, she continued to flick through the type-written sheets. One caller had claimed the killings were linked to the ongoing situation in the Middle East. Well, it made a change from the North, Claire supposed. Two people were sure they had seen Eugene Cannon begging in the city centre in the weeks before his death. Claire put those to one side; they had the smell of truth off them, alright. Another caller claimed he'd seen Cannon get into a screaming row with another man in the middle of Supermacs, which would be brilliant if the incident hadn't happened the day after his body had been found.

A man had phoned claiming he'd killed Eugene Cannon. With a poisoned dart, apparently. Ah, God love him. Still, he'd have to be phoned back. And referred on to another, more suitable, organisation, probably.

She blinked and rubbed her eyes. It was all needle-in-hay-stack stuff, the usual feeling of all of the information being matted, messed up, unclear. But at least it felt like they were doing something. She was knackered, though; she'd been up twice the night before with a snot-nosed Anna, and, after the week he'd had, she hadn't had the heart to wake Matt when it came to his turn. Reminded of their last row, she took a quick look at her phone: turned on and fully charged. She wasn't going to make that mistake again. Poor Anna, though. Red-eyed and wet-nosed that morning, her daughter was clearly in the early stages of another bloody cold and had grizzled miserably when handed over to her ever-cheery minder. It would have been nice to have kept her home, thrown a duvet over the two of them, watched some daytime TV. But there wasn't a hope of that happening today.

As if it felt her scrutiny, her phone buzzed. Oh, please, no – but it wasn't the crèche number, just a text from Dean Evans, that young fella from Ireland 24.

Any update on Mannion/Cannon? Tnx. D.

Claire deleted it without answering. Dean Evans was becoming a bit of a pest, actually. There was a time he'd been good about not calling her, not using her personal number unless he really needed it. But now he was texting most days, and ringing as well, looking for an update, a heads-up or God knows what else. Fair enough, he was a friend of Liz Cafferky's, probably worried about her as well as trying to get a jump on the story, but that didn't give him any right to expect information before anyone else. And it had been cheeky of him, putting Eugene Cannon's name out there before they'd officially released it. Not a huge deal, not something she'd bother complaining about. But she'd noted it, and would hold off on the helpful hints for the time being.

Garda Whyte put another couple of pages on her table. More calls. A woman wanting to know if Tom Carthy was single. What were they, a dating agency? A man saying he had information but would only talk to Liz Cafferky, in person. Well, he could whistle for that. Jesus, did people have nothing better to do with their time? Claire rubbed her eyes again. She'd give her right arm for a coffee – not machine muck, but a proper hot vanilla latte or, better still, a white chocolate mocha, a large one. And a copy of the new *Vogue*. Ah, focus, Boyle.

A woman had phoned to say she thought her teenage daughter was dating Eugene Cannon, and could the guards do anything about it? She seemed to have missed the part of the story about him being dead. A man had complained that his car had been broken into six times and didn't the cops have anything better to do than looking after old men who had one foot in the grave? Ouch. Claire slapped that one down on the 'ignore' pile and scowled at it. People were lovely, just adorable, sometimes. And in this job you got a full insight into human nature.

God, even a cup of tea would do her at this stage. And a biscuit. A custard cream. Any method of getting sugar into her bloodstream. She lifted another piece of paper. Five more minutes and she'd be done for the evening. And then she read the details and all thoughts of a break disappeared. A call from a woman, claiming she had seen a man who answered to Cannon's description coming out of Tír na nÓg the afternoon before he died. OK, that was fair enough. They knew he'd visited the centre that day, but it was nice to have it confirmed. Hang on a minute, though. He'd been involved in an altercation with a much younger man, Garda Whyte had written in small, careful handwriting. Now, that was far more interesting.

After five hours of snuffling dogs and shuffling elderly men, even Flynn's enthusiasm was beginning to fade. He could have written a thesis on the front door of Tír na nÓg, he decided, described at length the precise part of the hedge the local cats used as a public toilet, and given a good guess as to the number of cracks in the path leading up to the front door. But he had seen nothing so far that seemed in any way connected with the death of Eugene Cannon or James Mannion. In fact, the only person he'd recognised had been Tom Carthy, who'd left the centre at around three and returned half an hour later clutching a plastic bag from a convenience store. Flynn used his superpowers of observation, and the zoom function, to deduce that Tom liked his milk low in fat. God, he was bored.

He yawned. Five more minutes and then he'd call it a day. He'd have to freshen up a bit, anyway, or he'd never get his head together for the pint-not-date with Diarmaid later. X indeed. He yawned again and looked closer at the screen. There was Tom, putting something in a wheelie bin. He still couldn't figure that chap out. What was he doing there? Clearly an intelligent man, a teacher – a fine-looking man too, in fairness to him. So why in God's name was he spending his days surrounded by oul fellas? Spending his inheritance on them, too, according to himself. Flynn rolled the tape on. He watched Tom return to the building. Watched a bird land on the path. Watched the bird shit on the path. Watched a man walk up the path. He paused the tape. OK, this might be something. He hadn't seen this dude before, anyway. The picture wasn't great, but you could tell, even from this distance, that he was significantly younger than the usual Tír na nÓg client. What was he doing? Delivering something? No, he was moving far too slowly for that. In fact, you'd almost swear he was reluctant to be there at all.

Philip Flynn watched as the man raised his hand, lowered it, and then repeated this action twice before finally knocking on the door. It opened. And the man on the path stepped back at just the right moment to allow Flynn to see Eugene Cannon on the other side.

CHAPTER TWENTY-THREE

They found him on the number forty bus. Sometimes it really was that simple. Flynn wasn't one of those guards who was sniffy about technology; after everything that happened in the Miriam Twohy case, he knew he couldn't afford to be. He'd signed up for all the courses, took his passwords seriously, even got himself an anonymous Twitter account so he and his little egg could listen into online conversations. Philip Flynn knew his way around the web, alright. But sometimes, even in these days of I.P. addresses and mobile-phone triangulation, the deep web and Europol, sometimes it was still all about the basics, and the legwork. You were told a fella got on a bus, and you found the bus, and you found the fella.

As soon as he'd realised the importance of what he was looking at, he'd shouted for Boyle, and the two of them had gone through the CCTV footage together. Within minutes they were sure that, yes, it had been Eugene Cannon who had answered the door to the man in the dark trousers and, yes, he had followed him down the path and exchanged what looked like heated words with him too.

But the camera's range only extended as far as the front gate, and that's where Boyle's caller came in – a woman who claimed to have witnessed a row between the two men, or men who looked very like them. She hadn't wanted to tell them a thing; that much had been obvious as soon as she had opened the door.

'My ma saw a bit about it on the news, said I should ring you.'

She was probably around the same age as Boyle, Flynn thought, but looked older – well, harder, anyway. A small, wiry person, she was dressed in a white vest top and tight-fitting stonewashed jeans and, as she sucked deeply on her cigarette, the veins stood out on her pale, muscular arms.

'She said that, on the telly, it said that anyone with information should contact you? But, actually, I've changed my mind; I don't want to get involved.'

She was nervous, Flynn realised, as she squinted at them through the smoke. Probably had good reason to be. It'd be nothing major – the lack of a television licence, maybe, or a kid who'd missed too many days off school – but he knew the type: people who didn't want to go dragging the law in on top of themselves. People who didn't see the Guardians of the Peace as their friends.

Fact of the matter was, though, neither he nor Boyle gave a bollix if every stick of furniture in her place had fallen off the back of a lorry. They needed to hear what Amy Leahy had to say. Her home, just around the corner from Tír na nÓg, was spotless, apart from the stench of cigarette smoke that clung to the heavy velvet curtains, the sofa and even to the hair of the large Alsatian who wandered freely from room to room. As Flynn watched her, Miss Leahy patted the dog's head absently and took another drag from her cigarette.

'I mean, I'm not really sure it's important at all, so . . .'

Flynn took another look around the room, trying and failing to come up with some way of convincing her to tell them her story. But that's when Boyle jumped in, although *jump*, in this context, was totally the wrong word. Her voice was gentle, almost diffident, betraying none of the urgency Flynn knew she was feeling. Instead, she sounded almost uninterested as she settled herself back into the armchair.

'It's tough, isn't it? Trying to remember what you did a few days ago. Jesus, I'm not sure what I had for breakfast this morning, never mind what I did yesterday afternoon.'

'Yeah.' The woman's eyes narrowed, but there didn't seem to be any double meaning in the detective's comment. 'That's what I told me ma. I mean, yeah, I told her Thursday night I seen two fellas arguing outside that centre, teer na nog, or whatever you call it . . .'

She pronounced the name as in 'eggnog' and it took Flynn a moment to realise what she was talking about.

'But I'm just not sure if I can be of any use to you at all.'

You're our only witness, so start remembering, is what Flynn knew Boyle wanted to say. But the detective simply leaned over and scratched the dog behind his ears. Her attitude towards this witness was one hundred and eighty degrees different from the one she'd adopted with Liz Cafferky, and it was fascinating for him to watch the gear change. Fascinating, and a reminder of how lucky he was to be able to learn from her. Not that he'd ever tell her that, of course.

Boyle nodded again.

'I know, I know. And, sure, it mightn't mean anything, anyway. But, look, the boss likes us to follow up on every call.'

She rolled her eyes and the woman smiled, for the first time.

'Ah, yeah, I know what you mean. I work for a fella like that meself! Feckin' eejit.'

She gave a sudden cackle and Boyle grinned at her.

'Ah, they're all the same. So, look, maybe you could give me a dig-out, yeah? Have a think about that evening, whatever you saw. Anything you can remember.'

The woman lit another cigarette from the butt of the last while Boyle kept talking in the same mild, measured tone.

'And don't worry about details or anything – anything you're unsure about – just tell us whatever you remember; we'll do the rest. You were coming home from work, I think you said on the phone?'

'Yeah. OK. Well, I always come that way on a Thursday. Usually, I get the bus all the way down here, but Thursdays I do stop off at Tesco to get a few bits.'

'So you had a few bags with you?'

The woman's face brightened. 'Yeah, well, that's why I remembered it. It was just starting to rain and I was walking along with me bags and, next thing, he comes barrelling out the gate and straight into me. Sent me flying and me bags went everywhere. Me milk just exploded and he stepped into me yoghurt – two cartons of it, the big ones. Went bleedin' everywhere. And then the other fella ran through it too.'

'The other fella?'

Flynn couldn't keep quiet any longer. 'At what stage—?'

A sideways glower from Claire and he fell silent again.

'Well, he was coming after him, wasn't he? Chasin' him out the gate, like. I was kneeling down, at this stage, trying to grab me stuff, and then the big fella grabs the smaller fella and says . . . Hang on, now, till I see what he said . . .'

She took another drag from the cigarette before continuing.

'"Did he send you after me?" Something like that, anyway. The smaller fella is kind of half crying and he says, "No, no, I don't know what you mean," and the bigger guy says, "Was it the brother that sent you? Because I swear to fuck—"'

Unsure how they'd take the expletive, she darted a quick look at the guards, but both nodded at her impatiently to continue.

'He was a country fella, by the sounds of it, the big chap. He was ranting and raving and saying something about his brother and how, I don't know, something like he'd come up here to get away from him? And the little fella was shittin' it.'

The dog came over again, startled by the rise in her voice, and whined, softly.

'And the little fella says, "It's not you! It's Elizabeth. I just need to see Elizabeth." Something like that, anyway, I was gathering up me stuff and trying to get away from them, to be honest.'

Claire's tone was so light, so delicate, she might have been asking for a drop of milk in her tea, but Flynn could hear the tension, taut as a violin string, that overlaid it: 'And do you remember what he looked like? The smaller man – the little fella? You said he banged into you – did you get a good look at him at all?'

'Black hair.'

The woman released a long stream of smoke and stared through it, as if she could see him in the haze.

'Kind of sweaty, if that makes sense? Really stressed-looking. About me own age, I suppose. Black slacks on him and shoes – he looked like a bar man or something. Like he was wearing a uniform. Old-fashioned clothes. And he looked like he was going to burst into tears.'

'That's brilliant, absolutely brilliant.' Boyle's voice was so soothing, she might have been reading a bedtime story. 'And did he run off then or—?'

'Yeah, he kept going down the road . . .'

The woman's voice trailed off, then she blinked suddenly and looked from one to the other, with surprise.

'He got on the bus! Jesus, I'm only after remembering that now. He got on the bus at the end of the road. I remember, now, looking after him and thinking, *You're better off, son, not to have this fella after you.* Yeah. He got on a bus. The other fella headed back into the house. That was it, then; I headed off to me ma's.'

The dog whined softly.

'Didn't even ask me was I OK, the big guy. Just turned around and headed back into the teernanogg place. Some of them country fuckers have no manners.'

Then she reached out for the dog again and pulled him towards her.

'Jesus, though, he's dead now, isn't he? That's the fella who died, isn't it? Oh my God. You don't think—?'

'Ah, sure, it's all guess work, at this stage.'

Flynn could hear the effort Boyle was putting in to keeping her voice steady.

'And do you remember, at all, what time of the evening this was?'

'Half five.'

The woman's voice grew fainter.

'Half five, because I looked at my watch and I was thinking, *Shit, I'm going to be late picking up the kids*. That's why I told her in the first place, me mother, about what happened. I always pick up the kids at half five on the dot on Thursdays to let her go to bingo. So I had to tell her why I was late. Fuck it, though. Did he kill him, did he? That scrawny fella – did he do it? Oh, Jesus . . .'

The dog growled as Boyle rose to her feet. 'You've been brilliant, really brilliant.'

Keeping her hand on the dog's head, the woman looked up at them. 'C'mere, did he see me? Am I in trouble now?'

'No, no, not at all.'

'Here, do I have to go to court or anything? Oh, I knew I shouldn't have called you.'

'Ah, sure, look, don't worry about that for the moment.'

Flynn shot his boss a look. The witness would almost certainly have to go to court; he knew – and he knew Boyle knew – that she had given them their best lead yet. But right now their main aim was to find the bus, and the man, and avoid becoming the Alsatian's evening meal.

'I'll give you a shout in a few days.'

Claire was almost doing a comedy walk now, backing through the house at speed, the woman following her, the dog bringing up the rear.

'I don't want any trouble, now.'

'It's all fine. You've been a brilliant help. Oh, and by the way –' Claire stopped dead in the centre of the hall and reached into her briefcase – 'just wondering – is this the man you saw, do you think?'

She held out the still image, taken from the CCTV footage. The lads in tech had done their best and, although it was still grainy, they'd managed to catch him, full face, just before he looked up at the door.

The woman glanced at the page and nodded immediately. 'Yeah, that's him, alright.'

'We'll be in touch.'

The dog's snout was the last thing Flynn saw as he followed Claire back to the car.

A movie would have had a montage sequence right at that point, Flynn reckoned. A few pictures of him making some calls and then staring at a screen, maybe a scene where he stuck his head in his hands and looked knackered, or punched the desk in frustration, that sort of thing. Or maybe there'd be a bit showing him and Boyle going door to door and holding out a sheet of paper, and people nodding and scratching their heads and saying, 'Maybe,' and, 'Yeah,' and, 'No,' and, 'Possibly,' and, 'I don't think I've seen him.'

In reality, it took three days, which was actually pretty speedy for the real world. Three days to find out which buses stopped in that area at that time of the evening, and requisition the CCTV and then sit through it. More bloody grey pictures. But their man had been quite easy to spot, in the end. It had been impossible to miss him, truth be told, the way he'd jumped on to the bus and flung money at the driver. Even distanced from the scene by the graininess of the picture, you could see he was upset. Hassled. Then he'd stood near the door for the entire journey, right in front of the camera, fair play to him, so it was no bother figuring out when he got off, either. And after that, well, Flynn hated using the word *simple*. But it was, really. The bus stop where he got off turned out to be near a row of shops and it was just a case of going from door to door, picture in hand, asking about him.

And the young, bored-looking Chinese girl behind the counter in the newsagent's said, 'Yes,' the minute they showed her the photo of him, and, 'Yes,' again when they asked if she knew where he lived. He'd dropped his wallet one morning, she'd told them, and she'd followed him outside and seen him go through a metal gate on the other side of the road, a gate that led to flats above yet more shops in this small inner-city enclave.

Sometimes, Flynn thought, it was as simple as getting on a bus and asking the right questions. And finding the people who could answer them.

CHAPTER TWENTY-FOUR

Stephen was on the internet when they arrived. Looking at pictures of her, as it happened. So that made it easy for them.

The Tír na nÓg Facebook page hadn't been updated for days, so he had just Googled her name instead and then sat back, surprised and delighted at the number of pages that crowded the screen: links to articles in the papers and clips from the TV news; a discussion on a message board about her; another discussion about the killings at Tír na nÓg and how it was all really obvious who was doing it, only the guards were too thick to figure it out. The second post on that thread had been deleted by the moderator before Stephen got a chance to read it. It would have been interesting to see how close to the truth it came.

She even had her own hashtag on Twitter, #LizCafferky; there were loads of people talking about her there and someone had set up a fake account too, @charideegurl, in what appeared to be a feeble attempt to slag her off. The picture was of the back of some other woman's head but you could tell they meant her, alright; the little bit of writing at the top was about how she wanted to save the world, one sob story at a time. The account, which wasn't very funny, only had thirteen followers and Stephen had no intention of adding to their number. But it was a pleasant way to spend time, nonetheless, reading about her. She was everywhere.

It wasn't just Elizabeth, either. You couldn't click on her name now without Mr Mannion's coming up alongside it, or that other chap, the one Stephen now knew was called Eugene Cannon. The photograph they were using was old and looked nothing like the man Stephen had seen, but the papers said it was him and who was he to argue with them? Stephen had never been very good at arguing and he wasn't going to get any better at this late stage. That was how he felt when they knocked on his door too: passive, reluctant to disagree with anything they were saying. It felt as if everything that had happened so far had been inevitable, and this? Well, this next stage was inevitable too.

There were two of them: a tall, quiet man and a busy, angular woman who spoke quickly, too quickly, about evidence and footage and search warrants and possible cause. For one mad moment, Stephen considered holding his hand up gently in front of her face the way his mother used to when he came home from school, full of some story or another, and saying, Take it handy, now; don't be rushing; sure, you have all the time in the world. *But he didn't dare, and he didn't think she'd appreciate the advice, either.*

Instead, he just stood by the wall and watched them search his home. He'd felt embarrassed when he saw it dawn on them that the 'flat' was just one room. The man guard said they'd start the search 'in here' and then stopped dead when he realised there wasn't actually anywhere else to go. The woman guard muttered something about how she thought 'these places' had been banned years ago, when Stephen, trying to be helpful, opened the door that led to the toilet, in the little partition between the two-ring cooker and the fridge. And when they raised their eyebrows and asked if this was the only bathroom, he'd told them about the shower room he shared at the end of the corridor and how it was handy being on shift work because there was never usually anyone else in there. Then he realised he was talking too much, and stood back against the wall, feeling exposed, and angry that they had made him feel this way.

He knew they felt uncomfortable around him too, but he was used to that. He hadn't slept properly in days, hadn't washed, either. Just got up when he woke, dragged on the same clothes as the day before, turned on his computer and thought about her, and everything that had happened. The girl from his job had called him the day before to tell him that there was a formal warning in the post. Her voice had been a lot less friendly this time. Without a proper medical certificate, she told him, he was in danger of dismissal.

Well, there was no point in worrying about that anymore.

So, they searched his home: the sofa bed and the chair, the box of magazines in the corner, the cupboard over the sink where he stored his food, the WiFi modem – the man guard spent a long time over that; Stephen thought about offering him the password but then decided he might sound cheeky. They even rifled through his clothes, and the woman guard had called the man over when she'd found the scrapbook stored in with his shoes. It wasn't like he'd hidden it, or anything. He'd just wanted to keep it safe. But she acted like finding it was a big deal, put on gloves, took some photographs, the whole shebang. Meanwhile, the big chap was examining his computer. He didn't have to be a genius to figure out what was going on there, either. Sure, the minute they knocked it off sleep mode they could see that his screen saver was a picture of her. He hadn't ever thought anyone would see it, that was *all. There were no big mysteries to be found in his search history, either. Most of the searches were about her: Elizabeth Cafferky. Liz Cafferky Tír na nÓg. Elizabeth Cafferky help. Elizabeth Cafferky boyfriend. Well, a man could dream.*

And this was a bit like a dream too, he realised. Standing here, in his room, his home, answering their questions. Saying yes and saying no. It seemed to make them happy, every time he got one right. So he kept it simple. Yes, he had called to Tír na nÓg that evening two weeks ago. Letters to Elizabeth? He'd rather not discuss that, thank you. He hoped being polite would still count for something; he was trying to be as helpful as he could, under the circumstances. Yes, he did know James Mannion, or had known him, many years ago. He'd known him in school; Mr Mannion been a teacher there. The lady guard had widened her eyes then and made a kind of a whistling sound through her teeth and said, 'Jesus, are you Stephen? Stephen Millar?' And Stephen had said yes, although it had been many years since he'd used that name. He used his mother's maiden name now, Stephen Ford; he felt more comfortable with it. But by then she wasn't really listening, she had got all excited and, pretty soon, so had the tall chap and they were talking about arrest warrants and bringing him into the station. He realised that trying to answer their questions hadn't done him any good, so he'd have to take a different approach, if things had any hope of turning out OK.

CHAPTER TWENTY-FIVE

'I just don't think it's a good idea. You'd be too obvious out there, too exposed. Those letters might have been bullshit but—'

'Yeah. Totally. You're right. I don't know what I was thinking.'

Liz folded the flyer, made a paper aeroplane and aimed it at the bin. She wasn't particularly surprised when it fell well short and took a nosedive on to the carpet instead. It had been that sort of day. That sort of life, really.

'They were talking about it in the office today; they reckon there might be hundreds there. I'll probably be working at it, even. A couple of politicians are saying they are going to turn up as well; it makes them look good, you know – the whole touchy-feely thing.'

In the absence of anywhere to sit, Dean had propped himself against the windowsill and was tugging anxiously at his ear.

'I just don't . . . It's one thing doing a few interviews, you know, but this? This is totally different. I'd worry about you, to be honest.'

'Yeah. You're right. Forget it; it was a stupid idea.'

Liz looked around the bedroom, every surface covered either by her clothes or by mystifying pieces of electronic equipment, all belonging to Dean, and all of which he insisted were vital to his survival as a freelance journalist. Liz reckoned, if they ever found themselves under attack from aliens, he'd be able to build his own satellite communication system, no bother – providing the little green men left them some electricity, of course. But, Christ, it made the place feel cluttered.

When Dean had invited her to stay with him for a couple of days, he had neglected to mention the fact that he shared his house with three other people, two of them students, neither of them particularly tidy and none of them keen on the idea of a body on the sofa in the already-cramped living room. So Liz had spent the last four days sleeping in Dean's bed while he lied about being more comfortable on a chair. It had been kind of him to take her in, but she couldn't go on like this. She needed to get back to her real life. Whatever the hell that was.

She looked across at the crashed aeroplane again. A large red 'V' could just be seen peeping out from the fuselage.

A Vigil for the Voiceless.

It was a good name, she thought – said it all. It was incredible, really, how quickly the whole thing seemed to have come together. Just a couple of days ago, a small picture of James Mannion's funeral had appeared in one of the daily papers. Delayed by the investigation into his death, the service had been sparsely attended but moving, thanks, for the most part, to a sincere priest who tried to say nice things about a man he'd never met. However, a photograph taken from the car park, which had been printed in the *Dublin Daily*, had made the crowd look tiny and there had been something almost pathetic about the sight of the mourners, most of them elderly, shuffling alongside the funeral car. There had been no floral tribute on top of the coffin – no *Dad*, or *Husband* formed in pink carnations – just a small wreath with a misspelt card proclaiming love from *all at Tirna Noge*. Liz had felt saddened all over again when she saw the picture, and it seemed she wasn't the only one to have that reaction.

The following afternoon, a caller to one of the country's most listened-to radio shows had declared herself *moved to tears* by the photograph and had asked if there was any way she could pay her respects to a man who had died in such a violent and lonely way. Another caller asked for Mass cards to be sent to Tír na nÓg, while a third suggested a city-centre vigil be held, in memory of James and all elderly people who die alone. One caller had mentioned Eugene Cannon's name too, but, since details of his criminal past had been written about in a couple of the tabloids at the weekend, far fewer people wanted to brave the autumnal chill to pay tribute to him. But James's death, it seemed, had struck a chord and, by the end of the radio show, a vigil had been planned, to take place at the Spire on Dublin's O'Connell Street the following Saturday afternoon. One of the women who had spoken on the radio had phoned Tír na nÓg afterwards to ask if Liz could be there.

'To represent his friends,' was how the caller, Noeleen Kavanagh, had put it, her soft midlands accent gently persuasive on the phone.

'Maybe you can say a few words about him, whatever you think, yourself, really. But it would be nice to have you there.'

Liz had initially agreed to go along, but it now turned out that Dean was dead set against the idea.

'This guy, this Stephen – you don't know if he's for real or not, but do you really want to take that chance?'

'I suppose not, no.'

She shook her head, slowly. Her friend was right. As the guards had pointed out, her name and address were in the phone book, her place of work freely available on Facebook or through Google. She wasn't at all hard to track down and the notes could have been the work of some nutcase trying to freak her out.

But they could have been real. And it would be foolish, very foolish, to appear in such a public place if they were.

Still, though, she thought, as she moved a bundle of unsorted laundry to one side and sat down heavily on Dean's bed, at least speaking at the vigil would have given her something to focus on, something to work towards. And, God knows, she needed that. Camping out in her friend's house was really starting to depress her. She missed her home, her bed, her security and her privacy. It had been great of Dean to take her in but she craved solitude, a bath, a night alone. And work was stressing her out too because Tom was acting so weirdly.

Tom: somebody else who seemed totally drained by the events of the previous few weeks. When the guards told Liz they'd prefer if she didn't stay in her own place for a while, her first thought had been to call her boss for advice. But all she'd got from him was a long string of negatives. No, he hadn't any idea where she could go. No, she couldn't doss down in Tír na nÓg, it wouldn't be any safer than her own place. And no, he couldn't lend her money for a hotel. She hadn't even asked him if she could stay at his place because it was obvious what the answer would be.

Not that she had any idea where that was, anyway. Liz had been working with Tom for over two years and considered him one of her closest friends. But she didn't really know what he did outside Tír na nÓg, and, truth be told, had never thought to ask. There couldn't have been much to find out, anyway. Tom was never away from the centre – opened it up every morning and shut it after the last man had left at night. He was never sick, hadn't taken a holiday in the two years she'd been working there. But, in the past few days, all that had changed, too.

Half the time he wasn't in the building and, even when he was, he spent hours in the office with the door closed, breaking his own cardinal rule. He had even taken to turning his mobile off. That didn't make sense, either. The landline at Tír na nÓg was diverted to it every evening; Tom was a one-man twenty-four-hour helpline and, although Liz had seen him lose car keys, wallet and, once, an entire birthday cake on the journey from the kitchen to the sitting room, she'd never seen him without his mobile, and usually a charger trailing out of it too.

But, for the past few days, he'd been out of contact more often than not and, even when he was in the centre, you could tell his heart wasn't in it. Liz had found him the day before, standing at the front door, foot on the step, nostrils twitching like a horse getting ready to bolt. He had started when she came up behind him, reddened, muttered something about making a call and then pushed past her, back in the direction of the office, leaving what she could have sworn was the faint scent of stale tobacco wafting after him. And Tom, as far as she knew, didn't smoke.

His absence, both physical and emotional, unsettled her. The clients sensed it too and had taken to huddling around Liz like needy toddlers, tugging at her sleeve and wondering when Daddy was going to come home. She was starting to wonder that herself. It had been four days since she'd last had a proper conversation with her boss and supposed best friend. If she were to stop and think how that made her feel, she didn't think she'd be able to get going again. So she had to keep moving.

But she wasn't going to lose herself in drink this time. She'd love to. God, there were times when she wanted nothing more than to uncork a bottle and turn off her thoughts for a while. But the memory of the three-day hangover she'd inflicted on herself the last time was keeping her from going there, for the moment, anyway. That and the fleeting look of distaste on Dean's face the last time she'd suggested going to the pub. Maybe she had been imagining it? Paranoia from the hangover, maybe? But the thought of his disapproval and, worse, his pity, was enough to keep her sober, for the moment.

She needed something, though – something to keep her going, to distract her from the murders and Tom and how shit everything was these days. She needed something to do, something practical to stop her thinking and worrying and panicking. Something that didn't involve getting rat-arsed. She needed a project and taking part in this vigil was very tempting. If only she could risk it.

She walked across to the crash scene and unfolded the page again. A white page, red writing.

Vigil for the Voiceless.

Liz was sick of staying silent.

'We could collect money, Dean. If I did it. Pass around a bucket, or something. God knows, the centre could do with it.'

She reached for the coffee Dean had handed her earlier, savouring its bitter kick. The only stimulant now left to her, the coffee tasted how she felt: sharp, toughened up. She couldn't really explain it, but, despite everything that had happened, Liz realised, she was actually feeling OK these days. Clearer than she had done in years. Cleaner. Stronger. Weirdly, it was the interview with the guards that seemed to have finally sorted things out in her head. For the last two years, she'd been ter-rified that someone would find out about how bad things had been, how far off the rails she had gone. She had been afraid to even think about that night, that girl, the flash of the blue lights above the roofs of the houses, the mist of rain on her face, her feet slapping through the puddles, the tumble into the taxi and the fear of turning around. She had buttoned it away but, every so often, the memory poked through, terri-fying her. But now she had talked to someone about it. And not just someone. The guards. She had told them everything. And they had just shrugged, and written a few things in their notebooks, and told her to go home. The sky hadn't fallen in. Turned out she had a choice, after all. To go back to the crap, or head towards the future she'd worked so hard to secure.

Dean frowned again. 'I suppose what you could do—'

But her phone interrupted him. Liz answered it, listened for a moment, then gave a muttered, 'Thank you,' and hung up. She grinned across the room at him.

'You can stop worrying, Dean. I might just have a story for you too. They've arrested him. That was the guards – you know, that Philip Flynn guy? He says they've arrested the guy they think wrote me the letters. Stephen. They're going to start questioning him today. Everything is OK.'

Ignoring the frown on her friend's face, she looked at the flier again and read the time and the date. She took a deep breath. And smiled.

CHAPTER TWENTY-SIX

He decided, after the fourth cup of tea, that it was better not to look at them, not to make eye contact at all. Or maybe it was the fifth. The cups themselves had been taken away but he could count their number in the fur on his tongue, the bitterness at the back of his throat. At some stage during the evening, the liquid had stopped quenching his thirst and had started to make him feel parched instead. Parched, desert, deserted. Alone. Words swam in his brain. He was so tired. Best not to look at them. Best not to answer them. Best for them not to know things. Best for her.

'You're going to have to start talking at some stage, Stephen.'

No, I'm not. The solicitor they had called for him had told him that much – told him it wasn't necessarily the best course of action, but that he could keep his mouth shut if he wanted. Fine, so. It was exactly what Stephen wanted. Or, more to the point, what was needed.

It was late, or was it early? He didn't own a watch, and the guards had asked him, much earlier, to turn off his phone. They'd told him too that he was entitled to a rest break, but he'd been so terrified of being left alone in a cell that he'd refused. Then they'd introduced him to the solicitor, a stocky man in a brown suit whose Brylcreemed hair had shone under the lights. The handkerchief in the man's breast pocket was damp from the sweat on his forehead, which reappeared as soon as he tried to wipe it away, and he had an over-eager expression on his face, as if Stephen and his problems were all he could think about right now. But Stephen, once he'd found out what he needed to know about staying silent, had ignored him too, and told him to go away. Then he simply allowed himself to be led back to the yellowing room with its high, windowless walls, closed himself up to their questions, and looked at his hands.

'We can sit here as long as you like, you know. You're just making things difficult on yourself.'

Could a room be yellowing? Stephen pondered on this, blocking out their words. He was beyond scared – just dazed now, numbed and lost in his own head. He was making them angry, he knew that. He hated it when people were angry with him. But there was nothing else he could do.

'Does the name James Mannion mean anything to you?'

Despite himself, he caught the guard's eye, and then pulled his gaze away from hers again.

Mr Mannion. It must have been, what, three months ago now that he had last met him? Thirty years after everything had happened. Stephen had just climbed off the bus and was heading for home after an early shift when he'd seen him rounding the corner. He hadn't recognised his former teacher at first. The hair had been the same, white now, obviously, but still strong and wavy, worn long at the back and swept off his face. But everything else had changed. Mr Mannion's shoulders were stooped now, his face unshaven. Like any other old man you'd pass on the street. Until he'd looked at him and said, 'Ah, Stephen.' The voice was the same as he'd remembered.

Oh, Mr Mannion, if only you had let things be.

But that hadn't been his way, had it? Not back in the Rathoban days and not now, either, it seemed.

'Hello, Stephen. It's good to see you again.'

'Stephen? Stephen? Can you hear me? Flynn – do you think we need a doctor in here? Do you think he's conscious at all?'

'I can hear you.'

The woman cop looked really pleased when he said the words, like she'd finally achieved something. But Stephen was only trying to avoid their talk of doctors and, when it became clear they weren't serious, he fell silent again. There was a blackened piece on one of his fingernails and he thought he might lose it – wondered, if he left it, would it fall off in its own time?

'You're going to have to start talking to us, Stephen.'

No. No, I'm not.

He turned his hands over, studied the calluses that had formed where finger met palm. Awkward, heavy hands. Mr Mannion had reached out and grasped them, clumsily.

'Are you in a hurry, Stephen? Or will you let me buy you a cup of tea?'

Then the two of them had hovered awkwardly at the door of a café; more decisions; you, no you, I insist. Stephen won the meek half-argument and directed Mr Mannion to a corner seat before buying two mugs of tea and a package of biscuits in plastic wrapping. It was one of those places Stephen rarely visited, loud and too bright and confusing, with food in one place and a coffee machine in another and no sign for where you were to stand if you only wanted a cup of tea. So it had taken him ten minutes to place his order and then he'd tripped over someone's handbag on the way back and slopped the drinks out all over the tray. Mr Mannion had just smiled and said it didn't matter. Stephen felt eleven years old again. Nothing had changed.

'You look like a man who works with his hands?'

The calluses. That broken nail. Yes, Stephen had told him, raising them, showing him the weals. He did shifts in a factory, moving boxes from one side of the room to another. It was a computer factory, although what was inside the boxes meant little to Stephen. He just carted them around. Heavy lifting. In films, that meant all lads in on it together, having the crack, chatting about the match on a Monday and where to go for pints on Friday evenings. In reality, of course, it meant not fitting in and always saying the wrong thing. Not understanding the jokes and laughing in the wrong places. Sometimes, it meant a day or two spent being nice to a new fella and him being nice back, before he copped on to the fact that you were an eejit and joined the rest of the pack in despising you. It paid the rent.

'It's an alright job. I get by.'

'I see.' Mr Mannion picked up his tea and then dabbed at the wetness it left behind with a hanky he took from his inside pocket. 'I had always hoped you'd go to university some day. You were good at maths, if I remember correctly? I thought you'd do honours maths – did you do honours maths, Stephen?'

Stephen shook his head and saw disappointment in the older man's eyes. You see, Mr Mannion? Everything was ruined that day.

'We moved to England shortly after . . . after you left. My father opened a business over there and we went with him. They had a different system. I went to school for a while, but you don't have to, after you're sixteen. It didn't suit me. I got out as soon as I could and came

252

back here – to Ireland, I mean. Not to Rathoban. I've never been back there.'

'We know he taught you in Rathoban, Stephen. But have you seen him since? Have you had any contact with James Mannion over the past few months?'

'I'm sorry. I've nothing to say.'

They had sat together in the café for almost an hour. A waitress came and tried to hurry them along, but Mr Mannion wouldn't let her. He was kind of funny about it, actually. Told her she couldn't take their cups, they weren't finished with them, but could she clean the table, please? No, not with that cloth, not the one she'd been using on all the other surfaces. With the clean one – the one hanging off the back of her trolley. Stephen knew by looking at her that she wanted to tell him where to go. But there was something so polite about Mr Mannion, so reasonable, that, despite his scruffy appearance, she did what he asked.

They chatted for a while about the weather, about the town. And then Mr Mannion slapped his hand gently against his chest.

'I'm afraid I'm not a well man, Stephen.'

Seeing his former pupil's discomfort, he lifted his hand again and held it out in front of him, as if stopping traffic. Or an argument.

'It's OK. You don't have to say anything. I'm sixty-eight; it's not a bad innings. And they say it'll happen quickly. I'm not going to go for any of their oul treatments. If your time is up, it's up.'

Stephen nodded. He didn't know what to say. He had never been good at social occasions.

'I'm sorry.'

Mr Mannion smiled. 'Thank you, Stephen. That's kind of you. You're the first person I've told, actually. There's a freedom, in saying it out loud.'

And then he'd looked at him. 'I had hoped we'd meet again one day.' He picked up the spare packets of sugar from the tray and stacked them neatly on the table. 'I had hoped I'd bump into you on the street, maybe. Or in a park or something. I had this idea that you'd have a clatter of kids with you and a big car. And a beautiful woman. Don't laugh! A beautiful woman, and I'd say to myself, "There's Stephen; he did OK."'

Stephen wanted to get up then, wanted to just walk away, get out of there before things got more awful. But there was a lump of dough in his throat and he didn't think he'd be able to get his legs to obey him. So he stayed.

Mr Mannion sighed.

'How are things, Stephen? Really?'

Stephen couldn't remember the last time someone had asked him that. The doctor, maybe? With that clinical way he had of looking over his glasses. No one who hadn't been paid to do so, anyway. He coughed into his hand and trapped a sob in his fist.

'Ah, Stephen, I didn't mean to upset you.'

Mr Mannion reached across, touching his arm gently. Stephen flinched.

'You haven't, it's grand, I . . .'

A tear rose up from the corner of his eye. Jesus. He was making a holy show of himself now. But Mr Mannion didn't look angry. Instead, he withdrew his hand and lifted his tea to his lips. The cup was shaking and it took him three tries to get it safely back on to the table.

'Things haven't gone so well for you, so.'

Stephen shook his head, mortified, embarrassed and angry in turns. It wasn't like Mr Mannion himself was swanning around in a Mercedes. You could read his own struggles in the shabby overcoat and the frayed *cuffs that peeped out from underneath the sleeves, his exhaustion obvious from the greyness of his face.*

His former teacher spoke again: 'Can I give you some advice?'

Terrified of how he'd sound if he allowed himself to answer, Stephen simply nodded.

'There are good people in the world, you know. People who can help you.'

'Yeah.'

The word came out as a grunt and Stephen coughed and tried again.

'Yeah. Doctors and that. I've tried them. They've nothing for me.'

'Ah, lookit.' A sigh, a shrug, an exhalation. 'There are a lot of people out there. You just have to find the right one.'

'Doesn't seem to have worked for you.'

The words hit home and, for a moment, Stephen was happy to see pain dart across the older man's face.

But Mr Mannion's gaze remained steady. 'I've had a few tough years, I won't deny that. But I've met good people too. I go to Tír na nÓg now; have you heard of it?'

Stephen shrugged. The name was vaguely familiar, nothing more. But the old man was looking more animated.

'They're the good guys.'

His smile widened when he said it – the good guys – the way old people smile when they think they're saying something the young folk will appreciate. His hand shook as it raised the hanky to his mouth to dab the edges, and Stephen felt all of his anger drain away.

'They're good people. Here –' Mr Mannion reached into his coat pocket and pulled out a crumpled newspaper dated a couple of days before – 'here's an article about them, look.'

The girl in the picture smiled up at him and something shifted inside Stephen.

'That's Liz. She's in charge over there, her and Tom. Oh, I'm not saying . . .' Mr Mannion slid the paper towards him. 'I'm not saying you have to talk to them, or anything. They're mainly for oul fellas like me, not young men like yourself, with your life ahead of you. But it's good to know, you know, that there are people out there. Do you know what I'm saying? People who can help. I found my sanctuary; you can find yours. I'm an old man, Stephen, and I'm on the way out, so I can say these things. You don't look happy, son. You don't look like life has been kind to you.'

But Stephen was only half listening. Instead, he stared down at the paper and gently touched Liz's face. Elizabeth, he'd call her. It suited her better.

'I've thought about you often.'

Mr Mannion's voice cracked on the end of the sentence and Stephen could hear a rasp in his throat as he struggled to catch his breath before continuing.

'What happened . . . Look, I don't need to tell you that it ruined my life. But all these years I've been hoping it hadn't ruined yours. But, looking at you today, Stephen, I'm not sure about that.'

Stephen could hear tears in the old man's voice now and he focused his gaze on the newspaper, embarrassed and ashamed, praying he'd stop talking. Christ, God, what good was this going to do anyone? But Mr Mannion had more to say.

'Life is short, Stephen. I know – it's a terrible cliché. I used to tell you boys not to put clichés in your essays, didn't I? But sometimes they are clichés because they are true. You should talk to someone, Stephen. Bring it out into the open. Let yourself have a good life, the life you deserve. Tell the guards, maybe?'

Stephen let another small noise escape from him, a squeak this time, that same sound that used to cause so much irritation, so long ago.

Mr Mannion shook his head. 'OK, so, not the guards. But someone, Stephen. Find someone to tell.' Then he pushed the paper away, grabbed his hand and pulled it towards him. Forced him to look into his blurred, blue eyes. 'What happened shouldn't go unpunished. I knew it then, Stephen, and I know it now. It's up to you. You're still a young man. You can put it behind you. You can end it, Stephen. It's in your hands now.'

There was pressure on his hand, firm pressure, and then Mr Mannion dropped it, levered himself slowly to his feet and walked out the door.

Oh, Mr Mannion. Why did you have to come around that corner, that day? Why did you stop and talk to me? We could have walked on, the two of us, sick and miserable and safe.

'You have to talk to us, Stephen.'

The cross woman, the senior guard, raised her voice and forced his gaze upwards.

No. No, I don't.

I've been saying nothing for thirty years.

CHAPTER TWENTY-SEVEN

'Waaahhh!'

Instinctively, Claire's head whipped around, but the cry belonged to someone else's child. Grand, so. She bent down and stroked her daughter gently on the cheek.

'More ups-a-daisy?'

Anna might have been, in her mother's eyes, at least, the most advanced infant in the greater Dublin area but, at just seven months old, a verbal response was still beyond her. No matter, the grin of pure delight on the baby's face was evidence enough that she was enjoying herself. Claire smiled back and gave the swing a gentle push.

It was a stunning day: warmer than usual for early November, the chill of the last week forgotten and the sun so bright that most of the other parents in the park were wearing shades. Claire had forgotten hers and squinted slightly as she allowed her gaze to roam lazily around the playground. These places had certainly changed since she was a child. She remembered one park, in particular, that she used to visit with her cousins on her yearly trip to Dublin: a large expanse of green and concrete with what seemed to her a huge and exotic play-ground at its centre. A row of swings, a slide even taller than her uncle and a high metal horse on top of which too many cousins used to balance precariously and scream uproariously.

She also remembered the year the smallest cousin slipped and was dragged to and fro across the gravelled ground, her leg wrapped around the horse's flank, for what seemed like minutes until her shocked mother was able to get to her side; could recall with perfect clarity the red rash on the little girl's legs, seconds before the pin pricks of blood poked through, and the black gravel embedded in her knees and hands. Later, there had been the miserable bus journey home and, later still, the smell of Dettol and the consoling treat of chipper chips for dinner, served in front of the TV.

Claire shook her head, surprised at how close the memory was to the surface. Stretching out her foot, she poked at the springy, multi-coloured safety surface she was now standing on. They weren't all good, the old days.

The swing's momentum carried it back towards her and, as Anna glided through the air, Claire bent down and tickled the baby on her tummy. She couldn't have been able to feel much under the heavy-quilted snowsuit, but chuckled, anyway, a hearty baby belly-laugh that Claire couldn't help but return. Another tickle brought forward a high-pitched squeal. Brilliant. Hard to believe such a tiny person could make such a gloriously rich sound.

Claire straightened up again and gave the swing another push, a little harder this time. It was mad, really; she'd lived minutes from this park for three years and hadn't stepped inside the playground until this morning. Needs must, she supposed. After yet another argument with Matt, she'd been in a hurry to find somewhere to go.

Anna had woken several times during the night and, although it had been her 'turn' to see to her, neither parent had had anything approaching a decent night's sleep, and they had both been groggy and grumpy when they'd finally dragged themselves out of bed that morning.

Aware that she still owed him for her unplanned overtime the previous week, Claire had offered to let Matt go back to bed. Or at least that's what she had intended to say. But her gruff, 'Just go back to sleep, will ya,' hadn't had the desired effect.

'Are you telling me what to do now?'

'I'm telling you to stay in bed; it's my turn; I have her.'

'You're damn right it's your turn; you've hardly seen the child all week.'

'Yeah, that's right, I was off sunbathing while you changed nappies twenty-four seven. You're such a saint.'

Well, thought Claire, grimly, as her husband stomped into the bathroom, leaving Anna wailing in her mother's arms, that escalated quickly. But, she reprimanded herself, she did owe him one. Actually, in the point-scoring competition their marriage seemed to have evolved into, she owed him several. But when he didn't, as she expected, go back to bed, but instead appeared, minutes later, in running gear, her temper had flared again.

'You're going running? I thought you were exhausted.'

She regretted the words as soon as they left her mouth, but she was tired, and frustrated and annoyed, and Matt was the only person there.

Her husband was equally irritable. 'What's it to you what I do?'

'Just that you can't be that tired if you want to go running. I'll remember that, the next time you claim you "slept through" her crying.'

She pushed the child up further on her hip and rummaged in the dishwasher for a clean bowl.

'So, how long will you be?'

'What's it to you?' he said again, his head bent over as he laced up his runners.

'Well I'm expecting a work call . . .'

Matt looked up, his eyes narrowed. 'Are you on today, or not? I mean, do you just want me to take her? Is that it? Jesus, if you're expecting a *work call* . . .' He reached out and made a grab for the little girl whose bottom lip was beginning to tremble again.

Claire hugged her closer. 'Don't be so bloody childish; I'm just wondering when you'll be back, OK? Just a simple question. Oh, just get out.'

The slam of the front door had been his only reply.

At least, she thought, looking around the playground, the weather had stayed fine for his run. Hopefully that would put him in a better mood.

'Are you enjoying that, pet?'

She reached down and gave the swing another push. Still rattled by the row with Matt, she had only walked to the playground because she was too stressed to stay around the house any longer. Even after she'd arrived, she had assumed her daughter would be too small to use any of the equipment and had looked around, almost embarrassed, as she lifted Anna out of the buggy and settled her awkwardly between the metal safety bars of the baby swing. It was almost as if she was looking for permission, waiting for another mother, an experienced mother (a real mother) to tell her yes, she's old enough – swing away. In the end, of course, nobody even turned to look at them. Meanwhile, Anna seemed enchanted with this new experience, and took flight.

She was, Claire realised, well on the way to sitting up on her own now. Where had her newborn gone? Her little girl grinned up at her again, impossibly cute in a furry hat with rabbit ears, which Claire had spent far too much money on and didn't regret in the slightest. A beam of sunlight struck the baby's face, causing her to frown suddenly, and, in the expression, Claire could see for the first time the child she would soon become.

But not yet. Claire gave the swing another gentle push. Anna was still a baby, still her baby. And, despite all the shit with Matt and everything else, at least today she was getting to enjoy every minute of her.

And, God, she needed that. She raised her head slightly, closed her eyes and turned her face towards the winter sun. It must have been a week or more since she'd properly felt daylight on her skin. A week of leaving the house before day-break and dashing home again through the drizzle and tension of rush-hour traffic, arriving just in time to give Anna a bath or, at the very least, plant a kiss on her cheek before Matt tucked her into bed. The worst of both worlds. In her pre-baby days, she'd have stayed in the office late every night while working on a case like this, persuading herself it was time well spent, that she was avoiding rush-hour traffic while getting extra work done. Even – and it was only now she was admitting this to herself – even on the days when there was very little to do. She'd enjoyed the reputation she was getting of being the first in and the last to leave.

Now it was all about getting home and grabbing time, never enough of it, with the baby before she fell asleep, and, usually, working again late into the night while the monitor crackled beside her. Truth be told, she was getting just as much work done now as she had before the baby arrived. But no one could see her doing it. Did that make a difference? She'd find out soon enough, she supposed. Claire had always hated the word *juggling*, or, more specifically, the magazine articles that seemed to equate working mothers with circus performers, but she was beginning to see what they meant now as she darted from work to home and back again, tasks from both worlds jostling for space in her mind. It was worth it, though, to get the little baby kisses at the end of the evening, and the work done at the same time.

Tickle, giggle, push.

Course, the other frustrating fact was that, when it came to the Mannion and Cannon murders, she could have actually spent a couple of days in Lanzarote the previous week and still ended up with the same result: sweet feck all. Eugene Cannon had been dead for more than a week, James Mannion for nearly three, and the Gardaí – or, more to the point, Claire herself – were still no closer to finding out what had happened to either of them.

The interview with Stephen Millar – or Stephen Ford, as he was now known – had been a disaster. Thanks to the CCTV footage and his admission that, yes, he had argued with Eugene Cannon some hours before his body was found, she and Flynn had had enough cause to question him about Cannon's violent death. But, despite keeping him the full twenty-four hours allotted by law, they hadn't learned much more. Ford said he had gone to Tír na nÓg to make a donation, having heard 'that nice lady' – Liz Cafferky, Claire presumed – speaking about the centre's work on the radio the week before. That was also the reason he'd been looking at pictures of her on the internet. Claire hadn't bothered to hide her smile when he came out with that one, but Ford hadn't reacted, just stared straight ahead, reciting the facts in a monotone.

He had wanted to give her the money, he said, because she sounded genuine. So when Cannon, or the man he now knew to be Eugene Cannon, had opened the door and told him she wasn't in, he didn't want to leave the money with him and, instead, had turned and left, deciding to come back another day. That's when Cannon had grown angry, Ford said, following him back down the path and insisting he leave the money with him. Ford had felt intimidated, and simply ran away.

On the surface, at least, the story sounded plausible. Claire felt he was leaving something out but had nothing other than instinct to go on, and the D.P.P. wasn't a big fan of cases based entirely on intuition. So, they'd released Ford and immediately rearrested him in connection with James Mannion's death. Then things had turned even stranger.

When questioned about his former teacher, Stephen Ford had had quite literally nothing to say. Claire had never seen anything like it. Even the so-called 'Hard Men' usually cracked in the end – whether through clever questioning or simply out of sheer boredom – they said something, anything, in the hope that it would allow them to leave the station and go home. But for hour after mind-numbing hour, Ford had said nothing at all. He'd just stared past them at the wall.

Ford didn't seem, to Claire, to be a stupid man, nor, in fairness, a particularly difficult one. But once the topic of James Mannion was introduced, he shut down completely. If she had to make a guess as to what he was feeling, she would have said it was fear, but she had no idea why he was so terrified.

Claire had felt the defeat like a dull thud inside her stomach as they'd finally admitted they'd have to let him go. She'd seen her emotions mirrored on Flynn's face – frustration mixed with rage that they still had nothing – and had muttered about preparing a file for the D.P.P., while unsure if they had enough to do that, even. The whole episode had been a total disaster.

At least Stephen Ford wasn't the gloating type. In fact, he hadn't said anything at all when they'd told him he could go. He'd just stood up, looked at them with the same dead-eyed stare he'd adopted throughout the questioning, and waited patiently for someone to open the door. He'd stopped by the front desk on the way out, then, and asked the sergeant the way to the nearest bus stop. Claire wasn't surprised that he hadn't the money for a taxi or, indeed, the phone number of a friend willing to pick him up. There was something lonely about him, something pathetic. Stephen Ford was the type of man you just knew had been bullied in school. He was probably still bullied, daily, in a thousand tiny, mean ways. A pale man with a slight build, he looked like a person who'd never get served at a busy bar and would always have his place in the taxi queue stolen on a rainy day.

Even his clothes gave the impression that he'd stopped caring years ago – that was, if he'd ever started. A cheap blue shirt, the same type a kid would wear to school, was tucked too tightly into black trousers, worn shiny at the knees. The school-uniform impression continued with his shoes, which were large, laced, lumpy and scuffed, and turned up slightly at the toes. His greying hair was sparse on top, curly tufts springing from a pink scalp, and cut tight at the sides, but worn long and straggling at the back, a clump of greasy ringlets covering his collar. He was the type of man you wouldn't want to touch; after shaking his hand, you'd want to wash your own.

But, regardless of how he looked, his ability to stay silent in the face of everything she threw at him showed a strength of character Claire couldn't help but admire.

A file is being prepared for the D.P.P. – the sentence that ended every news report when the journalist had nothing else to say. Well, this file would be a bloody thin one. What did they have, really? Confirmation that Stephen Ford had argued with Eugene Cannon on the day he died. Cannon was a crook; it was highly likely there was a list of people who wanted to do him harm. What else? Confirmation that Mannion had taught Miller thirty years ago; sure, half the men in Rathoban could say the same. Confirmation that he'd been looking up pictures of Liz Cafferky on his computer; again, there was a strong chance many of the men in Rathoban could plead guilty to that one, and in other towns around the country as well. And with both of the letters destroyed . . .

Finally bored of the swing, Anna started to whimper and Claire lifted her out. Pushing the buggy with one hand, she carried her baby daughter towards a bench at the side of the playground. The letters to Liz Cafferky had been signed *Stephen*. The letters, that was, that she claimed to have received. But then she'd destroyed them, and, with them, any chance of linking them to Ford. At least the first one had been seen by Dean and a number of others at the centre. At this stage, there was no evidence to suggest that the second one existed at all.

Anna grizzled again and Claire smoothed her hat back from her forehead and nuzzled the soft downy skin of her forehead.

'Are you hungry, lovey?'

Ah, there was plenty of baby left in her yet, Claire mused, as she propped her against her shoulder and reached down with her other hand to the bag hanging off the back of the buggy. She just wasn't sure how she was going to . . .

A shadow fell over her.

'Here – give her to me!'

'Hi.' Claire looked up but didn't smile as Matt took the baby and eased himself down on the bench beside her. 'Good run?'

'Great, thanks.'

He stretched his long legs out in front of him and gave an exaggerated sigh.

'Bit rusty, you know, yourself. But it was nice to get away.'

You're not exactly chained to the kitchen sink, was what she wanted to snap. But the time spent with Anna had lifted her spirits and, given that it looked like her husband was willing to put the row behind them, she decided to do the same.

'Great.' As she was speaking, she filled the clean bottle from the formula carton and handed it to him. 'Want to feed her?'

'Sure.'

Matt grinned down at his daughter, but she was too hungry to respond and tugged at the bottle, whimpering until he was able to get her into a comfortable position and start the feed.

'I thought we might go out for brunch later? After she's finished?' He nodded down to where their daughter was now sucking pleasurably at the bottle, its level diminishing before their eyes. 'She'll probably conk out after this.'

'Brilliant idea!'

Claire stretched her own legs out and sighed. Matt was right; after all the fresh air and excitement, Anna would sleep for an hour or more. There was a new café opened right outside the main entrance to the park; they could even grab a paper and—

Deep inside her pocket, her phone buzzed.

Anna twitched and gave her mother an accusatory glare as the bottle fell from her mouth. Before Matt could put it back, she reached for it herself and jammed it back in, sucking frantically before settling into a rhythm again.

'Little Madam!' Smiling broadly, Claire reached into her pocket for her phone. And then stopped laughing. 'I'm sorry, I have to—'

'Go on.'

Instinctively, she moved away from her husband and daughter to take the call, stood up straight, deepened her voice. There were two men, the voice on the other end told her. They were on their way to Collins Street and wanted to speak to Claire, and only to Claire.

'OK,' she replied and then looked back to the bench, to where her husband and child were looking like the stars of some classy advert on TV. 'But I have to check something first.'

As she walked towards them, Matt looked over Anna's head and narrowed his eyes. 'No brunch, so?'

'They want me to come in.' She sat back down on the bench and looked squarely at him. Ready for the row.

But instead her husband simply shrugged. 'Go on, then.'

'You're sure?'

'I'm not going to offer twice. And, Claire?'

She bent down to give the baby a kiss then looked up at him again.

'Good luck with it, OK?'

She wasn't quite sure what they were advertising, her tall, broad-shouldered husband and his equally gorgeous and adorable daughter, now sitting straight up on his lap and looking lazily around. But she'd buy it in a heartbeat.

CHAPTER TWENTY-EIGHT

'Will you say a few words, so?'

Noeleen Kavanagh was a small, pink-nosed dormouse in her mid fifties, friendly and eager in black quilted coat and green bobbled hat. She had to stand on her tiptoes to reach Liz's ear.

'They'd really appreciate it.'

'I'm not sure.' Liz shrugged, then dug her hands deep into her pockets. Her breath froze in the air in front of her and, behind the haze, she could see that the crowd was growing. There must have been two hundred people there, maybe more, huddled together on the traffic island at the centre of O'Connell Street. Dean would know the exact number, she thought. He was out there somewhere, filming a report for the evening news, picking out the people holding candles and the signs that would look best on TV, asking others, 'Why are you here?'

It was a question Liz herself wasn't sure she knew the answer to.

Smiling vaguely down at Noeleen Kavanagh, she lifted her head and looked out over the crowd. It was amazing to see so many people standing quietly at the centre of the city's main thoroughfare. Out on the pavements, life on O'Connell Street was going on as normal. Pedestrians were playing dodge the chugger, gangs of teenagers were cramming into burger joints, and queues of harried commuters jostled for position at the street's many bus stops.

But here, on the pedestrianised area at the centre, all was still.

Liz inhaled and felt frosty air cut through her nostrils. It was a beautifully clear winter's day and, in the gap between glove and sleeve, cold air tickled at her skin. It would be a miserable night to be sleeping on the streets, she thought, suddenly, Tír na nÓg and its clients never far from her mind. But a lovely day to stand still, and to breathe.

Behind her, the Spire rose steeply into the blue sky. Some Dubliners had complained when the 120-metre-high needle had been erected at the top of O'Connell Street over a decade before. It had been too new, too modern, too bloody shiny to replace Nelson's Pillar, blown up decades before Liz was born. But most of the capital's citizens now loved the monument. The Spire gave the city centre a much-needed focal point. Tourists gathered there to read maps, new residents of the city met up with their fellow countrymen there on nights when home seemed very far away, and today a crowd had gathered there to remember James Mannion, a man few of them had ever met, but whose death had touched them in some way.

Most carried mobile phones; some were already filming the proceedings, although very little had happened as yet. Earlier, there had been an abortive attempt by a middle-aged man in a trench coat to say a decade of the rosary, but, other than that, the crowd remained silent. A murmur of conversation began, tapered off and then swelled again, and Liz became aware of a growing sense of impatience. *We turned up*, they seemed to be saying. *Now what?*

'They're waiting for you.'

Noeleen pressed a loudhailer into her hand and Liz resisted its pressure for a moment. But already the people at the front of the crowd had noticed what was happening, and began to mutter to their neighbours.

'That's her, now. That's your woman.'

'What's her name?'

'Elizabeth something.'

'Ah, yeah, I recognise the face.'

'Shut up, now, and let the lady talk.'

'Quiet now, let's hear what she has to say.'

Two, three, four camera-phones were raised and readied. Liz coughed, then lifted the loudspeaker and spoke into it, hearing nothing but a muffled whisper.

Noeleen Kavanagh nudged her arm. 'It's the little button, there – look.'

'Hello, I . . . Oh.' Her head jerked back as her voice, simultaneously loud and tremulous, boomed into the air. The crowd fell silent and, for a moment, she wondered if she could escape. But 120 metres of shining steel stood in her way, and the crowd was expecting something.

'I'd like to . . . thank you for coming.'

Jesus, what was she? A bridesmaid at the world's grimmest wedding? Liz's voice trembled, then she looked down at the smile on Noeleen's face, the bobble on her hat waving furious encouragement, and the sight of it gave her just enough courage to continue.

'James would have . . . James would have been amazed to see you all here today. And very surprised. He was . . .'

And then she stopped speaking again. How to describe him? What could she say? She had known James Mannion for less than a year. Truth be told, he hadn't been the easiest person to get on with, particularly towards the end. But she could hardly say that to them, now, could she?

Could she?

'He was much loved – he was a lovely man . . .'

But her words sounded false, evaporating with her frosty breath into the blue sky, and the people in front of her were shuffling their feet, checking their watches, wondering if they'd have time to pick up a few bargains in the big Penneys across the road. Liz's hand tightened on the megaphone. Well, if it was honesty they wanted . . .

'Do you know what? James Mannion wasn't always an easy man to get along with.'

She couldn't have felt more awkward, more exposed, but the cold had chilled her blood to such an extent that she wasn't blushing, and that knowledge lent her courage.

'He was a complex man, a complicated man, maybe. An educated man. He could quote from any Shakespeare play. He had an opinion on everything. But I'm not sure if I'd call him a nice man. He'd correct your grammar, soon as look at you. He would!'

She paused as a couple of polite titters escaped from the crowd.

'And if you misplaced an apostrophe . . . Jesus! A sign saying that *potato's* were on sale would put him in a bad mood for the rest of the day.'

Several more titters now, and a couple of hearty laughs. Noeleen Kavanagh's hat was bobbing appreciatively.

'He liked cats, and hated dogs – couldn't talk about them, even; couldn't stand people who talked about them. He would walk away in the middle of any conversation, actually, if he didn't agree with what you were saying.'

She paused, looking at her hands, now rock steady on the megaphone.

'He was clever. He was a genius at chess, and Scrabble, and any other game you could mention. But socially . . . socially, he wasn't able to cope at all, really. I saw him in the supermarket once. I was a couple of people behind him in the queue – he didn't know I was there. I saw him pack his bag, slide the money across to the girl, take the change, leave, all without saying anything to her. He just wanted to do his shopping and go home. Or go somewhere like Tír na nÓg, where nothing was expected of him. That's what we gave him, you know? Somewhere he could be himself.'

A couple of hundred pairs of eyes were fixed on her now, and no one was muttering anymore. Liz gave a brief smile, and continued.

'That's a funny phrase, when you think about it. We say it all the time, you know. "Just be yourself." We say it to kids, if they are worried about something. "Just be yourself." But that's bullshit, really. What we really mean is, be the version of yourself that is acceptable to other people. Be what the world wants you to be. Act correctly. Don't step out of line. We don't have much space in this world for people who are different. James was different. And I think, I hope, that in Tír na nÓg we gave him space to be that way.'

For a moment, the crowd stood motionless. Then came a handclap, and another. Then a cheer.

'Hear, hear!'

A sudden burst of loud applause felt almost violent and her hands fumbled with the loudspeaker, looking for the off switch.

Noeleen reached up and took it from her, before speaking into it herself.

'Ladies and gentlemen – Liz Cafferky!'

Liz moved backwards, her knees suddenly weak. If Noeleen hadn't taken her elbow, she would have tripped over her own feet and headbutted the Spire, which was not the kind of finale she was aiming for.

'Lovely speech.'

Still stunned by the crowd's reaction, Liz simply smiled weakly at Noeleen, who was still holding her arm.

'I was just glad to help.'

The phone in her pocket jangled and she took it out, saw Dean's name. Answering, she could hear applause and loud conversation all around him and had to strain to hear what he was saying.

'Nice job! . . . interview . . . me?'

'What?' She pressed her finger into one ear, jamming the phone into the other, but there were people clustering around her now, their faces pushed into hers.

'. . . talk to me?'

'I can't hear—'

'Here – can I get a photograph?'

She blinked as a camera flashed in her face, and then a second young man stood beside her, snapped a grinning selfie and walked away again.

'. . . very crowded. Don't go off, OK? I—'

Then Dean's phone signal disappeared altogether.

'You're a great woman, love! Are you taking a collection, or . . . ?'

'I'm not sure.'

The woman pressed a fiver into her hand. Over her shoulder, she could see that a bucket was being passed around the crowd.

Noeleen was tugging on her arm. 'There's a few people over here want to talk to you, look—'

'I'm sorry.'

More people were crowding around her now and Liz couldn't see a way out. Despite the intense cold, sweat had broken out on her forehead and she felt panicked, overwhelmed.

'If I could just . . .'

But nobody was listening to her. Instead, they approached her with demand after demand.

'Can I talk to you about my father? I really feel he needs—'

'There's a lad over there says he's collecting money for you, but you'd want to watch that fella, he—'

'—photo? Just look over here. Excellent!'

Hands clawed at her arms.

'I'm sorry, I really do need to . . .'

A teenager in front of her raised his phone to snap yet another picture and, in the gap he created when he raised his arm, she saw her chance to escape.

'I'm sorry, I can't. I have to – go!'

She ducked her head, manoeuvred her body through the space and then pushed her way into the crowd.

'Please – excuse me – I have to . . .'

Hands clutched at her coat but she kept moving, pushing herself forward to the edge of the traffic island and then across the road, ignoring the red man, darting through the lines of cars before, finally, out of breath and flustered, reaching the other side. Pulling the hood of her coat as far forward as it would go, she strode quickly down the street, passing a bank, a disused ice-cream parlour and Clerys department store before she dared to look around. Most of the crowd was still in the centre of the traffic island; it looked like she'd got away with it . . .

Then a figure loomed over her.

'Elizabeth, I need to talk to you. Can you come with me? Straight away?'

CHAPTER TWENTY-NINE

Her first instinct was to tell him she didn't have time to talk. Or rather, didn't have time to talk to him. Tom had been blanking her for days; what right had he to turn up now, at a moment when she really needed some head space, and demand her attention?

But then Liz took a closer look, and her boss's fragility frightened her. His shirt hadn't been ironed, the skin around his eyes looked equally creased. He looked exhausted, and something else too. Frightened? Maybe.

'Can we talk?' he asked again. The tentative, strained voice didn't seem to belong to him and, worried, Liz tried to make her reply sound as normal as possible.

'Sure. You want to go for a coffee or something?'

Tom nodded. 'Yes. Please. And –' he sighed, then reached out and touched her shoulder awkwardly – 'I'm sorry I haven't . . . haven't been much use to you these past few days.'

'Ah, Tom.'

The look of absolute helplessness in his eyes shocked her and, without thinking, she flung herself at him and buried her face in his shoulder. Tom held himself rigid for a moment and then relaxed into the hug.

'I'm sorry,' he said again, pulling away slightly. 'I should have talked to you before now.'

'C'mon. It can't be that bad? Will we need scones as well as coffee? Jam and cream?'

A reference to his sweet tooth usually made him smile, but not this time.

'I'm sorry,' he said again, before taking a step back and looking down at her.

It was an expression Liz had never seen on his face before: sadness, mixed with defeat. He didn't look like Tom at all; it was as if something about him had changed, something fundamental. Then she dismissed the thought. She was on edge, hyper after the vigil and the crowd's reaction, lacking in sleep and any perspective. She was seeing things that weren't there. Tom never changed – that was the joy of him. He was just having a bad day, or a bad week, or something. She looked across to the traffic island again. The vigil crowd were beginning to disperse and there was a green bobbled hat heading in her direction.

'Actually, now would be the perfect time to escape. Let's grab that coffee.'

They strolled together down the street, past a tall uniformed guard who was standing with his back to a window, solemnly watching the crowd disperse on the other side of the road.

'Afternoon.' Unsmiling, he nodded at Liz and then directed his gaze upwards to where Tom was walking close beside her. 'Mind yourself, now.'

'Ah, I'm in good hands.'

Fair play to that detective, Liz thought to herself. What was his name again? Flynn. The guards didn't have the budget to put her under twenty-four-hour watch, she knew that much. And the truth of it was, they didn't have any reason to. She'd burned the letters and hadn't left them with any physical evidence that she was in any trouble. But, when he'd dropped her back at Tír na nÓg after she'd been to the station that last time, the Flynn chap had given her a funny look and told her to 'be sensible'; and she had the feeling that he'd asked a couple of his colleagues to keep their eye out for her too. There had been too many sideways glances from cops at the vigil, too many double takes and suggestions for her to 'mind yourself, now' for her to have been imagining it. Well, that was nice of him, Liz decided. It felt good, being minded. And now Tom was here too. It didn't matter what sort of humour he was in, he was by her side again. For the first time in ages, she felt safe.

'We might get a seat in here?'

She followed Tom into a large coffee shop on the corner of O'Connell Street and Talbot Street and allowed him to lead her to a table by the window.

'God, I'm knackered after that.'

'Can I get you a coffee?'

Their words collided and Liz felt a tension between them, a nervousness in the air. They hadn't really spoken in days, she realised. But, what matter, they just needed a few minutes in each other's company and they'd be grand, back to normal again.

SINÉAD CROWLEY

Chatter about the vigil broke the silence until the coffees arrived and then, when the waitress had gone, she looked at him. 'So are you going to tell me what's up? You have me worried, Tom, and the clients can feel it too. You haven't been yourself for days.'

He picked up a spoon and stirred his coffee. 'I know. I'm sorry.'

He fell silent then and grabbed a long thin packet of sugar, squashing it so hard between his fingers that the paper tore and grains trickled on to the table.

A sudden, terrible thought struck her. 'You're not sick, are you? Oh, God, Tom, it's not . . .'

But he shook his head. 'No. Nothing like that.'

And then, more silence. Anxious to fill it, she started to gabble.

'Was it just the Eugene thing freaked you out? I mean, I don't blame you, it was awful, and the guards have been around the whole time and—'

'I just needed a bit of time, Elizabeth.'

It was the way he said her name, Elizabeth, that really frightened her. Like there was something really serious approaching and she wouldn't be able to get out of its way. She gabbled nervously, hoping to drag some normality back into the conversation.

'I know, we all need time sometimes, don't we? No harm at all, get away from everything, get a bit of head space. Anyway, sure, the lads have been a bit worried about you, but they're grand, you know, yourself.'

'Elizabeth. Liz.' Tom stretched his hand out and reached for hers. The movement was clumsy and he succeeded only in grasping the tips of her fingers. She let them rest in his for a moment before pulling away.

'So, yeah, if you want to, like, take a break or something—'

'Elizabeth, I need to tell you something.'

Tortured. That was the only word she could use to describe the expression on his face now – tortured, his features pinched and pale. He needed a friend, that was obvious. Or, more to the point, needed her to be his friend. But that was his job, wasn't it? To pick people up, dust them off, send them on their way again? Not hers.

The silence between them grew heavy. Liz was starting to regret that she hadn't suggested they go to a pub – somewhere crowded, with a TV in one corner and a crowd of noisy after-work drinkers in another. A bit of distraction. Instead, they had nowhere to look but at each other.

She forced a smile. 'So, what can I do for you?'

Tom brushed the sugar from his fingers. 'You know I told you the story of my dad? How he got sick, and why I started the centre?'

Liz nodded. 'Sure. Yeah.'

She had, in fact, heard the story several times. Tom trotted it out on a regular basis to prospective donors anxious to get information about where their money might be going; or to new clients curious about what motivated this tall, broad-shouldered man who seemed to be offering them sanctuary and wasn't asking for anything in return. He'd keep it simple, tell them how his dad had got sick and then left him a few bob when he died, and that he, Tom, had decided to use it to help other men of a similar age. It was a straightforward enough tale, Liz always thought, but the telling of it used to make clients feel at ease.

'Well, there's a bit more to it than that.'

Tom rubbed a hand across his face, the skin wrinkling beneath his fingers. He looked old, Liz realised, as well as knackered. She had never asked Tom his age. What was he? Fifty, maybe? She had never really thought about it before; it had never seemed particularly important. They were mates, nothing more, so what did age have to do with it? Sure, she'd heard the slagging in the centre sometimes, was aware that some of the men thought the boss fancied her, or even assumed that they were already in a relationship. But the rumours never bothered her, because they were so far from the truth. Liz knew Tom didn't think about her in that way. That wasn't false modesty, just the way things were. Over the past few years, Liz had been around enough men who wanted to get into her pants to be able to recognise, very quickly, one who didn't. Once, after a few pints, Dean had described Tom as her 'father figure'. That had been a little closer to the truth than Liz was comfortable with and she'd moved the conversation on, not wanting to think about it at all.

Tom picked up his coffee, using the cup to warm his hands. 'I told you my dad had Alzheimers, and that was why I started Tír na nÓg, didn't I?'

Liz nodded.

'Well, that's true, but it's not the whole story – just the Ladybird version, you know what I mean?'

Tom's attempt at a smile was even more disconcerting than his earlier strained expression and Liz didn't attempt to return it, just nodded again at him to continue.

'Well, the bones of it are exactly as I told you. Mam died suddenly and I went home to look after my father. I was an only child, so nobody thought there was anything strange about it. The neighbours thought I was some sort of saint, you know? Jesus. If only they knew.'

He reached his hands up to his face and pulled at the skin around his eyes. He looked, Liz thought, more like a client of Tír na nÓg than the man in charge.

'The fact of the matter was, I had to get away. Dad getting sick was just the excuse. I was . . . I was getting a bit too fond of the gee-gees, if you know what I mean?'

Liz stared at him, blankly.

A flush of red crept across his pale face. 'The horses, I was into the horses. Gambling. I was in trouble, Liz. Serious trouble.'

'OK.'

She couldn't think of anything else to say, but many things were starting to make sense, now. The sympathy Tom had for the men at the centre, for her. Maybe it had been empathy, all along.

His secret out, Tom's words began to tumble over each other as if he was afraid to stop their flow.

'I was in way over my head. I was a teacher; it's a decent enough salary but it wasn't enough for me. I had a house, sold it, lost the money. Rented an apartment, lost it. Moved into a horrible bedsit, but I was still having problems making the rent there. You understand, don't you?'

A memory struck Liz: the sound of a cork popping; the glug of the first glass of wine as it flowed into the glass; the spice hitting the back of her throat; the instant sense of relaxation and, more than that, the peace. She understood, alright.

Tom was still talking.

'You know what it's like to want something so, so badly, even when you know it's no good for you. To crave it. To think about it all the time . . . In a way, gambling is the worst addiction of all, I think, because there is always the promise that one more shot is going to fix everything. You fool yourself into thinking there's a science to it; you're out there, studying the form. I thought I was a bloody expert! I used to buy the racing papers – you know, the specialist ones? I wrote everything down, all the tips, watched the telly, listened to the commentators – all the shite – even the oul lads down the bookie's who reckoned they had a sure thing – I listened to them all. And, every so often, you'd get a win, a small one or a decent one, and you'd think, Yeah, I'm on a roll now. I'm grand. But you're never grand.'

He paused for a moment and looked out into the body of the café. A lone waitress, back bent, was cleaning a table and, from behind the counter, they could hear the jangle of a till.

Tom sighed. 'So, when the chance to move home came, I saw it . . . Well, I saw it as a sign, I suppose. I could move in with Dad, who knew nothing about what was going on with me. There's only one bookie's shop in the village and I didn't want everyone seeing me going in and out and knowing my business. So I thought moving home would do me the world of good. Sure, I hadn't a feckin' clue.'

He reached into his pocket, took out his phone and laid it on the table between them.

'First thing I did when I got home was get the broadband installed, just for a bit of company, you know? Something to do in the evening. And then I discovered you don't have to go to the bookie's anymore. They'd followed me home.'

He picked up the phone, tapped it and looked up at her.

'Swipe of a finger; everything has an app now. So things got worse, not better. I got a credit card, and that filled up and I got another one. And then –' he put down the phone again and placed his hands flat on the table as if to brace himself – 'I used his. Dad gave me power of attorney; I had access to every penny he had. And I used it. I spent his money, Liz.'

She had been listening intently, as if to a story, just another sad story being shared by one of the lads in Tír na nÓg. But now her stomach rolled over.

'I spent every fucking penny he had. And, as long as I presented a nice happy face to the world, nobody knew. Dad was getting very ill at that stage. I was looking after him, you have to believe that.'

He shot her a quick, fierce look.

'I really want you to believe that, even though I don't suppose it matters a damn whether you do or not. But I took good care of him, honestly, I did. When the nurse would call, or the doctor, he'd be fresh-faced and shaven and they'd ask me had he a good night, and I'd say grand . . . but then I'd close the door on them and I'd make sure he was settled and, God help me, it would all start all over again.'

He slammed his hands on the counter to the rhythm of the final words.

'It would start – all – over – again. They'd ask was I coping OK? And did I know there was help out there? And I'd smile and put on a serious face – you know, serious but coping – and say, "Well, it's not easy, but he's my father; it's important I do it for him," and they'd go away. I'm not blaming them; I'm a bloody good actor. Or maybe you've guessed that by now.'

The waitress was cleaning the table next to theirs and un-ashamedly listening in, but Tom either hadn't noticed, or didn't care.

'Then he died. He died, God rest him, and suddenly there were all these people around. Relatives – they all turned up then – aunts and uncles and cousins I hadn't seen in years, the whole lot of them down on top of me. I hadn't a bloody minute to myself. After the funeral, I realised I hadn't placed a bet in three days. So I tried to go another day. And another one. It wasn't easy, you know that – Jesus, Liz, you know that more than anyone. But I did it. I knew I couldn't keep going on my own, and I didn't want to go to counselling – the thought of it, telling some young one or young fella my story – no, that's not me. So I came up with a plan. I knew he'd left the house to me – sure, what else was he going to do with it? – and, if I stayed there, I'd only get myself into more trouble. So, I sold it. And I came up here, and opened Tír na nÓg. Invested every penny I had in it, so I couldn't do anything more foolish with the money. Surrounded myself with fellas who were just like me – they thought I was supporting them! But we were helping each other, really. And it worked, it really worked, for two years. For two years I didn't put a foot wrong.'

When he exhaled, his breath was shaky but he seemed determined to finish the story.

'Then Greg died. You remember . . . ?'

Liz gave a brief, hard nod.

'I'm sorry, of course you do. I was low – lower than I had been in a long time. I blamed myself – for everything, for shutting the place at the weekends and not answering the phone . . . Anyway. There's no need to go over that again. But his brother came to see me; do you remember the brother? Big, well-dressed man. Some sort of builder, the well-to-do kind, and he gave me a massive donation – I mean, it was huge. I didn't want to take it; I felt, all along, I'd failed Greg. But he insisted. It was all cash. I walked to the bank that afternoon and I had to pass the bookie's on the way. I was walking past – I swear to God, I was walking past – but the door just swung open and I got this blast of warm air and noise and energy and, before I knew it, I was inside. I only put on a tenner. And I won fifty. So, sure, that was a sign, wasn't it?'

He spat out the word *sign*, moisture landing on the table between them.

'And I had two more small wins. More signs.'

He sat back in the chair suddenly and ran his hands over his dishevelled hair.

'Ah, you can guess the rest. I lost it all. Every penny. And everything in petty cash – everything we had. I was sure you were going to find out – there wasn't money in the account to cover the next electricity bill and I knew you opened all the letters. So I was panicking. And then Dean turned up at the door, looking for someone to do a television interview about the place; some politician had mentioned it to him, he said, and he wanted to find out more. I wasn't up to it; it was all I could do at that stage to keep my head together in front of you and the men. But, you know Dean . . .'

A ghost of a smile warmed his face briefly, and then disappeared again.

'He told me it'd be good for us and that it would bring in a few bob. He's a smart man, Dean. I think he knew that there was something . . . that I was struggling. When I said I didn't want to do it, he asked if there was anyone else around. I mentioned you, and, well, that's Ireland for you, isn't it? He asked if you were the same Liz Cafferky he knew from school. One of those mad coincidences. And we both reckoned you wouldn't do it if you felt like you were being set up, so Dean said he'd make it look like he had just kind of wandered into you, you know, just bumped into you on the street. And, well . . .'

But Liz had stopped listening and was sitting, motionless, in the chair.

'You set me up? Both of you? You tricked me?'

'Ah, now, I wouldn't say it was like that, exactly—'

289

'Really? And what the fuck would you say it was, Tom?'

The waitress was staring openly at them now.

'It seemed like a good idea . . .' The pitch of his voice had risen; there was a whine there, a childishness she had never heard before. 'It worked, didn't it? Dean got his story and, yeah, we made money out of it.'

'Which you spent.'

'Well – yes. But not all of it. I mean, we kept the centre going, and—'

'You absolute piece of shit.'

'Don't say that, Liz.' Tom stared at her, horrified. 'Please don't say that. I told you all of this because I thought you were my friend. Please, Liz. I need you—'

Liz scraped her chair back from the table. 'I have to get out of here.'

'Don't go. I'm sorry – I can explain.'

'I've had weirdos writing to me, you know that? Probably following me, and all sorts. I could have been in serious trouble and you did that! You and Dean, putting me out there on the TV. On the internet. And all for what? So you could get your jollies down the bookie's? Christ almighty, Tom.'

Her voice cracked on the last word and she turned to go.

'I can explain.'

But she didn't want to hear any more, and ran out of the café, careering into tables on her way, not caring what the waitress thought. The café door slammed behind her and she stopped dead. Where could she go? She couldn't go back to Dean's place; after all he had been in on it, too. She could go

290

home but she felt like that space had been violated, as well. The pub across the road had never looked so tempting. Lost in misery, it took her several minutes to hear the noise coming from her pocket. She took the phone out and checked it. Four missed calls? Someone was keen. As she held it in her hand, it rang again and she answered it without thinking.

And it turned out that, yes, the day could get worse. Felim sounded terrified.

'I'm at the centre and I think we've been broken into. Can you come? Straight away?'

Throwing the phone into her bag, she hailed a taxi. Tom was a problem she'd have to think about later. Dean was a shit. But she owed it to the clients to keep the centre going – at least until she figured out where to go from here.

CHAPTER THIRTY

'I just want you to understand one thing, detective, before we get started. I'm here . . . I'm here out of my own free will. Is that clear? I'm helping you with your enquiries, that's all.'

Richie McBride sat up straighter in his chair and smoothed down his suit trousers, fussily. He might have been far from home, Claire thought, but he was still going to make a good stab at controlling his environment.

Well, good luck with that, councillor.

'I'll be delighted to hear what you have to say, Mr McBride.'

The younger of the two men in front of her shifted miserably on his chair. In the luxurious surroundings of his own office, Gavin McBride had looked a little overweight, big-boned, well built, carrying a few pounds or one of any number of non-threatening euphemisms. But here, perched on the edge of a small, Garda-station standard seat, his belly sagged on to his thighs and his pristine white shirt collar was leaving red ridges in the skin around his neck.

'Detective, I really must insist that—'

'I'll handle this, Gavin.' Again, the tone was that of the

chair of Rathoban Council. Richie McBride gave a mournful half smile. 'The thing is, detective . . .' Somehow he managed to make the word sound uncertain, like he was using the title just to humour her. 'The thing is, I might have misremembered something I told you on the phone a couple of days ago.'

'Oh, yes?' Apart from a twitch of one eyebrow, Claire kept her face and voice neutral.

McBride smiled again. 'You asked me, I think, if I had heard from Stephen Millar in recent times.'

'I did, yes. Stephen Millar, who now goes by the name Stephen Ford.'

The man paused and shifted his wristwatch higher on his wrist. 'I may have given you the impression that I hadn't, in fact, heard from him.'

'You did.'

McBride steepled his fingers under his nose. 'Well, I was . . . um . . . busy at the time you called me. I think, casting my mind back, I would have spoken to him more recently. Yes.'

Claire felt any vestiges of patience drain out of her. She had a murder to solve, two of them, in fact, and a baby who she wanted to get home to, preferably before she started school.

'Can you just tell me what you came here to tell me, please? You did speak to Mr Ford, is that right?'

The older man paused for a moment and then, clearly incapable of coming up with a more convoluted answer, nodded. 'Yes. He contacted me a couple of months ago.'

Beside her, Claire could hear the scratch of Flynn's pen on his notebook. She herself had grown totally still, her gaze focused on McBride, her skin prickling with the certainty that they were finally going to get some useful information out of him.

'Mr Millar was looking for advice on a personal matter.'

McBride was now refusing to meet her eyes.

'He wanted to know if he could make a complaint, a legal complaint, about something that happened over thirty years ago.'

He took his glasses off and rubbed the bridge of his nose before continuing. His eyes were red, she noticed, the skin beneath them sagging.

'I must apologise, detective, for misleading you the other day. I thought . . . Well, to be honest with you, I thought things would be better left alone. That's what I told Stephen Millar too, when he came to me: that there was no point in digging up the past. But my son, here, says I've made a mistake. So here I am.'

A look passed between senior and junior. Suddenly, subtly, Claire felt the balance of power shift between them. McBride senior coughed, the sharp bark echoing around the room.

'Stephen, um, phoned me, out of the blue, about three months ago. He said he wanted legal advice. I told him I was retired, that I could put him in touch with several other people, if he liked, people up in Dublin, nearer to where he lived. But he said he wanted to talk to someone he knew. I would have done legal work for his father, many years ago. He would have been a big businessman in the town – a lot of employees. Lar Millar kept all of his business local; he was good that way.

Anyway, Stephen said he had found my number in some old documents he'd kept from his parents' house. He sounded quite distressed, to be honest with you.' He coughed again. 'Do you think I could get a glass of water?'

Silently, Flynn disappeared and then returned a few moments later.

McBride's hand shook as he lifted the plastic cup.

'He wanted to know what the statue of limitations was for suing someone. Somebody who had hurt him.'

Flynn stopped writing. 'Statute of limitations?'

'Yes.'

McBride took another sip of water before continuing.

'Those were the words he used. Poor Stephen. It sounded like he'd heard them on television, or something. He wanted to know what would happen if someone had injured him thirty years ago – if he could still bring them to court. He wanted to know what his options were.'

'Sure, he could have gone to the guards at any stage.'

'Yes. But I told him that he couldn't.'

Claire kept her voice low. 'So you lied to him?'

'Well, I mean, a lie –' McBride shrugged, some of the old bluster returning – 'I mean, it's very black and white to say "lie", isn't it? I was just giving him the advice I thought he needed, that's all. In my day . . .' He sat up straighter in the seat and met her eyes. 'In my day, we had a phrase: let sleeping dogs lie. No one believes in that anymore. It's all about tribunals and investigating and closure and all that nonsense. Much good it does anyone, raking up the past. But that's what's in vogue now, it appears. According to my son, anyway – and, God knows, he's the expert.'

The colour had returned to his face now and he shot McBride junior a resentful look.

'I just didn't see the point of Stephen Millar raking up oul stories from thirty years ago, that was all it was. Sure, what good would it do him? Or anyone else? So I told him he'd no option, that he should leave things alone.'

Claire shot a quick look at Flynn. This was good; it gave them an excuse to recall Stephen Ford for questioning, at least. She'd had a feeling McBride had been holding out on them, and now she had proof. But there were a couple of other issues she had to clarify as well.

'Mr McBride – why are you telling us this now, when you lied before?'

McBride frowned. 'Well, um, you came down asking about James. I didn't know what to say; I didn't want to get involved. I thought Stephen had listened to me; I didn't think what we had said was important. I thought I had handled things. But then it was on the news, that another man had died and—'

'I told him he had to come down.' Gavin McBride's voice sounded weary, almost resigned. 'I'd no idea – I'd no idea he was this involved. I'm sorry. I hope it's not too late.'

Despite her growing excitement, Claire forced herself to keep her own voice even: 'Why did you lie to him, anyway? About James? Why did you tell him that nothing could be done after thirty years? It's not true – plenty of historical abuse cases have been investigated.'

'Because there's something else I need to tell you.'

Suddenly, Councillor Richie McBride seemed to have left the room. In his place was an older and frailer man, wrinkles fanning out from behind the metal frames of his glasses. He took the glasses off and dug his finger and thumb into the corners of his eye sockets. He looked smaller too, Claire thought, deflated somehow. Here was a man, she thought, who was desperately trying to hold on to the power he once had but was seeing it evaporate. Here was a man who was afraid.

CHAPTER THIRTY-ONE

'Thanks, I'll get out here.'

Liz threw money at the taxi driver and slammed the car door behind her. She had expected to see evidence of the break-in as the car drove around the corner – Garda tape, maybe, or a police car parked outside the house. But Tír na nÓg looked the same as it always had, its front garden deserted, the gentle swish of the leaves on the hedge as she brushed past them the only sign of life. The cops must be on their way, she decided, and thought for a moment about waiting for them out on the road. Then she reconsidered. She needed to get inside. Felim had sounded so worried on the phone.

The front door was locked and she scrabbled in her handbag for her keys, rooting through receipts, tissues, wallet and past her phone before finally closing her hands on the bunch and withdrawing it, hands suddenly shaking. It took her three goes to get the key into the lock and, when the door finally opened, she half stumbled, half fell into the hall.

'I'm here!'

'Oh, thank goodness!' Felim's head poked out of the sitting

room, his face flushed. 'Oh, Elizabeth! I'm so glad you came. I couldn't get in touch with Tom. I was so worried. I didn't know who else to call.'

'It's OK, Felim, you did the right thing.'

'They must have come in through the kitchen window.' Speaking quickly, the old man led her down the corridor and into the kitchen at the back of the house, where the windows still stood wide open.

Shaken, Liz looked at Felim. 'Jesus. You must have got some fright. Oh, my God – you don't think they're still here, do you?'

Felim shook his head. 'God, no; I wouldn't have asked you to come back if I thought that. No, I had a quick look around after I called you. The place is empty. I'm not sure if they've taken anything, either; you'd know more about that than me.'

'Yes.' Liz stepped backwards and out into the hall again. It didn't look as if anything had been disturbed, but, with the house in its usual messy state, it would take a while to figure out if anything was missing. Anyway, she thought bitterly, it wasn't like there would be any money on the premises to take. Tom had made sure of that.

The doorbell interrupted her thoughts and made Felim jump.

'Oh! That'll be the guards. I'm sorry, love, I'm in a heap.'

'Here, you take it easy; I'll deal with it.'

Liz pointed him in the direction of the sitting room. The last thing she wanted was for him to collapse, or have a heart attack or something. At the risk of sounding flippant, they'd lost too many clients recently.

'Go in there. They'll probably want to talk to you, anyway.'

Taking a deep breath to calm herself, she walked down the hall and towards the front door where a figure could be seen, blurred by the glass.

'Thanks for coming; we're not sure when it happened but . . .'

It took her a moment to realise that the man wasn't wearing a uniform and that there was no squad car parked outside.

'I'm sorry, I . . .'

'Elizabeth, I need to talk to you.'

His stench was almost unbearable. As the man moved towards her, Liz took a step backwards as the full force of the smell hit her. He couldn't have washed in days. Jesus, where were the cops? He reached out his hand and she saw the stains under the armpits of his shirt, caught the rottenness of his breath as he moved closer.

'It's important!'

His hand was on her arm. She tried to tug it away and he clamped his other hand on top of hers. Suddenly, she was reminded of a dance they learned in school, the luascadh, an Irish dance which involved one partner swinging the other at great speed around the dance floor. Repulsed by him, she took another step backwards and he moved with her until he was inside the hall door.

'Get away from me.'

'I need to talk to you.'

There was a rustle from behind her and she turned her head with relief. 'Felim! I need some help here?'

'It's alright, Elizabeth.' Felim moved towards them and, in one quick, fluid movement – she was surprised, in fact, at how quickly he could move – he pulled the younger man fully into the hall. He was still holding on to Liz's arm and she collided with the wall as she tried to stay upright.

'Hold on, I don't think . . .'

And then the other question occurred to her, too late. The obvious one, the one she should have asked immediately – the one that had been driven from her head by Tom's revelation and her own distress. How had Felim discovered the burglary? The centre wasn't open on weekends; he had no reason to be there.

Suddenly her hand was released and she felt herself falling forwards as the man at the door darted past her and launched himself at Felim. But Felim, who was by far the bigger of the two, simply pushed him out of the way and, reaching upwards, gave the door a heavy shove, slamming it shut.

'What are you doing?' Liz's voice rose in a shriek, but the younger man was talking too, and his words washed over hers, so it took her a moment for her to process what he was saying.

'Daddy. Please don't touch her. Please leave her alone.'

CHAPTER THIRTY-TWO

'It was Stephen's own father he wanted to sue. Lar Millar.'

'But you said . . .'

Claire looked at Richie McBride in disbelief. All of his gruff bluster had evaporated. Climbing down from a pedestal he'd been living on for thirty years hadn't been easy.

'I know what I said. I'd say I was sorry now, only I don't think you'd believe me.'

'Why don't you just tell us everything, Richie? From the beginning? We're all sick of the messing around.'

Gavin's voice was sharp and Claire noticed, with interest, the use of his father's first name. McBride senior sank down even further in his chair.

His son was still talking, the bitterness in his voice unmistakable: 'Or maybe I'll start off, yeah? Maybe I'll be able to jog your memory.'

He'd make a good barrister, Claire thought, as he began.

'I'll try and keep this as short as I can, detectives. I got the practice audited a week ago. I've been thinking of taking on a partner; things have been going pretty well and I thought it was time. But we needed to get the books done first: an intensive audit, a spring clean. The guy I hired went back over financial records from years ago, and then he came to me saying that something was wrong.'

Richie McBride was paler now than the pages of the notebook in Flynn's hand, but he said nothing, just fastened and unfastened the strap of his watch, the metronomic clicking providing a strangely appropriate soundtrack for Gavin McBride as he began to unravel his father's thirty-year lie.

'There was a period in the nineteen-eighties the accountant just couldn't figure out. You could see from the books that things were in bad shape for a while – that's no surprise, I suppose; everyone took a hit back then. But then – and I'm not an accountant, but even I could see it quite clearly when he pointed it out to me – suddenly things were fine again. He explained it really well; I have the details here, if you want to see them. But what it boils down to is, someone stepped in. Someone fixed things. It was clear the business got a cash injection from somewhere, only there was no record of the source. So I asked Dad.'

All three looked across at McBride senior but his gaze remained fixed on the floor.

Gavin McBride sighed. 'I asked him and I didn't believe his answer. So I asked him again and—'

Abruptly the clicking stopped. Ignoring his son, McBride senior looked directly at Claire. 'Lar Millar lent me money when I needed it. He was a good friend. He stood by me.'

'And you stood by him too, didn't you, Dad?'

Claire could hear the disgust in the younger man's voice. McBride shrugged but said nothing.

'He scratched your back; you scratched his! I swear to God—'

'I had no option!' Richie McBride's voice rose to a shout. 'My son, the big man. You think you have all the answers, don't you? Well, I'm telling you, I had no choice. I had five children, a mortgage, your mother wasn't well and my business was in trouble. Yeah, that business – that fine, thriving business I handed over to you on a plate – the one that has you sitting back and talking bullshit about partners! I built that up and handed it to you, so don't you talk to me about back-scratching!'

His voice was shaking now, spittle gathered on the corners of his lips.

'My business was going to the wall and I needed cash. I had just been approached to stand for the council too; I couldn't do that if I was unemployed. I was in a bad way. Lar Millar was one of our biggest customers and, yes, I asked him for help and, yes, he helped me out. He just needed help on . . . on a legal matter in return.'

'Stop fucking lying, Dad!'

She had anticipated the anger, but Claire was shocked to see tears in Gavin McBride's eyes.

'You lied, for Christ's sake! You lied to the school board and you lied to Mum and, if you didn't lie outright to the entire town, well, then, you did the next best thing: you covered something up and you let a good man lose his job, and his name!' He looked at Claire in despair. 'Some of it I've had to guess. But it looks like Dad was taking backhanders from Lar Millar for years.'

They both fell silent and looked at Claire, who frowned.

'So where does James Mannion come into this? And Stephen?'

'James . . .'

Richie McBride took a deep breath and held it for a moment. Contrasting emotions flickered across his face. Anger at his son's actions. Guilt at whatever had happened in Rathoban thirty years ago. Reluctance to give any more information than he needed to. And then, and Claire could see it as clearly as if a light was turned on, he came to a decision. It wasn't out of any sense of justice, she knew that, but Richie McBride had been a lawyer for a long time; he knew how deep his involvement was, and how it would look when things came to court. He couldn't hope to get away with it and, at this stage, honesty was his best chance of retaining some sort of dignity.

'James Mannion came to see me one night. He was worried that Lar was . . . had displayed violent tendencies. Towards his son. Maybe his wife too.'

'And why did he come to you?' Flynn's voice was calm, but Claire could hear the tension in it.

'Things were different back then, detective. People didn't speak about these things. There weren't the stories you hear now, on the news and that. Sure, we all knew Lar was fond of the drop but we weren't sure of anything else and if we heard rumours, we kept them to ourselves. People just didn't interfere. James had thought about going to the guards, but he didn't know anyone in the barracks. He thought that maybe, as a solicitor, I'd know what he should do . . .'

'And you went straight back to your mate and told him everything.' Gavin spat the words out. 'I'm right, amn't I, Dad? That's how it went.'

McBride senior gave a resigned nod.

'Yes, I told Lar what James was saying. I owed him a favour. Jesus, I didn't mean any harm by it. Don't look at me like that, Gavin! I thought James was probably exaggerating, that Lar had just given the young fella a few slaps or something. Things were different in those days. And I knew, if it got out that someone in the school had been asking questions, that it would do Lar serious damage. He ran a factory in the town; he was a big employer locally. Lot of families depended on him. So, yes, I warned him – warned him that James had been talking. And he—'

'He marched straight into the school and told everyone that James Mannion had dropped the hand on his son.'

Flynn had stopped writing now. Three pairs of eyes were fixed on Gavin McBride.

'I had a chat with Mum last night, Dad; we filled in the blanks between us. She's just as pissed off as I am, by the way. Probably more so. Anyway, detectives, this much I know: Lar Millar went straight to the school and told the headmaster James had interfered with his son. Mum said it was known around town that James was gay, or rumoured to be. It was never spoken about; no one mentioned that sort of thing in those days; sure, it was still illegal, apart from anything else.

But people knew, alright, or suspected it. So it was very easy to accuse him of child abuse. Everyone believed it, straight away. Isn't that right, *Daddy*?'

McBride didn't move, and Gavin continued after a moment.

'He used to give the kid lifts home and that; people felt there was evidence there. And I suppose, the way things were . . .' Beads of sweat were now rolling down his face. 'When it came to it, he didn't feel he could fight it. It was Lar Millar's word against his. The big man around town, and his solicitor backing him. So James Mannion took what must have seemed like the simplest option. He got the fuck out of Rathoban and never came home again.'

Claire nodded, slowly. 'And that's why his father cut him out of the will. He believed the story.'

'Yeah.' Gavin nodded. 'I've been thinking about this all night. The timing all makes sense and everything. You've been there, detective; you know what a small place Rathoban is. It's easy to see how simple it would be to ruin someone's life. I just can't believe . . .'

His voice cracked on the final word and Claire could see how hard he himself had been hit by the revelation. It wasn't just that his father had lied. It was that his own business, his life and that of his family was all built on those lies.

But she didn't have time to sympathise with him now.

She looked across at Richie McBride who was, once more, fiddling with his watch strap. 'So that's why you told Stephen not to chase his father, not to look for a prosecution. You were still protecting him, after all these years.'

McBride dipped his head. 'I thought . . . Thirty years had passed; I thought the whole thing was best forgotten.'

Click, as he fastened the strap of his watch again.

'There's something else too, I might as well tell you. I contacted Lar a few months ago, after Stephen called me. The Millars emigrated to England soon after everything that happened with James. But Lar always made sure I had his address; he still had fingers in a few pies over here. So I called him and told him Stephen had been in touch. The next I heard, James was dead. I told myself it was a coincidence, James was an old man, it was just one of those things. But then you came to see me. And I saw that interview on the news, with the superintendent, and another man dead—'

'Stop fucking lying!'

Gavin McBride's voice bounced off the walls and the other three jumped.

'Don't even go there, Dad! Don't make out like you decided to come here or that you came to some decision. If I hadn't gone through the books, you never would have said anything!'

'Hold on.' Fascinated as she was by the disintegration, in glorious Technicolor, of the McBride family, Claire needed to take back control of the situation. The name Lar Millar meant nothing to her. He'd be, what, in his early seventies now? 'Do you have a photograph of him?', she asked. 'Of Millar?'

Gavin McBride shook his head. 'I don't think so.'

'*You* must do.' Flynn leaned towards the older McBride.

'When we were in your sitting room, it looked like there were pictures of half the town up on the wall. Your *hall of fame*.'

Given everything that had emerged, Claire forgave him the note of sarcasm.

Richie McBride nodded, slowly. 'I would do, now you mention it. I opened the new wing of Lar's factory, when I was Mayor. But I don't . . .'

Brilliant. Claire mentally went through the checklist. They could get someone from Rathoban station to call out to the house, maybe scan the image through.

Flynn interrupted her thoughts. 'Is your mother in?' he asked McBride junior. 'Does she have a smartphone?'

Gavin McBride's brain was moving as fast as Flynn's; he grabbed his own phone from his pocket and dialled.

'Mum? I need you to do something for me, OK? Yeah, we're with the guards now. I'll tell you later. I need you to do this first. Can you stick on Skype? Yeah, now. Brilliant. I'll call you back on it, OK?'

He hung up and looked across at Claire.

'The brother lives in Sydney. She learned how to use it when he had the first kid.'

His phone beeped and he pressed the Skype icon.

'Hi, Mum. Yeah, that's brilliant. Listen, I need you to go down the end of the room, OK? We're looking for a photograph from Dad's wall . . . Yeah, just walk down and hold the computer up. That's brilliant, Mum.'

He held his phone out and Claire watched as the familiar room swam into focus. Marvelling for a moment at how technology was changing her job, she kicked herself for letting Flynn come up with the idea first. But then a small photograph came into focus and she forgot about everything else.

'I've seen him before,' said Flynn quietly. 'At Tír na nÓg.'

CHAPTER THIRTY-THREE

Perception is everything. Was that a well-known phrase, Liz wondered? Or just something she had made up? The words danced in her skull and she dwelled on them for a moment, happy to focus on something that wasn't in the room. Perception is everything. It was true, anyway. A place of security could become a dungeon; a kitchen chair, a cage.

She shifted on the chair, testing the strength of the belt, feeling it bite into her wrists. Felim had taken it from Stephen's trousers, telling his son, with no small amount of pride, why he had done so.

'Makes sense, you see, to use something of yours. So, when they find her, it'll look like you had it all planned out.'

His voice was the same, that was the weird thing. Liz could still hear the softness in it, the low midlands burr. The reasonable tone. It was a gentle voice, a voice that had once soothed her.

The hand that had opened a packet of crisps to help her through her hangover, was now holding a knife to her throat.

Across the room, Stephen moaned softly. It hadn't taken much for his father to persuade him to hand over the belt.

Just the sight of the knife, and the promise that he would kill Liz if he didn't do what was asked. So Stephen had looped his belt around her wrists, fastened them to the back of the chair, and left plenty of what his father termed 'good, decent finger-prints'. Then he'd crept back across the room again. Because his father had told him to.

They were in the office. It was the only room in Tír na nÓg without a window, Felim explained, his head cocked to one side. He was taking all of this very seriously, he told them, as he turned off Liz's phone and tossed it in a corner. Hadn't come this far just to fall at the last hurdle.

'That's not my way, now, is it, son?'

'No, Dad.'

A terrified squeak. A boy's voice, coming from a man's body. It was obvious the sound irritated Felim. But for Stephen not to answer would have irritated him too and Liz could see the strain of the dilemma in the younger man's eyes. That's what it must have been like for him, she realised, growing up as Felim's son – knowing that every decision made would be the wrong one, every road taken would lead to pain.

And Felim O'Hagan – or Lar Millar, or whatever the hell he wanted to call himself – was a man who knew how to inflict pain. As he bent over his son, looping a rope around his neck, Liz could see muscles rippling under the thin material of his shirt. He was taller than Stephen, broader too, she realised. He'd kept himself in shape. From the back, he could have been forty years old. She had never noticed how fit he was before.

They all look the same to me.

Tom had told her off, the day she'd said it. 'They're all individuals,' he'd told her. 'Don't patronise them; don't make that
mistake.' Christ, how right he'd been.

Stephen gave a low, terrified moan. Giving him a rough
shove in the small of his back, Felim forced him to stand on
a chair and pushed the other end of the rope through the gap
at the top of the badly constructed partition wall, hooking it
around a nail that had been left there by the negligent builder.
It was perfect for what he needed, Liz realised. He must have
been planning this for quite some time.

Noose in place, Felim stepped back to admire his handiwork.
Stephen, who was several inches shorter than his father, had
to keep himself balanced on his toes to stop the rope from
growing taut. He swallowed and his Adam's apple bobbed frantically, the rope shifting slightly and then pressing against it.
A cough, and he could breathe again. For the moment.

Liz closed her eyes. Felim had tied an old tea towel around
her mouth as a gag. The taste of soap scum and old-man hands
would once have made her nauseous, but she was far beyond
that now. Instead, she sucked at it, swallowing the saliva that
collected on the fibres, working at the cloth to try and get a
rhythm going and move the water down her throat, keeping
the passage clear. Suck, swallow. Breathe.

Her nose prickled and she thought, semi-hysterically, about
all the times she had considered hoovering this room and
decided not to. Well, that was a lesson learned. Dust lay on
every surface, on the files in the corner, the discarded coffee
mug on the table, the ancient computer whirring gently on the

desk nearby. Her nostrils were beginning to swell. She sniffed, violently. Please, Jesus, don't let me die of a stuffy nose. Please, Jesus, don't let me die.

Felim's eyes opened wide at the sound of the sniff and he smiled at her.

'It doesn't actually matter if you choke to death. It'll just be a change of plan, that's all. I don't mind how you die, actually, as long as it all makes sense to whoever finds you. Tom, I suppose. Poor Tom. He's had an awful few weeks of it.'

You prick.

She threw her weight forward in the chair, her breastbone colliding with the desk in front of her. The momentum caused the mouse to shift a fraction and the computer screen, knocked off sleep mode, glowed green. Turning his head, Felim darted across the room and pushed her backwards. He was wearing gloves, she noticed, plastic gloves, and, seeing her look at them, he gave her a thin smile.

'I left the kitchen window open last night, none of ye noticed. Got in that way this afternoon and I'll leave the same way. No CCTV out there! I've thought of everything. That's why I'm not killing ye straight away, by the way. I want there to be some evidence of a struggle; what you're doing there now, that jigging around, sure, that's perfect. When they find you, it'll be obvious what happened. Poor Stephen Millar, the weirdo, the abused child, flipped at last and killed the girl he was obsessed with. And then killed himself. And when the cops figure out the link between him and dear departed James Mannion – well, it'll be easy to believe that Stephen killed him too. I'm sorry you had to become so closely involved, my dear, but once you told the police about those letters, well, you involved yourself, really, didn't you? They know Stephen, here, was trying to contact you. And I don't want them digging any deeper into my boy's life, so it's best for them to think that this was what he had in mind all along.'

He stepped into the centre of the room so they could both see his face.

'But I don't think Stephen would do it straight away, do you? No, I reckon poor lost Stephen Millar would take his time about it. He'd talk to you first, Elizabeth. Try to tell you things. Make you feel sorry for him, instead of despising him like the rest of us. You see, I know my son, Elizabeth. I knew if I called him today and told him I was sorry, and that I wanted to meet him, to make it up to him, that I'd listened to James and –' his voice rose in a whine – 'that I'd *seen the error of my ways*, I knew he'd turn up, and here he is. And here we all are.'

No.

Unable to think of anything else to do, Liz threw herself forward again. But there was less momentum this time and the belt kept her anchored, chafing against her skin.

Felim grinned.

'Keep at it, love. That's the type of action we're looking for. Isn't that right, son?'

He turned his back on her and walked towards Stephen, whose legs were starting to tremble. Felim moved closer until his head was level with his son's chest.

'You really are a pathetic piece of shit, aren't you? I'm embarrassed you are my son. I always was. You used to think that was the drink talking, didn't you? Well, I've been sober twenty years and you're still a waste of space.'

Stephen swallowed and, when he spoke, Liz had to strain to hear him.

'It was you, wasn't it? It was you I saw in the hall here, behind that poor man who died, Eugene Cannon. I saw you the day I called looking for her. For Elizabeth.'

Felim nodded. 'Indeed it was. I thought the game was up when you spotted me. Any normal man would have confronted me, asked me what the hell I was doing there, miles from where I was supposed to be. But you didn't even have the guts to do that, did you? Instead, you ran away and told that Cork clown that you'd seen your father in the hall, and that he was a dangerous man, and that he was to tell your darling Elizabeth to keep away from me. Fool. What did you expect? Sure, Cannon came straight back inside and told me what you'd said. I said you were a madman, of course, that I'd never heard of you and that I hadn't a clue what you were talking about. But, do you know what, Stephen? Afterwards, I got thinking. What if Eugene Cannon wasn't as thick as he looked? What if, after you were found dead – and I knew already that you were going to be found dead, Stephen – what if he remembered that day and told the guards about it? No, it wasn't worth the risk. So he had to die too. All your fault.'

A single tear ran down the younger man's face and Liz looked away, unable to bear his terror. Her eyes landed on a euro-shop painting on the wall – a flowery blob, half falling out of a rust-coloured vase – and she wondered if it was going to be the last thing she ever saw.

But the thought disrupted her rhythm and, as she felt herself grow dizzy, she forced herself to concentrate again. Suck, swallow, breathe. In through the nose, and out, and in. She tried not to think of her nostrils as two balloons, filling up and joining together. She thought instead of a menthol cigarette she had tried once and the way the cold smoke had sliced through her windpipe, down into her lungs. Thought of pine forests. Thought of jumping into the sea. She'd go for a swim in the sea when she got out of here. When she got out of here. When she got out of here.

Felim had left his son's side now and was standing in the middle of the room again. He held himself poker straight, careful not to touch the desk or computer.

'I didn't set out to kill James, you know. I didn't mean to kill anyone. But you forced me to.'

'I didn't . . .'

Please don't say any more, Liz prayed. You'll only make him even angrier.

But Felim simply looked up at his son, and smiled. 'You didn't mean to, is that what you're saying?' His voice rose again, a whining imitation of an overtired child. 'You didn't meeeeean to? Sure, you never meeeean to do anything, do you Stevie? Well, what the fuck did you think you were doing, eh? Going to McBride, feeding him all that bullshit about how you were going to *report* me, how you were going to *tell on* me. Tell on your daddy? Don't make me laugh. McBride came straight back to me and told me what you were planning to do. Seriously, boy, what else did you think was going to happen? Richie McBride owes me. I have a long memory. He'd have had no business, no happy life in public service, no pretty pictures of himself in his mayoral chain without my help. He'd be destroyed if people found out how much money I gave him, money he didn't pay a penny tax on. He owed me, and he paid me back by telling me exactly what you had in mind!'

Liz, unable to bear the hatred on his face, looked away. Her gaze fell on the computer again.

Felim was spitting out the words now. 'McBride had Mannion's address too; you didn't think of that, did you? He gave it to me and I hung around outside for a while till I found him. No one spotted me. One of the neighbours, a darkie young one minding a clatter of kids, even said hello to me one day; I think she thought I was Mannion! We looked the same to her – which was useful, for what I had in mind. So, yeah, I found his house and I waited for him and then I followed him back here, to Tír na nÓg. I made a big deal of bumping into him here by accident – "Oh, my God, it's yourself, small world, amazing, really, how we all ended up here?" I told him I was sorry, and that I wanted to make amends – that I'd come back home and changed my name because I wanted to start again. He believed me, poor bastard. Asked me to his house, even, to talk in private. Told me that he'd met you and had tea with you and that he was worried about you. Poor pet. Said you looked like life hadn't been kind to you. Kind. Poor baby.'

He looked across at Stephen again.

'I told him I was sorry, and, you know, maybe that could have been the end of it. We could have shook hands like men, left it there. But then, James Mannion never was much of a man, was he? He wouldn't listen. He insisted he was going to go to the guards. Said he had no time left and he wanted to sort things out before he went, that it would be good for me if things were settled. Imagine! The cheek of him! He said it would be good for me to face up to things. That's when I knew I had to kill him. I've had a long life, Stephen, but it's not over yet. I could have twenty years left, more, and I'm not going to spend it with people muttering about me, saying I wasn't a good father, a good husband. Criticising me for doing things I'd every right to do.'

Liz was fascinated now, despite herself, listening to the story, hearing the pieces fall into place. But Felim – and she couldn't think of him by any other name – was still concentrating on the sweating, terrified Stephen.

'And then I saw your letter. You foolish, foolish boy. Sure, herself, over there, showed it to half the centre. *My darling Elizabeth* . . . What did you think you were doing? Did you really think she was going to pay any heed to the likes of you? I'll tell you, though, you did me a favour. Gave me a laugh – and a great idea.'

The second letter. Liz grunted, the gag blocking her words, and Felim looked at her.

'Yes. I wrote the second letter, Elizabeth. Brilliant, wasn't it? When they discover your bodies, there'll be a trail, there.

It'll all make perfect sense. Poor Stephen Millar, flips and kills the man who abused him all those years ago and then fixates on a young one and kills her too, and himself. I didn't know, Stephen, how many people you'd been shooting your mouth off to. I was afraid, if you were found dead straight after James, that people might start asking questions. But if people thought you killed Elizabeth, here ... well, then, it wouldn't matter who you'd told or what you'd said I'd done. No one would believe a word.'

Stephen's muscles must be screaming by now, Liz realised, as she gazed across the room. He'd been holding himself perfectly still for almost twenty minutes and the strain was etched on his features. If he relaxed even a fraction, the noose would tighten. As she stared at him, he shifted his head and his gaze met hers. She had heard, hadn't she, of people passing messages with their eyes? Was he trying to tell her something? Had he a plan? For a moment, hope flared.

Then, still looking at her, he muttered something too low for either of them to hear.

Felim moved closer.

Stephen spoke again, much clearer this time.

'I'm sorry, Daddy.'

And Liz felt all hope disappear.

CHAPTER THIRTY-FOUR

'I can't believe we don't have an address for him.'

'Can't you? I can. Jesus.'

Claire slapped her hand off the dashboard in frustration.

'Take the next right. No, this one! How long have you been living in Dublin, Flynn? Christ.'

She dragged her phone out of her bag again but Anna's face was the only thing on the screen. Where the fuck was Carthy? She'd left, what, three voice messages? And sent three texts in the last fifteen minutes. Surely he'd have enough sense to keep an eye on his phone, with everything that was going on?

Flynn braked suddenly and she braced herself with her feet as he rounded a corner. God, she hated being a passenger. She'd only let Flynn drive because she'd assumed Carthy would have called her back by now and she wanted to be able to give him her full attention. As soon as they'd realised who Stephen Ford's father was, they'd both galloped out of the interview room, abandoning the open-mouthed McBrides. But a quick glance through their files had confirmed that, although the man calling himself Felim O'Hagan had indeed been interviewed, along with all of Tír na nÓg's other clients, after James Mannion's murder, he had given 'no fixed abode' as his address, and this hadn't been investigated further. Claire didn't blame the Garda who had taken the statement. Three other clients had said the same thing and the process of re-interviewing them, in the wake of Eugene Cannon's murder, was still underway. They were a small team; there was a limit to their resources. But it was agonising to know they had the man they wanted, and no idea where to find him. And he *was* the man they wanted. Claire was sure of that now.

As Flynn turned on to the street leading to Tír na nÓg, her phone screen finally flashed, *Tom Carthy.*

'You were looking for me, detective?'

He sounded exhausted. Didn't even bother with the usual veneer of politeness that almost everyone adopted when speaking to the Gardaí. And his mood didn't improve when she told him what she wanted.

'Felim's address? God, I don't know. We might have it in the office somewhere. Liz deals with all of that, really, have you tried her?'

I have, Claire told him. Almost as often as I tried to get you.

'Do you know where she is?' she asked.

A thought flickered across her mind. Had she missed some-thing? Were they a couple? Was there something there she hadn't picked up on?

But the dull defeat in his voice indicated otherwise. 'No. I don't know where she is. We had a . . . a disagreement. I've been calling her myself but she must have turned her phone off.'

'Well, we need to have a look around ourselves, then. Can you come by and let us in?'

'To Tír na nÓg?'

Carthy's inertia was seriously beginning to piss Claire off.

'Yes, Tír na nÓg; we're outside there now but the place is deserted. You close on weekends, don't you?'

A deep sigh. 'I'll come as soon as I can. Half an hour, maybe. That's the best I can do.'

Darkness was falling. Claire replaced the phone in her bag and looked at Flynn. 'I can't be dealing with sitting here for half an hour. You wait here, yeah?'

The gate clanged behind her as she walked up the path. The place was an awful mess, really. Fair enough, Carthy didn't have much money, but he could have cut the grass or something. The place looked almost derelict. She kicked an empty crisp packet out of her way as she approached the scuffed wooden door and rang the bell, more in hope than anticipation. Nobody home.

She took a step to the side, peering in through the smeared window. The room in which she'd spoken to Carthy following Eugene Cannon's death was empty. Ah, this was pointless. She'd head back to the car and wait for him. Half an hour wouldn't make any difference at this stage.

CHAPTER THIRTY-FIVE

'I'm sorry, Daddy.'

Felim grinned. 'What was that, pet?'

'I'm sorry, Daddy.'

He moved closer to Stephen and looked up at him. 'That's better, I—'

And then the sound of the doorbell pealed through the room. Liz's head jerked around, Felim's too. And in the split second afforded to him by the distraction, Stephen Millar raised his knee and kicked his father squarely between the legs. There was a muffled grunt as Felim doubled over. Terrified, Liz stared at him. Then she realised the gift Stephen had given her: a couple of seconds. Would they be enough? They'd have to be. Reaching forward with the hand she had managed to wriggle loose from its binding, she grabbed the mouse to the side of the computer screen. It took a second to double click the icon, two more to wait for it to open and pray the password had been saved. Three, as Felim continued to whimper in pain, for her eyes to flicker over the page and pray she'd found the right place. Two more to type the words, and one to post them. And then, as Felim began to haul himself painfully and furiously to a standing position again, she closed the icon and settled back on the chair – with one precious second to spare.

Back in the car, Claire felt the phone in her handbag vibrate and reached for it. Maybe Carthy had unearthed something, after all? But the caller I.D. showed, *Dean Journo*. Oh, go away. Bloody nuisance. She let the call ring out without answering and climbed back into the car.

Then, immediately, a text message.

Call me. Urgent.

He was a bit of a pest, Dean, but honest enough at the back of it. Not one for false alarms. And it wasn't like she'd anything else to do for the next half hour.

'This is going to sound mad,' he said, as soon as he answered her call.

'What's going on?'

He sounded breathless, she realised. Almost nervous.

'I just saw this post, from the Tír na nÓg Facebook page? I mean, it doesn't make any sense; only Tom uses that account, really. But it was a status update, so it popped up on the feed on my phone.'

'And . . . ?'

Claire only used Facebook to keep track of the school reunions she hadn't attended, but knew enough to have a vague idea what the younger man was about.

'It had been posted from the centre,' he continued. 'I mean, it must have been, it was tagged there. But it didn't make sense, you know? Just two words: *help me.* I mean, it was probably someone messing, but . . .'

It was only afterwards she realised how corny her next words must have sounded.

'Flynn? Follow me. We're going in.'

Just breathing. That was all that mattered now. The inhale and the exhale. The ribbon of air whistling through her nasal passages. A stab of cramp caused her shoulder to twitch and Liz moved her arm reflexively, trying to ease the pain.

Recovered now, and very angry, Felim strode over to her, spotted her free arm and slapped her across the face. 'I told you it didn't matter how it happened, lovey. The end result is all I care about.' Then, very gently, he pinched the tip of her nose.

The dishcloth in her mouth contracted as she sucked at it frantically. There had to be a gap. Just a straw, just a needle of air. Just a pinprick. But already her head was pulsating, her vision starting to fade. She blinked, tried to see what was happening on the other side of the room, but all she could make out was a shuddering, all she could hear were gasps similar to her own. Black polka dots danced in front of her eyes. Red and black and pain. Was it Tom who would find them? He'd never recover from that. Oh, Tom. You saved me. Don't ever forget it.

Then she heard a thud, and a muffled shout. Was that the sound of wood splintering? It was coming from very far away.

CHAPTER THIRTY-SIX

Just breathing, that was all that mattered now. The inhale and the exhale. The hiss of the oxygen going into her lungs. The hug from the mask. There would never be another panic attack, Liz decided. There would be no more anxiety. Not now, now that she knew how beautiful it was just to be able to breathe.

Sergeant Boyle was leaning over her.

'I know you've been through a terrible ordeal. But if you wouldn't mind . . . ?'

The paramedic was scowling, but Liz removed her mask, and almost smiled.

'Sure.'

There would be a crash later, she decided. Probably tears. But right now she was high – more blissed out than she had ever been during the dark years of dependency – buzzing on the knowledge that she'd been rescued. High, and she didn't care how goofy it sounded, on being alive.

The detective was speaking again: 'You sent the Facebook message?'

'Yes.' Liz nodded, then replaced the mask and took another

blissful drag. Clean air, cool streams. What was that TV show, high up in the mountains? *Grizzly Adams*. All she was missing was the bear. She almost chuckled and saw the guard's eyes narrow. Hey, maybe she was a little out of it, but who could blame her? It had been like a movie. The room retreating and then the noise, and the shouting, the figures bursting through the door.

She blinked and remembered what she had forgotten.

This woman, Detective Boyle, and the other fella – Flynn, that was his name – they had been there. And Stephen.

Stephen and the look on his face when the office door burst open, and the way his head had jerked backwards.

No. Don't remember. Just breathe.

'We've arrested Mr Millar – Lar Millar. But we will need to talk to you when you're able.'

The cop was bent almost double, crouched into the back of the ambulance while the paramedic tutted and tapped his watch.

'We'll be leaving in a minute. This young lady needs to be checked out.'

'I know.'

Sergeant Boyle attempted a smile but she looked, Liz thought, exhausted. As well she might. Over her shoulder, a blue light pulsed through the darkness. The path outside Tír na nÓg was packed now with onlookers, Garda tape keeping the crowd outside the gate. Two separate sirens wailed, intersecting in the night air. It'd be all over the news, Liz knew. Before they'd put her in the ambulance, she'd seen the flash of at least one camera, the bobbing of several microphones. Dean would be out there with the rest of them. She'd been so angry with him when Tom told her the full story of why he'd asked her for an interview that first day. Now, none of that seemed to matter.

'Is he dead?'

There were probably more delicate ways to put it, but her throat was really hurting, numb nerve endings reawakening. With the pain came memory. And with the memories, fear. She just wanted to lie back now and let this nice man and his nice ambulance take her somewhere safe. But first she had to know.

Sergeant Boyle shook her head and allowed herself a proper smile this time. She had a nice smile, Liz decided. It made her look less fierce.

'All I can tell you is that there were no fatalities at the scene.'

The smile widened and she bent closer.

'But Stephen will be OK. He was hurt, but he'll be OK. That's all you need to know. We got there in time – thanks to your message. You did good, Elizabeth. Take care, won't you? And we'll talk properly when you are feeling better.'

Then Sergeant Boyle backed out of the low doorway and Liz put the mask back over her face – properly, this time – and allowed herself to drift away.

CHAPTER THIRTY-SEVEN

The absolute exhaustion. Even turning off the car engine seemed like too much hassle. The pain in her head was pinning her to the seat. It was all over, and Claire wanted everything else to be over too, for the rest of the evening. Control, alt, delete.

For a fleeting moment, she wished she was single. No Matt, no Anna. No one to ask her how the day had been. No demands, no questions. No hugs, even. She'd trade them all. Trade them for an empty house with a warm bath and a full bottle of red. Nineteen-eighties' Irish rock on shuffle. Rinse and repeat.

Then she dismissed the thought. She needed them, both of them. A kiss from Matt. The feel of Anna's hair, soft against her cheek. A pre-warmed bed. She turned off the car engine and eased herself and her creaking body out of the seat and up the path. She turned the key and slowly unlocked the door.

Then the smell hit her. The last thing she'd been expecting.

Good God, had someone been baking?

Her mother emerged, smiling, from the kitchen, Matt trailing in her wake.

'Ah, there you are, pet. That was a long day; we saw it all on the news. Go on into the sitting room, love, and I'll bring in your dinner.'

A flapping gesture from her husband: *Don't make a scene; go on inside; I'll explain.* Too tired, too astonished to protest, Claire allowed herself to be led to the sofa.

'The fuck?' No other words, just an eyebrow raise. But it was all she needed to do.

'I was going to call you, but I heard what happened . . .'

Her husband gave an apologetic shrug, but Claire's headache was building now, throbbing against her temples. This was supposed to be the bit where she came home, collapsed into the sofa, dropped a kiss on her sleeping baby, got a high five, maybe, from her husband. Opened a beer. Clearly, that was too much to ask. Instead, she seemed to have wandered straight into some sort of shaggin' family reunion.

'I've kept it warm for you.' Nuala Boyle bustled into the room.

She must have brought her own apron with her, Claire thought, in a daze. She can't have found that pink patterned monstrosity in here. And then, as the smell of red-wine-soaked beef hit her, her stomach gurgled traitorously. Beside her on the couch, her husband had opened a decent bottle and pushed a glass into her hand.

'I'll leave ye to it.'

Was that Nuala Boyle being subtle? Very few stranger things had happened, thought Claire, and this was coming at the end of a very strange day. She thought briefly about giving the plate back, leaving the house again, heading for the twenty-four-hour Maccy D's around the corner. But as the steam met her nostrils she abandoned the suggestion. Fine. She'd eat their last supper. Didn't mean she had to thank them, though.

'Tough day?' Matt's conciliatory tone. The one he used when he'd broken something or forgotten to set the D.V.R.

Claire chewed, but ignored him. She took a sip from the wine, a gloriously full-bodied Cabernet, and shivered as the alcohol hit her bloodstream. One of her wishes had come true, so. She was paying a high price for it, though.

'Listen, I've been meaning to talk to you . . .'

Was that nervousness in her husband's voice? Was Matt actually afraid of her? But before Claire could fully process his tone, the door to the sitting room opened again.

'She drank most of the bottle; she's back down again now. Ah, Claire! I see you're home!'

Claire doubted if Matt's mother owned an apron. Eimear's usual armour was in place: the bang-on-trend glasses, the power suit that had been her trademark look before the term had even been invented. All of which made the empty baby bottle in her hand look even more incongruous. This was too much.

Claire glared at her husband. 'Are you going to tell me what's going on?'

But it was his mother who answered her, in a tone of voice that had encouraged the signing of a thousand contracts. 'You must be starving. Finish your dinner, Claire, and then we can all have a chat.'

'Excuse me?' Claire put the plate on the floor but held on

to the wine. 'Are you telling me what to do? In my own sitting room? Seriously?'

'Ah, Claire, love, don't be like that ...' Nuala Boyle had reappeared in the doorway and was twisting her hands together repeatedly, a gesture Claire recognised well and which irritated her every time.

But Eimear Mackey remained calm. 'I know what this looks like.'

'I'll tell you what it looks like –' Claire drained her glass and grabbed the bottle off her husband – 'an episode of *Dr Phil*, that's what it looks like! What's the story, Matt? Finding it difficult to cope, are you? Couple of late nights with the baby and you go running to Mummy? Is that it? Good God!'

All of the day's tension fizzed up inside her and she was horrified to find tears in her eyes. She blinked them back and decided to be furious instead.

'If you have a problem with me or with how I look after my family, you come to me, OK? Not to my mother, or your mother.'

'Well, I'd have to be able to get in touch with you first, wouldn't I?'

'I can't believe—'

Matt raised his hand. 'Give us a minute, Mum, yeah?'

'Sure.'

The older women left and walked into the kitchen. Claire could have sworn she heard another cork pop before they closed the door.

She turned to her husband. 'What's she doing, giving Anna

ARE YOU WATCHING ME?

a bottle? Putting her back to sleep? How did you even know she was going to settle for her?'

Matt took a large draught from his own drink. 'Because she's been looking after her for days.'

Claire swallowed furiously and slammed her plate down on to the floor. 'You are joking me.'

'No.'

Matt shrugged.

'I needed time off; you didn't seem to want to give it to me. I told you I needed a break. So I called Mum. And she was glad to help. She's been here for an hour or two most evenings this week. Don't look at me like that, Claire! It wasn't like I was having an affair, or something. I went for a run. Just got a bit of head space, that was all.'

'And you didn't think to tell me?'

'And how was I supposed to do that? Your phone is never on and, even when you're here, you're not listening to me.'

'We talked about this, Matt!' Claire stared at her husband in disbelief. 'We talked it up, down and backwards before Anna arrived. Before I got pregnant, even! We knew it was going to be tough and you said you were cool with it. I'm the bigger earner of the two of us. I was the one who was going to keep working; you were going to go freelance and try and work your hours around her. We agreed!' The last word came out almost as a screech and she bit her lip, forcing herself to calm down.

Her husband's voice remained level, but his anger was still audible. 'Nobody tells you what it's like, being here all day. Not having a minute to yourself. I love Anna, but minding her and running the house and trying to get my own job done – I was cracking up, Claire. I was worried. I needed to get out, go for a run, clear my head.'

And what about me? she wanted to say. *When do I get time?* But her husband was still talking.

'Mum rang one evening, and she could tell I was in a bad way. She offered to come over.'

Claire's voice rose again. 'So it's all my fault, is it? Jesus Christ, Matt. It's not like I've been on the town; I saved some-one's life today.' She paused, wondering if that sounded as corny to Matt's ears as it had to hers. Well, feck him. It was the truth, wasn't it?

Matt gave a watery smile. 'I know that. And I'm really proud of you. But the fact of the matter is, I can't cope with Anna on my own and keep the business going too. You need the flexi-bility to be able to come and go as you please and I can't give you that. Not on my own.'

'So are you asking me to give up work? Is that it?'

Her husband looked shocked. 'Jesus, no. Was that what you were thinking? No.'

'He's asking you to accept help.' Eimear had re-entered the room, condensation running down the glass of white wine in her hand. 'Don't look at me like that, Claire! I've had a chat with Nuala and we've come up with a plan.'

Claire glowered at her. 'We don't need help.'

Her mother-in-law crossed the floor and sat down on the sofa beside her. 'Do you think that I didn't have any? I had my mum living with me when Mattie was small!'

'Really?'

Claire stared at her husband in surprise and he shrugged, helplessly.

Eimear nodded. 'Of course I did. I was widowed at thirty-four, Claire, I had two young sons and I was just starting out in my career. What did you think I did with them, stuck them in a filing cabinet?'

'Well, I . . .'

Would it be rude, Claire wondered, to admit she had never thought about it at all? But Eimear was still talking.

'And when they were older they went away to school, but I still needed help. Au pairs in the school holidays. Mum at weekends. I didn't do it alone, Claire, no one does.'

Nuala Boyle walked into the room quietly, as if apologising for being there, and took a seat across from them. Claire looked at her.

'So is this why you're here too, Mum? To tell me I'm useless and can't cope?'

'Not at all, love.' She took a sip from her glass and made a face. Claire's mother only drank wine at funerals and on Christmas Day. Claire wondered which category this evening fell into. 'I want to help, that's all,' she continued. 'Sure, your dad and me, we don't see half enough of the little one. I'd be down here every week, if you'd have me, with the free travel.'

'To prove I'm a crap mother, is it? That I can't manage on my own?'

Claire rested her head back on the sofa, exhausted again

now that her initial anger was fading. But her mother's answer woke her up again.

'No, love. So you can achieve what I didn't.'

Nuala laughed at the look of surprise on Claire's face.

'What did you think, that I enjoyed spending my days cleaning up after ye? Claire, my dear girleen. I love your father, and you, but there are only so many times you can clean the kitchen floor without feeling you are going to go out of your mind. I had to give up work when I got married, that was the law back then. So when I had a little girl I swore she wouldn't have to do the same. Let us help you, love. Eimear is happy to do the odd evening during the week and we'll travel down at weekends, or you can come up to us, have yourself a night away. Please, Claire. We all know what you did today. You're bloody brilliant at what you do. Don't throw it away.'

Claire looked at Eimear and Matt, their brows knitted in identical fashion. How come she had never noticed how similar they were before? Her own mother was smiling – Anna's smile. She saw it every morning, but had never admitted before where it came from. But it turned out that, no matter how far you sprinted, you could never outrun them. Families. Her instinct was to fight them, tell them she'd be fine on her own, that she'd manage. That she always had and always would. But she was just so bloody tired.

She yawned, and picked up the plate of stew again.

'Well. You can start by telling me what's for dessert.'

EPILOGUE

She had forgotten how to breathe. And then she remembered. In, out. In, out. Naturally. The way she'd been doing for months.

On the other side of the desk, Dean shifted uncomfortably. He was nervous, Liz realised. Despite having been given a staff job at Ireland 24 some months before, this was his first live studio interview. Liz resisted the temptation to lean over and pat his hand. To tell him not to worry, that they'd get through it together.

They were quite the double act now, herself and Dean. After she'd been discharged from hospital, after Lar Millar had been arrested and the details of what had happened that evening in Tír na nÓg began to emerge, everyone had wanted to speak to Liz Cafferky. All of the papers, all of the TV and radio stations. Some of the British channels had sent reporters too, carrying chequebooks and offering to fly her to London, offering crazy money. But Liz had called Dean up, told him she'd give him an exclusive. She owed him one, she told him. Or, more to the point, they owed each other. And then she'd told him everything. Everything that had happened to her in Tír na nÓg, and everything that had brought her to that point: the dark days, the drink, the drugs. The girl she'd abandoned in the alleyway, and how guilty that had made her feel. At least she didn't have to worry about her anymore. Sergeant Boyle had, as she put it, 'made a few phone calls' and discovered that the young woman had woken up in hospital the following morning with nothing bothering her other than a grazed chin, a huge lump on her forehead and the realisation that she needed to find new friends. So Liz had told Dean everything. It was the best decision she could have made. Turned out, if you didn't hide anything, then there was nothing that could be discovered about you. He in turn told the world and, the next day, she was free.

A voice in her ear: 'Are you happy, Elizabeth?'

She nodded into the camera, and winked at Dean. He was on the programme to discuss a major story he'd been working on – a report on a drugs gang who'd been operating out of Dublin. He hated being in the studio, preferred being out on the road. But his boss had insisted they do it this way.

Their boss, she should say. Ireland 24 had offered her a job almost as soon as she'd been discharged from hospital, but Liz had waited until the Lar Millar trial was over. On the day of his sentencing, she'd shaken hands with Stephen Ford on the steps of the court and wished him luck. She'd handed him Tom's phone number and told him he was the man to turn to for help and advice, if he wanted it. Tír na nÓg was now closed; it had been impossible to keep the centre open once Tom admitted he needed residential treatment for his gambling addiction. But her former boss had helped find the clients other resources, other places to go, and she knew he'd help Stephen too – if he needed it. Stephen had had his hair cut and bought a new suit for the day in court. He'd found a new job, he told her, and was using the books Mr Mannion had left him to start his studies again. There was a 'People of the Year' award planned to honour the bravery he had shown, in that dark, dusty room. Liz herself was going to present it to him. She was looking forward to the ceremony. The more live television experience she could get, the better, or so her agent said, anyway.

She smiled, and turned towards the camera.

'Four and three and two and one.'

'Good afternoon, I'm Liz Cafferky. Welcome to *Dublin Today*.'

THE END

ACKNOWLEDGEMENTS

To the ever supportive and enthusiastic Sheila Crowley at Curtis Brown, thank you for always having my back, and to Becky Ritchie for your help and constant good humour. To all at Quercus, in particular my wonderful editors Jane Wood and Katie Gordon, thank you for making my books the best they could be. To Helen and Declan at Gill Hess, thanks for your guidance on the other side of the publicity curtain during the *Can Anybody Help Me?* adventure, and to all at Hachette Ireland for your support with this book.

To my family and friends who came to the book launch, particularly to those who travelled long distances, your support means more to me than you will ever know. Go raibh míle maith agaibh. To my first readers, Caroline, Ciara, Mags and Treasa, thank you for your insights, advice and encouragement. Much love to you all. Thank you Eimear Cotter and Rick O'Shea for your help and support.

To the online crime-writing community, bloggers and writers, your books might be full of murky deeds but you are lovely people! Thank you for your encouragement and virtual friendship. I've met some of you in real life, and you're even nicer on the other side of the screen. Thanks to Jane Casey, Liz Nugent and Louise O'Neill. Stars, all. Special thanks to my RTE colleagues, especially Hilary McGouran, Laura Fitzgerald and Ray Burke for all of your support and good wishes.

To all at Dublin City Libraries, you provide a safe, warm space for people to tap into their lap tops for hours on end. All this, and free books too? I couldn't do it without you. And to all coffee shops who tolerate writers nursing one drink for hours at a time, thank you. Keep the kettle on.

To Conor and Séimí: People keep asking how I get anything done with you two, but the truth is, you inspire me. Grá Mór.

This book is dedicated to my husband, Andrew Phelan, with all my love.